AFFIRMATION

THE LEPIDOPTERA VAMPIRE SERIES

BOOK THREE

BY
SUSAN HODDY

Also By Susan Hoddy

THE LEPIDOPTERA VAMPIRE SERIES

ATTRACTION

AWAKENED

Prologue

SEVEN YEARS AGO

Sister Mongose, who was from the Bagnolet parish, tucked the small child into a wool-lined calico bag to keep her warm enough for her journey to the church, which was a couple of blocks away from the Gramaze mansion.

"Thank you, Mr Gramaze. She will be well cared for by a loving couple we have selected for her."

"I would expect nothing less," said William matter-of-factly, opening the front door for her. "Good night, sister."

"Good night," said Sister Mongose, nodding slightly as she walked on through.

The gates closed automatically behind her as the sister left the Gramaze property and walked quickly down the low-lit, snow covered sidewalk towards the church. With her white breath forming in front of her, she rounded the corner and Sister Mongose watched a car, which was driving on the other side of the road, pass by her, brake and then do a U-turn, screeching its wheels as it turned. Looking over her shoulder, she held onto the calico bag firmly and quickened her step, in hope of arriving safely with the child.

With metres to go until she reached the church steps, the tinted window car mounted the kerbed footpath and ploughed into the sister, which sent her shooting into the air. As she tried to hold onto the calico bag and shelter the child from any injuries, the pain she felt from the car mowing her down overwhelmed her, and the bag slipped out of her hands and dropped to the ground with a thud. As Sister Mongose's limp, broken body laid on the pavement and her mouth filled with blood, her vision became blurred and gradually faded into black as she watched the tail lights of the vehicle drive away.

Chapter One

PRESENT DAY

Her big blue eyes opened slowly, and seven-year-old Katelyn Goodwit tried to focus on the small white pendant light shade hanging from the ornate ceiling. Silently yawning, she took a deep breath, turned her head slowly to the one side and watched through the bars of her white, wooden cot the goings on around her.

As she lay there wondering and watching in anticipation of when it would be her turn for someone to come and check on her, Katelyn's tiny body shivered from the wet bed sheets and blankets. But the staff didn't seem to notice that she was awake and required help. They just went about their busy daily routine, at the government funded home for disabled children in Berne, Switzerland.

Restricted to lying on her back, Katelyn stretched her right arm and hand out fully between the bars of her cot, and tried to get someone's attention as they walked on by her.

"Hey...don't forget about me," said Katelyn.

But what came out of her mouth was a moan. Unfortunately, no one could understand what she was trying to say.

Instead, the male and female staff gently touched her outstretched hand as they walked by, and went about their daily routine of attending to the other children.

God, this is frustrating. They don't even understand me. I might as well be dead, thought Katelyn, as she tried to move her paralysed body. Even though her mind was sharp, her muscles and body felt like they were weighted down with a piece of iron.

If there was one wish I would like granted, that would be to be taken care of by someone who loved me and cared about me. But I suppose it's too much to ask for someone to foster me. I see so many other kids leaving with their new foster parents. But not me, humph, thought Katelyn, blinking slowly with saddened eyes.

"Good morning, Katelyn. My name is Susan, and I am going to be looking after you from now on." A tall, reddish-brown haired woman stood next to the cot and smiled down at Katelyn. "How are you feeling today?"

Surprised, she turned her head towards the voice and smiled. Katelyn couldn't believe someone was actually talking to her. The other staff and carers always made her feel comfortable and looked after her well, but they hardly ever spoke to Katelyn. Stretching her left hand out through the cot bars to make contact with her new carer, she made a grunting sound.

Humph, why do I bother even trying to speak. It always comes out the same, thought Katelyn, as she laid there looking up at Susan.

It must be so frustrating for you, thought Susan, holding Katelyn's tiny hand.

Katelyn didn't see her lips move, but she did hear Susan's voice.

What? thought Katelyn, her eyes widening.

"Today I am going to get you out of this bed, and put you into a wheelchair. I thought that you might like to go outside for some fresh air and sunlight. How does that sound to you, Katelyn?" said Susan, lowering the cot rail.

I would love to. Wow, this sure is exciting, Susan. If I could jump, I would be jumping up and down with joy at the moment, thought Katelyn.

I'm glad, thought Susan. But again, her lips didn't move.

Can you hear my thoughts? thought Katelyn, as she gulped and looked into Susan's eyes.

But Susan didn't bat an eyelid, nor did she answer. Instead, she pulled the wet blankets from Katelyn and helped her get ready for the day.

After breakfast, Susan lowered Katelyn gently into the wheelchair, and strapped her in.

Oh… I don't feel too good, thought Katelyn, as she struggled to swallow her saliva and lift her head up from her chest.

"Are you feeling lightheaded? Sorry, I forgot about that… it's because you have been lying down most of your life. Your mind and body are not used to sitting upright and are trying to work out what's going on. Give it a few minutes and the dizziness will disappear," said Susan, placing her hand on Katelyn's sweaty forehead.

She was right, because after what seemed like a long few minutes, the dizziness stopped.

"There… is that better now?" asked Susan, as she felt Katelyn's wellness return.

Yes. Thank you… you must be hearing my thoughts otherwise there is no way you would be able to guess how I am feeling, thought Katelyn, as she looked up to Susan's face.

Again, Susan didn't bat an eyelid, she just continued to make Katelyn comfortable.

"Right… are you ready to go?" asked Susan.

Yes.

Susan pushed Katelyn down a long, black and white checked tiled corridor, and as they approached the glass sliding doors to go outside, Katelyn's eyes started to water. Her eyes weren't accustomed to the bright sunlight, as most of her life she had spent inside. Pulling a pair of sunglasses from her jacket pocket, Susan gently placed the glasses on Katelyn's face.

"That better?" asked Susan, as she knelt in front of Katelyn.

Thank you… are you sure you are not hearing my thoughts? thought Katelyn, frowning.

But again, nothing came out of Susan's mouth.

When the glass door slid open, a gentle breeze hit Katelyn's face for the first time. Breathing in the clean air, she loved how it made her feel alive. Looking towards the blue sky, she felt the warmth from the mid-morning sun on her face, which made her skin tingle from its warmth. She hadn't even realised what she had been missing most of her sheltered life. Watching as something big flew above her, she cringed from the noise and expected it to fall out the sky.

What is that? thought Katelyn, looking toward the sky and then at Susan.

"It's called a plane. People fly from one place to another in them," said Susan.

Katelyn nodded and frowned at the same time, as she watched the plane fly further away from her.

Continuing to push Katelyn's wheelchair along the grey concrete pathway and down to the beautifully manicured green lawns and gardens, which were all out in full bloom, Susan explained to Katelyn about what she was seeing in detail.

Katelyn's eyes widened, and were mesmerised as she watched a long, narrow beaked bird flying in and out of the flowers and how the orange butterflies landed on the plants and retrieved the nectar with their tongues.

Positioning the wheelchair next to the garden bed, Susan helped Katelyn lean forward and showed her how to breathe in the wonderful perfume of the colourful flowers. As she breathed in each flower's perfume, Katelyn's face was full of wonderment, for she had never smelt anything so beautiful in her whole life before.

She was even fascinated by the clear water and how it cascaded over the rocks of the waterfall and landed into a blue and green rocky pond, with pink and yellow flowered lilies floating in the water below. Even the lush green grass seemed to excite her. Katelyn smiled and grunted as she took in her surroundings, and appreciated the opportunity she had been given by Susan.

"Isn't it beautiful out here? What more could we ask for?" said Susan, as she pressed the brake on the wheelchair and kneeled on the ground beside Katelyn.

Looking into Susan's eyes, Katelyn clenched her fists and tried to tell her how much she appreciated it. But her mouth only moaned.

This place is so beautiful and calming. Thank you for taking me out here today, and explaining everything. I am not used to this type of kindness, thought Katelyn, her eyes wide with appreciation.

"You are most welcome, my dear," said Susan, as she looked at her watch. "Soon it will be lunch time, Katelyn. We had better go on inside and see what they have made you for lunch."

Oh, Ok, thought Katelyn, wondering what type of mashed up food she would be having.

Pushing the wheelchair inside through a side sliding door, Susan entered a room Katelyn had never seen before. As she steered Katelyn over to one side of the room and stopped, Susan bent down next to Katelyn, and took off her sunglasses.

"From today onwards, you will be eating your meals in here with the other children. This is called the dining room," said Susan, watching Katelyn's reaction.

Katelyn gulped, and looked around the huge, white room, where other children, some in wheelchairs, were seated at wooden tables with white metal chairs. Each child had a bib on and was eagerly waiting for their food to be delivered by their carer. As she watched the other children interacting with one another, the noise level rose in the dining room and made Katelyn feel anxious.

Susan stood up and placed a hand on Katelyn's shoulder for support. "Let's go choose what you are having for lunch," said Susan, as she pushed the wheelchair over towards the bain-marie.

Katelyn looked up at Susan and swallowed hard.

As they stood in line, waiting their turn, Katelyn's senses came alive from all the different aromas of food.

Mmm, smells so good, thought Katelyn.

Susan smiled.

Not knowing what food Katelyn preferred to eat, Susan looked down at Katelyn and said, "How about we get you a spoonful of each dish in the bain-maries and see which ones you like?"

Katelyn smiled and nodded quickly. *Sounds good*, thought Katelyn, looking from Susan to the bain-maries.

Susan found an empty table on the other side of the room near a clear glass window, which had a view of a gazebo and the beautifully manicured surrounding gardens outside.

Once they were seated at the table, Susan started to show Katelyn how to eat with her hands and that she needed to chew her food instead of just swallowing it. Katelyn had always been spoon-fed previously, so she didn't know how to eat with her hands, let alone use a fork, spoon or knife.

Susan held open Katelyn's tiny hand and placed a matchbox sized piece of pumpkin into her palm and then closed her fingers around the food. Bringing Katelyn's hand up to her mouth, so she could take a bite, Susan talked her through the process of eating and chewing her food. With the help of Susan, and with the determination that she wasn't going to choke every time she placed food into her mouth, Katelyn eventually worked out how to feed herself.

Next, Susan showed Katelyn how to drink from a cup with a straw. Previously she had always been given a bottle with a teat on it to drink out of.

This sure is different to what I know and have been taught by the carers here. Why haven't they shown me how to eat and drink this way previously? wondered Katelyn.

"It may take you some time to learn how to eat and drink, but you will get used to it," said Susan, wiping down the table. "I will make sure of that."

After lunch, Susan wheeled Katelyn into the bathroom and positioned her in front of a mirror, which had a basin below, to show her how dirty her face and hands were from the food she had just consumed. As Katelyn looked into the mirror and stared back at herself, the tears welled up in her blue eyes and spilled over onto her cheeks. She had never seen herself in the mirror before and with the whole day being so amazing already, she was feeling a bit overwhelmed by it all.

"Let's get you cleaned up," said Susan, helping Katelyn to lean forward and place her hands under the tap.

Katelyn knew this was going to take some getting used to as she always had others bathing her previously, but she was determined to learn.

"Well, from now on, every day will get better for you. I will make sure of that, my dear," said Susan, as she listened to Katelyn's thoughts and brushed the food out of Katelyn's shoulder length, brown, wavy hair.

Thank you…what time do you have to go home? thought Katelyn. She didn't want the day to end.

"I leave around five o'clock each day. But don't worry, I will be back each morning around nine o'clock to share the day with you," said Susan, placing her hand on Katelyn's shoulder.

I knew you were hearing my thoughts, thought Katelyn, smiling.

Don't tell anyone, will you Katelyn? I want to keep this secret between you and me, thought Susan, looking at Katelyn's reflection in the mirror.

Of course I won't tell anyone… are you psychic? thought Katelyn.

No, I am not. But I do have special powers though, thought Susan. *I will tell you about them another day. Ok?*

Ok, thought Katelyn.

After her wash, Susan chose to take Katelyn to a secluded part of the property and park her wheelchair in front of a lake, under the shade of a tree. When she pulled out a book called *Gulliver's Travels* out of her bag and started to read it, Katelyn's eyes lit up with gratification.

I have never had someone read to me before. Thank you, thought Katelyn.

"You are most welcome," said Susan. *I can't believe how all these simple pleasures that I take for granted, have never been given to you. You poor child.* She shook her head.

When it came time for Susan to go home Katelyn thought, *You are definitely coming back tomorrow, aren't you?*

"Yes, I will be here tomorrow and the next day and always, if that pleases you, Katelyn," said Susan, laying her in her cot, and tucking her in.

I have really enjoyed our time together today, Susan. I can't wait to see you tomorrow. Thank you for a wonderful day, thought Katelyn.

"You're welcome, dear. See you tomorrow," said Susan, looking down at Katelyn and smiling.

Bye.

As Katelyn watched Susan walk away and out the doorway, she sighed. She missed Susan's witty company and wished it was already morning.

Weeks soon turned into months and with Susan coming to the children's home to care for Katelyn every day, just as she had promised, they soon became good friends. Susan enjoyed helping Katelyn learn how to eat, drink and take care of herself. She also started to teach Katelyn how to pronounce letters and some words, which made life a little easier and a lot less complicated, when it came to communication.

Chapter Two

I wonder where Susan is today, thought Katelyn.

She always looked forward to seeing her each and every day. Looking at the clock on the wall, and not knowing how to tell the time, Katelyn wondered what time it was. It seemed to her that it was way past nine o'clock; the time Susan usually came to care for her. But Susan hadn't been in to see her in the past couple of days. Instead, the other staff had cared for her each day.

Trying not to go through the 'what if's' in her mind, as she sat in her wheelchair, she opened the drawer beside her single bed to get out a colouring in book and some crayons. This always seemed to soothe her when she was worried.

I hope she is coming in today, thought Katelyn.

Struggling to colour in just one picture, Katelyn gave up and threw the books and crayons on the floor.

"Hey… that's no way to treat your stuff," said Susan, as she walked into the room with the General Manager of the children's home.

Katelyn looked up quickly and smiled as soon as she heard her voice.

Where have you been? I have been worried, thought Katelyn.

"Good morning, Katelyn. Sorry I am late. But I have some exciting news for you. I have been to the district court this morning and I have applied to get custody of you. How do you feel about coming to live with me so that I can care for you at my house instead?" said Susan, kneeling in front of Katelyn.

The news took Katelyn by surprise. With a smile from ear to ear and tears forming in her eyes, she couldn't believe what Susan had just said.

What... really? Are you sure...? I would love to. Thank you, thought Katelyn.

But of course, only Susan could hear her answer and how excited she was.

Yes, I am sure, thought Susan, as she looked into Katelyn's smiling eyes.

Katelyn started to laugh and smile. This was the only way she could communicate how happy she was to be leaving. Leaning forward, she gave Susan a hug.

"Once we finalise your paperwork and pack up your gear, you are welcome to go with Susan today, if you want," said the General Manager to Katelyn.

I can't wait, thought Katelyn, smiling.

"Give us about thirty minutes to finalise everything, and then I will be ready to take you home," said Susan, standing.

I feel like the most luckiest girl in the world today. Thank you, Susan, thought Katelyn.

Susan was thrilled to be pushing the wheelchair through the glass sliding door for the last time. She had always adored and gotten on well with most children in the past and was now happy that the queen had given her the authority to fostering Katelyn. Reading Katelyn's thoughts, Susan realised how pleased Katelyn was to be leaving the disabled children's home, and that she couldn't believe she was finally going to live with someone that cared about her and her welfare.

Waiting for them at the end of the sparsely snow-covered pathway was Susan's limousine. The chauffeur opened the door as they got closer to the black car. Lifting Katelyn out of the wheelchair, Susan carried her into the car, whilst the chauffeur collapsed the wheelchair and stored it in the boot of the car with her belongings.

Thank you, thought Katelyn, as she leaned in and hugged Susan tight.

"You are welcome, my dear. Hopefully I can provide a better life for you than you have had previously," said Susan, hugging her back and then placing Katelyn's seat belt on.

Katelyn didn't remember ever having travelled in a car before and even though Susan had reassured her that she would be all right, she still felt a bit apprehensive about the one and a half hour ride to Susan's house.

Reading Katelyn's thoughts and watching her reactions to the buildings and scenery flying past the car as they drove along the freeway, Susan placed her healing hand over Katelyn's to calm her.

Thank you, thought Katelyn to Susan.

Susan smiled, and said, "You're welcome."

The car pulled up in front of a large property that had a high limestone brick fence, with electric wire fencing surrounding the top part of the limestone, and Katelyn wondered what was behind the wrought iron gates. Watching the chauffeur carefully key in the code on the key pad located outside, she jumped as the gates opened up to let them drive in. When the house came into view, her eyes widened and she smiled.

"Beautiful," said Katelyn, managing to get at least one word out of her mouth.

Susan smiled, and said, "It sure is. And I am glad to be sharing it with you."

Excited, Katelyn couldn't wait to see inside, especially her own bedroom, that Susan had promised her.

Susan lived by Lake Zurich in Zurich, Switzerland. When the chauffeur pulled up at the front French door entrance of the house, Susan's two security guards were standing on the tiled porch waiting for them.

As the limousine stopped below them, the two guards walked down the three snow covered steps towards the car. Opening the door and climbing in, one of the security guards sat next to Katelyn and said, "Hello... my name is Mark, and my friend out there is Connor."

Katelyn's eyes opened wide as she watched Connor give her a quick wave. Mark put his hand out to shake Katelyn's hand, but she didn't take it. Gulping hard, she looked at Susan for support.

"It's all right, Katelyn. Mark and Connor are here to help you," said Susan, placing her hand over Katelyn's hand.

Katelyn smiled nervously.

"Mark will carry you out the car and take you inside, Katelyn," said Susan.

Oh... Ok, thought Katelyn, eyeing them off. She had never met many men in her short, sheltered life, especially ones this huge and intimidating.

Stepping inside her wood-fire heated house, Susan stood in the foyer and breathed in the inviting aromas of something delicious cooking in her kitchen, as she waited for Mark to bring Katelyn inside.

"I would like to introduce you to all my friends that work here. You've met Mark and Connor. They will protect you whilst you are here," said Susan.

Katelyn looked from Mark, who was still holding her in his arms, to Connor.

Protect me. Why do I need protecting? thought Katelyn.

"They are more like security. This lady here is Zoe," said Susan, gesturing to a grey-haired woman with an apron on. "She is our cook. Later on, we will sit down with Zoe and you can tell her what food you like."

"Nice to finally meet you, Katelyn," said Zoe, in a French accent.

Pretty, thought Katelyn, as she smiled politely.

"The man on your right is Adam and he is our gardener. He also cleans our swimming pool which is in the back yard," said Susan.

"Hello Katelyn," said Adam, holding his safari hat and bowing slightly.

Why is he bowing? thought Katelyn, frowning.

Adam is from New Orleans and it is customary to bow when you meet someone, thought Susan to Katelyn.

Oh. Ok, thought Katelyn, as she nodded.

"Now... Mark is going to carry you up to your room and Connor will bring your wheelchair up," said Susan.

Are you coming too? thought Katelyn to Susan.

No, my dear. I will be up shortly to see you. Don't worry, you are in safe hands with Mark and Connor, thought Susan to Katelyn.

"Ok," said Katelyn. She smiled politely at them both.

Walking up what looked like steep stairs to her bedroom, Katelyn placed both arms around Mark, cuddled into his shoulder and held on tight.

"Don't worry, I won't drop you, kiddo. I am here for you anytime you need me," said Mark.

Thank you, thought Katelyn.

"You are welcome," said Mark, smiling.

You can hear my thoughts, too, thought Katelyn, as she looked him in the eyes.

He raised his eyebrows up and down and smiled. "Yes. We all can hear your thoughts, Katelyn."

This sure will make life easier for me until I can learn to speak properly. You said all of you can hear my thoughts. Oh my, that is just a bit embarrassing, after what I thought down there, thought Katelyn, blushing.

Chuckling, Mark said, "Don't worry about it… I am sure everyone has already forgotten about it. By the way, we are all here to help you with learning how to speak, so don't hesitate to ask anytime you need help."

Thank you. You don't know how much that means to me, thought Katelyn, as she entered her bedroom in Mark's arms.

"Where do you want me to put your wheelchair, Katelyn?" said Connor, standing in the doorway.

Katelyn face lit up when she looked around the room to see where to place her wheelchair. Her eyes straight away noticed the huge queen-sized, four poster bed over near the window, that was made up with a light blue and white quilt, which had the Frozen Princess picture on it, with some scatter cushions on top. In fact the whole room was painted a pastel blue up the top and had blue and white wall paper down the bottom. Over to the right of the doorway was a white dressing table with an oval mirror and it looked high enough for her wheelchair to fit under.

Wow, thought Katelyn, with tears welling in her eyes. She had never seen anything so beautiful like this in her whole life and never thought that one day she would grow up in a house like this either.

"Do you like your room?" asked Mark.

Like it… I love it. So beautiful," thought Katelyn, looking around in wonderment.

"Would you like to sit on your bed?" asked Mark. "Maybe you can put the wheelchair next to the bed, Connor."

She nodded quickly and smiled at them both. Excited, she couldn't wait to feel what her new bed was like.

Setting her down carefully on the bed, Mark asked, "Will you be Ok to sit by yourself unaided or did you need me to sit next to you?"

I should be Ok by myself, thought Katelyn.

"Ok. Let's try it first," said Mark, taking his arms away slowly.

"Stop fussing over her, Mark. She is fine. Look…" said Conner, placing the wheelchair next to her bed.

Mark gave him a dirty look and said, "Better to be safe than sorry."

"Katelyn, Wynton will bring up your bags from the limo in a minute. If you need help to put your stuff away, you only need to ask and we will hear you," said Connor.

I think that I will probably have to ask for help with that, as I can't do those sorts of things yet, thought Katelyn.

"No problem. I will stay here and help you," said Mark.

Entering the room, Susan said, "How are we going in here?"

Thank you so much for my beautiful room. I love it. I feel like the luckiest kid in town, thought Katelyn.

"You are welcome. I was hoping you would like it," said Susan, sitting beside Katelyn and giving her a hug.

Knocking on the door as he stood in the doorway, Wynton said, "Where would you like me to place your bags, Katelyn?"

Looking around the room, she pointed to what she thought was the wardrobe. *Over next to the wardrobe. Thanks Wynton.*

Wynton nodded once and placed them inside the walk-in robe.

Turning to Susan, Katelyn thought, *Mark said he will help me put my clothes away. Is that Ok?*

"Of course, dear. Looks like you guys have everything in hand here. I have some business to attend to, so I will leave you and catch up with you all soon," said Susan.

Thank you, once again, Susan, thought Katelyn, giving her a tight hug.

Smiling, Susan said, "You are welcome. See you later on then."

Ok, bye, thought Katelyn, as she watched Susan walk towards the doorway.

"Well... I will see you later on, Katelyn. If you need anything, don't hesitate to ask," said Connor, standing in front of Katelyn.

Thanks Connor, thought Katelyn, as she held out her hands for a hug.

Connor wasn't an affectionate vampire. But for some reason that he couldn't comprehend yet, he didn't feel threatened around her and hoped they would become good friends. Kneeling in front of her, he leaned in and gave her a hug. "I will only be outside in the gardens on patrol. So if you need me for anything... well I am sure you know what to do."

Ok. See you later, thought Katelyn, watching him walk out the door.

"Would you like to have a good a look around your room? We can put your stuff away after that," offered Mark.

Ok, thought Katelyn, as Mark lifted her into the wheel-chair.

Wheeling her slowly around the bedroom, Mark listened to Katelyn's thoughts about the disabled children's home that she had previously lived in.

"I can't believe how they treated you at the home, Katelyn. What a horrible life you have had. Don't worry, your life will only get better here," said Mark, placing his hand on her shoulder.

Yeah. It wasn't the nicest of places. I felt lonely there, until I met Susan, thought Katelyn, looking up at Mark. *I am so lucky to be living here and to have my own room. I love how the glass door windows lead outside onto a balcony, so that I can see the gardens outside. There is so much light in here, and it makes me feel alive.*

"I'm glad for you. Let's show you your bathroom," said Mark.

As Mark pushed Katelyn through the doorway of the bathroom, her eyes lit up and a smile came over her face. *Wow,* thought Katelyn.

"Luxurious isn't it. Susan had your bathroom redesigned just for you," said Mark.

Looking up at Mark, she thought, *Really… this is amazing and it looks like my wheelchair will be able to fit in the shower as well. Oh, and I love the claw foot bath. Not sure how I will get in there yet. I sure feel spoilt here.*

After Mark helped Katelyn put her clothes away, he said, "Well… I had better go and see if Connor needs my help. I am sure you would like some time to yourself to take this all in. If you need anything, all you need to do is talk and one of us will come."

Thanks Mark. And thanks for your help putting my stuff away, thought Katelyn.

"You are welcome," said Mark, giving Katelyn a hug. Pushing her over to the window, so that she could see the backyard, he left to go out on patrol.

Look at the view I have. Snow covered green lawns and beautiful trees. Mountains in the distance. I can even see a swimming pool and a gazebo from here, thought Katelyn.

Knowing how lucky she was to be able to have such a grand house to live in, Katelyn knew she would always appreciate it and never take it for granted.

Knocking at her door, Susan said, "Can I come in?"

Katelyn jumped.

Of course you can come in. This is your home, thought Katelyn.

"Yes I know, but it's polite to knock first... let's go. I am going to give you a tour of the house. And after the tour, I am going to introduce you to your physiotherapist, and speech therapist. They will both be able to help you on a daily basis to speak and do some things eventually for yourself," said Susan.

Thank you, thought Katelyn. She didn't know what else to say. It was all so overwhelming to her.

Susan wheeled Katelyn around the house explaining each room in detail. The snow seemed to hold off too, as she also took her outside and showed her around the gardens and the swimming pool.

The more time Katelyn spent with Susan, the more she noticed that she always felt really good when she was in Susan's presence. She wasn't sure what it was about Susan, but she felt alive whenever Susan was near her or touched her.

Walking toward the house, Susan said "I think I just heard someone driving up to the house. I would say it is your physiotherapist and speech therapist. Let's go and meet them," said Susan, pushing Katelyn's wheelchair up the back ramp and inside.

"Come in ladies," said Susan, opening the front door. "Debbie, Wendy, I would like to introduce you to, Katelyn."

Stepping inside, Debbie said, "Hello Katelyn. Nice to meet you finally."

Can they hear me too? asked Katelyn to Susan.

"Yes," nodded Susan.

Nice to meet you too, Debbie, thought Katelyn.

"Hello Katelyn. My name is Wendy and I am pleased to meet you. Susan has told me a lot about you," said Wendy, hugging Katelyn.

Hi Wendy. Nice to meet you as well, thought Katelyn.

"Well, let's go inside and we can talk about what is going to happen," said Susan, pushing Katelyn towards the lounge room.

Debbie and Wendy sat on the couch across from Katelyn and Susan. Before they started to speak about their plan of attack for Katelyn, Susan said, "Would you ladies like a cup of coffee?"

"Yes, please," they both said together.

As Susan poured the drinks, Debbie said, "Tomorrow I will be starting physio exercise with you in a specially designed room upstairs. Also we will be doing some swimming exercise in the swimming pool outside, when it's a bit warmer. This will give you strength in your whole body and will stop your muscles from withering away. You will probably be sore most days and I am not going to lie, it will definitely hurt, but it will be worth the pain you will go through to become independent."

Swallowing hard, Katelyn thought, *Ok*.

Now she was nervous.

"Then I will be teaching you how to speak properly. We will start with the alphabet and once you have that down pat, I will teach you how to read books, and so forth," said Wendy, smiling at Katelyn.

This all sounds a bit scary. But I am looking forward to be able to do some things for myself for a change, thought Katelyn, looking from Debbie to Wendy to Susan.

"Debbie and Wendy will be boarding here at the house whilst you need the physio and speech therapy. I am sure you will get through this Katelyn. We are all here to help you," said Susan.

Thank you. I appreciate all your help, thought Katelyn.

After Debbie and Wendy left the lounge room to get settled into the house, Susan said, "What about if we go and see Zoe? You can tell her what types of food you like to eat!"

Mmm, my favourite topic - food, thought Katelyn.

Susan pushed Katelyn towards the kitchen, and as they approached the doorway, the aromas wafting from the kitchen sent Katelyn's senses into a frenzy. Entering the kitchen, Katelyn thought, *What is that nice smell?*

"I am cooking a roast lamb dinner for you, my dear. I hope you like it," said Zoe.

One of my many favourite foods. What time is dinner? thought Katelyn.

"It's at seven o'clock and we all eat together, in the dining room," said Zoe.

I can't wait. That smell is making me hungry already, thought Katelyn.

"Let me get a pen and paper and I will write a list of what things you like to eat and drink, my dear. I can go shopping for the items we don't have this afternoon," said Zoe, walking over to the drawer.

Am I going to wake up from the best dream I have ever had? I can't believe all the opportunities I am being given and how nice everyone is to me, thought Katelyn, as the tears welled in her eyes.

"Do you remember wishing for this to happen?" said Susan.

Yes, I do actually, thought Katelyn.

"Well... what you don't know is that I was listening and that's when I decided that you are the one who needs my help the most. I want you to have a good start in life, Katelyn. When you were at that disabled children's home I could see that it was not going to happen there. They never had enough staff to cope with looking after everyone, so it then meant that you were not looked after correctly," said Susan.

I can't thank you enough Susan and one day I will repay your kindness; I promise, thought Katelyn.

"By just growing into a healthy and happy young lady, is all I ask," said Susan, bending down and giving her a hug.

"So... what sort of foods do you like, Katelyn?" asked Zoe.

I like most foods. Except for Brussels sprouts or mangoes, thought Katelyn.

"You are easy to please, my dear," said Zoe.

"Zoe cooks all our meals here. She also does the food shopping. So if you want anything different you just need to let Zoe know and she will get it for you," said Susan.

Ok, thought Katelyn.

"Well... now that that is all sorted, we might get you bathed and ready for dinner," said Susan.

Ok. See you later on, Zoe, thought Katelyn.

"Yes, I will see you later," said Zoe.

Katelyn was used to going to bed straight after dinner each night at the children's home, and tonight was no different. She was overwhelmed and exhausted from all the events of the day.

Thank you for a lovely day, thought Katelyn to Susan, as she tucked her in.

"You are most welcome," said Susan. "Would you like to sleep with a light on tonight? Or will you be all right in the dark?"

I will be all right in the dark. I am used to it, thought Katelyn.

"Ok. See you in the morning," said Susan, leaning into to give Katelyn a kiss good night on her forehead.

Good night, Susan, thought Katelyn, hugging her back and smiling.

When the light was turned off and the bedroom door was shut completely, Katelyn lay in her comfortable bed looking up at the ceiling. She was tired, but her mind was racing with all the events of the day.

I wish I had a body and mouth that worked. I can't wait for tomorrow, so I can start my treatment, thought Katelyn, anxiously.

Eventually drifting off to sleep, Katelyn dreamed of what her life would be like, now that she had a family that loved her and wanted to take care of her. Finally, her life had taken a turn for the better and she was glad about that.

Chapter Three

Katelyn woke to the sound of knocking at her door.

"Good morning, sleepyhead. How about we get you up and have some breakfast?" said Susan, walking over to Katelyn.

Yawning, Katelyn thought, *Ok. What time is it?*

"It's 8.40. How did you sleep?" said Susan, sitting on the bed.

Good, thanks. This bed is so much better than the one I had at the children's home. So comfortable, thought Katelyn.

"That's great… today is the first day of your treatment plan, my dear. We had better get you bathed, dressed and get some food into you so you are ready for Debbie and Wendy," said Susan.

I am looking forward to it, thought Katelyn.

After breakfast Wendy found Katelyn and Susan in the library. "Are you ready to start your speech therapy today, Katelyn?" asked Wendy.

Katelyn grinned and thought, *Yep. Can't wait to start.*

"I will leave you both to it," said Susan, watching Wendy set up her class with Katelyn.

"Ok… do you know any of the alphabet?" asked Wendy.

Yes. But my mouth won't let the sounds come out so that people can understand me, thought Katelyn.

"Right… from now on, you are not allowed to mind talk to me. When you speak with me, I want you to use your mouth only," said Wendy.

Ok, I will try thought Katelyn.

Pushing Katelyn over to a table, Wendy sat next to her and placed a book in front of Katelyn that had the alphabet in it. Each page had one letter. "Let's start. I want you to listen and watch how my mouth says a letter. Then I want you to try and say that letter too. It's a case of getting your tongue and lips to sound it out," said Wendy.

Katelyn nodded.

By the time their two hours of speech therapy was up, Katelyn was able to sound out some of the letters with her mouth. She knew it wasn't going to be easy, but she was willing to give it a go.

"You did very well today Katelyn. I am very proud of you. Tomorrow we will go over these letters of the alphabet you have learnt today again and also learn some new ones. Each day we will do the same, until you can sound out all the letters of the alphabet. From there, we will go onto words," said Wendy.

"Thank... you," said Katelyn, plainly. Smiling, she felt proud of herself for pronouncing the words correctly, instead of thinking it.

"It looks like you ladies are finished in here," said Zoe, walking into the library.

"We sure have," said Wendy.

"I have come to let you both know that lunch is ready, actually," said Zoe.

"Ok. I just need to pack everything up and then I will meet you both in the dining room," said Wendy.

"No problem. I can take you down to the dining room, Katelyn," said Zoe.

"Ok," said Katelyn.

"Well done, Katelyn. First words are always the hardest, you know. How did your first session go with Wendy?" asked Zoe, walking to the dining room.

Thanks... yeah, I can only say a few letters so far. But I am looking forward to doing some more tomorrow. Wendy told me that I did really well today, thought Katelyn.

"Excellent... we are having fish and vegetables today. Let's get you set up for lunch," said Zoe, pressing the brake on Katelyn's wheelchair at the table.

Katelyn noticed that the dining table was set up for more than two people and wondered who else was having lunch with them today.

"Hello Katelyn," said Mark, as he entered the dining room and sat in the seat next to her.

Hi Mark, thought Katelyn. *Who else is having lunch with us today?*

"Everyone eats together for lunch and dinner in this house," said Mark.

Oh. Ok, thought Katelyn.

"How did your speech therapy go this morning?" asked Mark.

It went well, thought Katelyn.

Soon enough, the long table was full. Katelyn loved to be able to eat and have a conversation at the same time with other people. She still had to pinch herself, as to how lucky she was to be living in such a beautiful house with wonderful people.

After lunch was finished, Debbie found Katelyn up in her room, sitting next to the window in her wheelchair.

"Are you ready to make a start on your physio therapy, Katelyn?" asked Debbie.

Sure, thought Katelyn.

Debbie wheeled her into the room that had been specially designed for Katelyn to do her physio in each day, which was on the ground floor of the house. It was set up with all types of equipment for Katelyn to use. The first machine that Debbie carried her over to was a walker. Strapping her in, so Katelyn was in a standing position, Debbie showed Katelyn how to use the machine.

"This actually helps you build the muscles in your legs back up," said Debbie, helping with the movement of the machine legs.

Feels strange, thought Katelyn.

"Yeah, it probably will at first. But you will get used to it," said Debbie.

Next Debbie concentrated on the upper half of her body with another machine. "This one helps to build up her strength in your arms and back, so that you will eventually be able to wheel yourself around in the wheelchair and at least get yourself dressed."

After an hour of intense physio Debbie could see Katelyn was getting tired.

"What about if we call it quits for today? We don't want to make your muscles too sore for our next session," said Debbie.

"Ok," said Katelyn, quickly.

Debbie looked at her with wide eyes and said, "You spoke."

Smiling, Katelyn thought, *I can only say a few words at the moment.*

"You will get there. Actually you did really well today in the physio. Well done," said Debbie.

Thanks, thought Katelyn.

"It's a lovely day outside. Why don't I take you out there and we can catch up with Susan?" said Debbie.

"Ok," said Katelyn.

Placing her back in the wheelchair, she pushed Katelyn outside to the shaded gardens, where they found Susan.

"How was your therapy today, dear?" asked Susan.

It was really hard, Susan. I am feeling a bit sore now. But I know it will be all worth it in the end. I'm just going to take every day as it comes, thought Katelyn.

"That's the right attitude to have, Katelyn. You keep that type of thinking up and it won't take long at all before you can do most things for yourself," said Susan.

I am looking forward to that day, thought Katelyn.

"Well, I might leave you ladies to chat. I will see you both at dinner. Bye," said Debbie.

"See you later Deb," said Susan looking at her watch. "Hmm, where has the day gone...? We had better get you bathed and dressed for dinner."

Katelyn looked at Susan and thought to herself, *wow she is such a lovely person to have as a foster mom.*

Frowning Susan said, "Do you consider me to be your foster mom?"

Yes I do. Well, isn't that what you are to me? thought Katelyn. She had forgotten, for one moment, that Susan could read all of her thoughts.

"I never thought of it like that. I just thought I would be a foster carer to you, Katelyn. I never thought you would think of me as your mom," said Susan.

Well I do think of you as my foster mom. I love you, very much, thought Katelyn.

Susan bent down and hugged her.

"I love you too, Katelyn. And I am hoping to give you a great life here with me, so that one day you can grow to be an independent, healthy, happy adult," said Susan, who was overwhelmed, but at the same time glad to be called Katelyn's mom.

Chapter Four

Fifteen Years Later

As the years went by, Katelyn learned, with a lot of hard work and determination, that she could achieve anything. With Susan by her side, she endured many hours of pain and frustration and eventually learnt how to speak with her mouth, and use her upper body. But for some reason which was unknown to Susan - a Lepidoptera healer - Katelyn still couldn't walk without assistance.

It had been fifteen years since Katelyn had come to live with Susan and the others. It had been a dream come true for her. As she sat waiting for her final class to finish for the term, her mind wandered back to what life had been like since she left the disabled children's home in Berne and went to live with Susan: learning to eat and drink, the long drive to Susan's house, learning to read and write, physio, Susan officially adopting her when she turned ten years old, puberty, college, and now university. She sure had been through a lot and come a long way since then.

It was her last day at university before they broke up for the year. Katelyn only had one more year left of her course. She was studying to become a psychiatrist, and then, with the help of Susan, she was looking forward to starting up her own practice.

"See you when I get back, Fiona," said Katelyn, waiting in the university parking lot to get picked up by Wynton.

"Have a good time on your holiday to Bagnolet, Kate. I sure will miss your ugly mug," teased Fiona, giving her a hug.

"Yeah, I will miss you too," said Katelyn, hugging her back. "I am so excited about going. I have never been out of Switzerland before. Mom has family and friends in Bagnolet, and it will be nice to finally meet them."

"France… they say it is a romantic country. So you never know," said Fiona, smiling.

"Yeah right. Maybe for you. But I don't think any man is going to look twice at me, Fiona," said Katelyn.

"You never know," teased Fiona. "Anyway, looks like my ride is here. So take care, babe."

"Bye," said Katelyn, watching her best friend walk away.

Arriving home, Wynton helped Katelyn out the car and into her wheelchair. Entering the house, Susan was waiting for her. "Hello, sweetheart. How was your last day?"

"Great. There weren't many lectures today, so I mostly sat around chatting to my friends. I can't believe I only have one year to go before I graduate. Scary hey, how fast time has gone?" said Katelyn.

"Sure is," said Susan, thinking back to when she first met Katelyn in the disabled children's home. "Sweetheart, you will have to excuse me. I just need to make a call to the Gramaze house, so I can let William know what time we are landing. He is organising for a car to collect us from the airport. I will catch up with you later on."

"No problem. I have lots of packing to do anyway. See you later on then," said Katelyn.

"Would you like a lift upstairs, Katelyn," asked Mark, walking past them.

"Yes, please," said Katelyn.

Once they were at the top of the stairs, Mark placed her wheelchair on the marble landing, so that Katelyn could wheel herself to her bedroom. Ever since her upper body had gained strength, she always like to do things for herself.

"I will be back soon to collect your bags," said Mark.

"Ok. Thanks for the lift, bro," said Katelyn, wheeling toward her bedroom door. Over the years, Katelyn had grown very close to Mark, and he had become like a brother to her. He was always there for her as a friend, confidant, and protector.

Showering and finalising the outfits and shoes she was taking on holidays, Katelyn shut the suitcase lid and zipped it up. Even though Katelyn was a quiet, academic woman, she still liked the latest fashion and makeup, to make her look good.

"Knock, knock," said Mark.

"Come in," said Katelyn.

"Bags all packed?" asked Mark.

"Yep. You can take them now," said Katelyn.

Picking her two suit cases up, Mark said, "Bloody hell… what do you have in here? A lump of lead?"

"A girl can never have too many clothes and shoes to match you know, when we are on holidays," scoffed Katelyn.

"Females… I will never understand you all," said Mark, walking out with the bags shaking his head.

Knocking on her door, Susan said, "You all ready to go, Katelyn?"

"Yes, Mom. What time does the plane leave for France?" said Katelyn, excited.

"It leaves in about three hours. So we need to get moving," said Susan.

Checked in and waiting for the airline to say they could board the plane, Katelyn said, "How long is the fight?"

"It's only one hour, dear. Then it's about another hour to Bagnolet from the airport. Shouldn't take us long at all," said Susan.

"I can't wait to meet your family and friends, Mom. I'm looking forward to some sightseeing as well," said Katelyn. She was looking forward to hearing some stories about them, too. Their world really intrigued her.

"They are looking forward to meeting you too, sweetheart," said Susan, remembering back to the day when she told Katelyn all about the Gramaze family and friends in Bagnolet and how long she had known them all.

By then Katelyn had already figured out that all the people who lived in her house where Lepidoptera vampires anyway. She always thought it was strange that they could all read her thoughts, but never wondered why, until one day when Mark was injured in an attack by a Debauched vampire. When Susan had to heal him with her powers, it was then that Katelyn was informed about their race and world. Over the years, Katelyn had come to accept it.

Taking her seat on the plane, Katelyn could feel her stomach doing somersaults. Checking the pocket of the seat in front of her, she looked for the sick bag. She had never been in a plane, let alone flown before, and it was making her feel nervous.

Susan took her seat next to Katelyn and watched how she was dealing with the thought of flying. Placing her hand over

Katelyn's, she said, "Don't worry, dear. We won't be in the air long. Just try breathing in and out slowly."

"Thanks, Mom," said Katelyn, putting her head on Susan's shoulder.

Susan was right, the plane flight didn't take long at all and before they knew it, they were in the limo and driving to Bagnolet.

Katelyn noticed that Susan was quiet in the car, as she watched her look off into the distance, through the window.

"Everything Ok, Mom?" asked Katelyn.

"Huh... yes, sweetheart, everything is fine. I was just thinking about the last time I was as the Gramaze house."

"Oh. Ok."

"Yeah, the last time I visited them was when William was drugged by the Debauched vampires and he started to lose all of his abilities. It sure was a scary time for William and his coven. Fortunately, I was able to heal him."

"Right... so he is still a Lepidoptera now?"

"Yes. He was totally healed by the time I left. And according to the phone call I had with William earlier today, things seem to be going well there now. I haven't seen them all in such a long time and I am looking forward to catching up on all the gossip," said Susan, smiling.

"Oh. Ok," said Katelyn, nodding.

Pulling up to the front gates of the Gramaze house, Katelyn watched the driver punch the code into the key pad. When the gates opened and they drove through, Katelyn said, "Their house is similar to ours on the outside."

"Yes. All Lepidoptera houses are somewhat lavish, dear," said Susan.

"But I think that this beautiful house and grounds are impressive; not that ours aren't," said Katelyn, looking through the driver's window as they approached the house.

"Wait until you see the inside; it's just as lovely," said Susan.

When the car came to a stop at the front doors of the house, Katelyn noticed Renee and William, who she recognised from photos, were waiting for them. Once Mark helped Katelyn out of the car and put her into the wheelchair, Susan introduced them.

"Katelyn, this is Mr. and Mrs. Gramaze," said Susan.

"Please just call us Renee and William. It's so nice to finally meet you, Katelyn. Susan has told us so much about you over the years. Come inside and meet our family," said Renee.

"Hello, Katelyn," said William, as he put his hand out in front of him for her to shake.

Holding her hand out, Katelyn shook Renee and William's hands. "Hello. It's nice to meet you both."

"How are you, my friend?" said William, shaking Susan's hand.

"Good. Thank you for asking," said Susan, smiling. "You have met Mark and Connor before, haven't you?"

"Yes. Come in, my good friends," said William.

Renee and Susan linked their arms and walked inside together. They certainly had a lot to catch up on, not having seen each other for years. Renee would always be grateful to Susan for saving her partner's life and his abilities years previously.

"Would you like me to push you inside, Katelyn?" asked Mark.

"Yes, please. Thank you," said Katelyn, looking up at Mark. Following them inside, she couldn't help but notice what a beautiful house they had.

Standing in the foyer, William introduced each of his coven. "Katelyn, this is Annabelle, Grayson, Samantha, Christian, Danielle, Lamiae, Michael, Violette, Temperance, Sherrie, and Nicky," said William, pointing to each of them as he said their names. They all shook Katelyn's hand and also gave a warm welcoming hug to their old friends Susan, Mark and Connor.

"Deveron, Brock and James are out on patrol at the moment and you should be able meet them all later on," said Renee.

"Ok. Wow, there sure are a lot of people that live here," said Katelyn, with her eyebrows raised.

"Yes, dear. We are one big family," said Renee. "Lamiae will show you all to your rooms upstairs, if you like, and the chauffeur will bring the bags up to you soon."

"Thanks, Renee," said Susan. "Mark, could you please carry Katelyn upstairs for me."

"Yes, Susan," said Mark.

"I can take Katelyn up to her room, if you like. I was going to ask Katelyn anyway if I could show her around the house," said Annabelle.

"That sounds great, Annabelle. Thanks," said Katelyn, smiling.

Susan nodded and smiled at Annabelle.

After Annabelle and Katelyn hung Katelyn clothes in the wardrobe, and placed other items into drawers, Annabelle said, "You ready...? Let's go."

"Ready when you are," said Katelyn.

As Annabelle was showing Katelyn around the house, Michael and Violette found them.

"Hey, Katelyn... we were wondering if maybe tomorrow night you would like to come and see the sights of Paris with us? It's just that the view at night is more breathtaking than during the daytime," said Michael.

"Sounds cool. I would love to," said Katelyn, smiling. "What time tomorrow night did you want to go?"

"How about after we all have dinner; would that be Ok?" said Michael.

"I am looking forward to it. Mom said we were staying for about four weeks, so what is there to do and see around here?" said Katelyn.

"There is plenty to do and see. You won't be bored that's for sure," said Annabelle. "Actually guys, I can hear Lamiae saying dinner is ready. Hope you are hungry Katelyn, as Lamiae has cooked something special for your visit."

'Cool. I am starving," said Katelyn.

Wheeling into the dining room, Katelyn couldn't help but notice the long wooden table and how it was set up for dinner with fine white china plates, silver cutlery and crystal-clear glasses. It all looked so elegant.

Taking their places at the table, Katelyn noticed three other guys walking into the room that she hadn't met yet. William then introduced them as Deveron, Brock and James.

Taking a chair next to Katelyn, Deveron said, "Hello. Nice to meet you Katelyn."

"Hi Deveron. Nice to meet you too. How was it out there on patrol tonight?" said Katelyn.

Frowning, he said, "Not too bad... so... you know what we are and do, then?"

"Yeah. Mom has informed me about you all," said Katelyn.

"Oh. Ok," said Deveron. He was a bit puzzled as to why a human would be told about the Lepidoptera coven.

Katelyn enjoyed the attention Deveron was paying her over dinner. Most boys throughout her life had been nice to Katelyn but had never wanted to spend time getting to know her.

Wow... Deveron is really easy to talk with, thought Katelyn.

"Thanks," said Deveron.

"What...," said Katelyn, frowning and wondering what he was talking about. It then hit her. "Please don't read my thoughts. That's rude."

"Sorry. I didn't mean to invade your thoughts. It's just I am not used to having someone around who can't stop me from hearing their thoughts," said Deveron.

"You mean you can't read anyone else's thoughts in the room without them letting you?" said Katelyn, with raised eyebrows.

"That's correct," said Deveron, nodding.

"Hmm... I wish I could do that sometimes. It sure would come in handy," said Katelyn.

He chuckled and said, "How long are you here for Katelyn?"

"About four weeks, I believe," said Katelyn.

"I will have to make sure you have some fun whilst you are here," said Deveron.

"Thanks Deveron. You are too kind. I know you are busy with patrols and everything. So please don't let me get in your way," said Katelyn.

"You are not in my way and I wouldn't ask if I didn't want to see you have some fun," said Deveron.

"Oh... Ok. Thanks. Actually, Violette, Michael and Annabelle are taking me out to see the sights tomorrow night. Would you like to come with us?" said Katelyn.

"I will have to check with William first to make sure that is Ok. We have patrols each night, and he would have to find someone else to take my place if I don't go. I will ask William now if you like," said Deveron.

Before Katelyn even got another word in. Deveron said, "William has just said yes to me going with you tomorrow night. So yes, I would love to come."

"Cool," said Katelyn, high-fiving him.

"What are you doing tomorrow?" asked Deveron.

"I am not sure. I haven't spoken with Mom yet," said Katelyn.

"I am going to play a soccer game at the park and I was wondering if you would like to come and watch?" said Deveron.

"Sure. I would love to go," said Katelyn. "What time are you all going?"

"I think around four o'clock in the afternoon," said Deveron.

Mom, Deveron has asked if I would like to go to a soccer game tomorrow and also Michael, Violette and Annabelle have asked me to go sightseeing tomorrow night. Is this Ok with you? thought Katelyn.

Susan looked at Katelyn across the table and nodded yes to her.

"Thanks, Mom," Katelyn mouthed.

Susan just smiled at Katelyn because she had been listening to her thoughts and she knew what she was going to ask anyway.

"Mom has said that it's fine for me to go, but I'm sure you heard that," said Katelyn turning to Deveron.

"Yep, I heard. That's great," said Deveron. "Well, I must go have a shower and get changed out of these patrol clothes."

"Catch up with you later on, Deveron," said Katelyn.

"Sure," said Deveron, standing.

After dinner, they all went into the sitting room for some refreshments.

"How is your health now, William?" asked Susan.

"Good, thanks to you," said William. "It only seems like yesterday since that happened. I was lucky to have you around, to heal me, Susan. The drugs they injected into me nearly cost me my abilities and my future."

"Yes. I remember how badly you were treated by the Debauched. Do you still have much trouble with them these days?" asked Susan.

"Nothing we can't handle here," said William.

"That's good, my friend," said Susan.

As the night went on, Katelyn listened closely to all the adventures the Gramaze family and Susan had gone through. She found it enlightening and couldn't get enough of their stories. Even the gory details didn't seem to scare her; they only made her more interested in the Lepidoptera vampires' way of life.

Chapter Five

Pulling on his denim jeans and white t-shirt, Deveron took a quick look in the mirror. With blue eyes looking back at him, he flexed his biceps up and down to see what they looked like. Pleased with his body, he then decided to give his messy brown hair a comb and splash on some cologne.

Remembering his conversations tonight at the table with Katelyn, he smiled. He still couldn't believe that after all these years, a girl could make him feel special.

She certainly is a heavenly sight, thought Deveron.

Knowing the Lepidoptera laws on interaction between humans and vampires, he also knew he wouldn't be able to pursue Katelyn even if he did like her.

Feeling a bit sluggish from the workout he'd had with a Debauched vamp tonight on patrol, Deveron decided to go down to the kitchen and get some blood out of the back fridge. Heading down the stairs at vampire speed, he heard Katelyn's voice in the sitting room. Even the sound of her voice excited him immensely. How was he going to be able to keep his distance from her for four weeks, let alone keep his thoughts to himself? If William ever found out he liked Katelyn, even from afar, there would be hell to pay. Continuing onto the kitchen, he found Lamiae in there cleaning up.

"Good evening, Lamiae," said Deveron.

"Hello, Deveron. What can I get you?" asked Lamiae.

"Nothing. Thanks, Lamiae. I have come to get a drink," said Deveron, walking over to the fridge.

"Oh. Ok. Katelyn seems very nice, doesn't she?" said Lamiae.

"Yep," said Deveron, trying not to give away how he felt an instant attraction to her.

"You are going to have to try harder than that, Deveron," said Lamiae, smiling at him.

"Huh," scoffed Deveron, swallowing hard.

"I saw you tonight at the table. You were drooling all over her. Luckily William didn't notice," said Lamiae, with one eyebrow raised. "Don't worry, your secret is safe with me."

"Are we sure she is human, Lamiae?" asked Deveron.

"Why do you ask?" said Lamiae.

"It's… well… as soon as I met Katelyn, I felt we had some sort of connection. Strange I know… if she was a Lepidoptera then I would understand the attraction," said Deveron, sitting down at the island bench in front of Lamiae.

"Why don't you ask her? Or better yet, ask Susan," said Lamiae.

"Mmm, I'll think about," said Deveron, confused as to what to do. "Well, I will see you later, Lamiae. Mum's the word, hey."

Lamiae put her finger to her mouth and gestured that her mouth was a zipper.

When Deveron entered the sitting room, he looked at Katelyn and their eyes met straight away. Smiling and trying to be polite, Katelyn wheeled over to where Deveron stood.

"Feel better now?" asked Katelyn.

You certainly look better. Mmm hot body or what? thought Katelyn.

"Sure do," said Deveron, trying not to read her thoughts.

Slapping herself, she thought, *Stop that Katelyn. You don't even know this guy yet. He wouldn't look at you either as you are in a wheelchair. You're just friends. Oh shit… I just remembered… he can read my thoughts.*

"Would like to go outside? The nights here are nice and warm at the moment and we have a great view out the back of the house," said Deveron.

"Ok. That would be nice, Deveron," said Katelyn.

"Would you like me to push you, or…" asked Deveron.

"No, that's Ok. I can wheel myself. You lead the way," said Katelyn.

Susan watched Deveron and Katelyn leave the room.

Following him through the house, she thought, *What a nice gesture to ask me if I wanted to do something with him.*

The glass sliding doors at the back of the house were already wide open when they arrived. Wheeling outside into the warm night air with Deveron, Katelyn's face lit up when she noticed how beautiful and the clear night sky was, with the stars shining brightly.

"Beautiful, isn't it?" stated Deveron. "If I ever have a bad day or need to cheer up I always come out here at night and this does the job."

"Wow… I can't believe how clear it is. Really beautiful. Thank you for bringing me out here. You are so lucky to have this," said Katelyn, watching the stars twinkle in the black night sky.

"You are welcome," said Deveron, kneeling beside her. Mesmerized by her beautiful smile, he couldn't help himself, he had to tell her. "By the way Katelyn… I wanted to tell you that I was listening to what you were thinking in there. About how I wouldn't look at you because you are in a wheelchair. Well, you have that wrong."

Her cheeks turned crimson red, and she didn't know where to look.

"You heard what I thought? I keep forgetting about that. God, I am so embarrassed," said Katelyn.

"Don't feel embarrassed. For the record… if I didn't want to spend time with you, then I wouldn't. You are a beautiful lady, Katelyn and… well… I want to get to know you more," said Deveron.

"Thanks… I too would like to get to know you some more. It's just… it has taken me all of my life to get to where I am now. I probably will never be able to get out of this wheelchair and walk. So you see, for me when a guy takes interest in me, I am not sure if he likes me as just a friend or if maybe after a while he really would love me, for just me. Do you know what I mean?" said Katelyn, nervously fidgeting with her fingers.

"Yes. I am now starting to realise why you were thinking the way you were inside. I must apologise for reading your thoughts again, Katelyn. It's pretty rude," said Deveron.

"That's Ok. Can we just forget about all that? I would love to spend some time with you Deveron, and get to know you more," said Katelyn.

"Sounds good. Would you like to step out of your chair and sit over there next to me?" said Deveron, pointing to a cozy, wood paneled, double seat that had cushions on it.

Katelyn felt her heart skip a beat, and her hands became sweaty. "Are you sure you want to do that with me, Deveron?" asked Katelyn.

Deveron didn't listen to her answer, he just scooped her up into his arms and carried her over to the double chair.

"Does that answer your question?" said Deveron, smiling.

Fumbling with her fingers in her lap, she looked up, to see him staring into her eyes. Quickly looking away, she thought, *I would love to kiss those sweet lips.* With her stomach doing somersaults, she glanced back at him for a second.

Reading her thoughts, he leaned into her and put his arm around her shoulder.

With her mind racing, she gulped, and leaned into his muscular body. Placing her head on his shoulder, she breathed in his scent: peach.

Why would he want me? thought Katelyn.

Deveron quickly pulled away and said, "How could you be so self-doubting? You are such a beautiful lady; no matter if you are in a wheelchair or not. So please don't think that I am playing games here, because I am not. To tell you the truth, Katelyn, ever since I walked into the house tonight and sat down beside you, I have had this pulling feeling toward you. Even when I was in the shower tonight I couldn't stop thinking about our conversations... can I ask you something?"

"Yes. What is it?" said Katelyn, looking into his deep blue eyes.

"Are you sure you are not a Lepidoptera vampire?" said Deveron.

Puzzled by what Deveron had just asked her, she said, "I am quite sure I am human. Why do you ask?"

"Well... it's just that our kind don't ever feel this way about someone unless they are turning or are going to be Lepidoptera vampire," said Deveron. "Can I see the back of your neck, Katelyn?"

"What... why do you want to look at the back of my neck?" asked Katelyn.

"If you are going to turn into a Lepidoptera vampire, then your butterfly tattoo will start to appear," said Deveron.

Frowning, and wondering what in the world he was talking about, she decided to turn around, and lifted her hair up off her neck.

"Well?"

"Katelyn it's..."

But he was interrupted by Susan, before he could get another word out.

"I think we should get you back inside, Katelyn," said

Susan, from behind them.

How could you, Deveron? thought Susan, as she stood in front of them, scowling at Deveron.

Deveron was startled by Susan's voice. Looking embarrassed, like he had been caught out doing something he was not meant to be doing, he bowed his head to Susan.

"What is going on? I know you too are mind talking to each other and I want to hear what you are saying," said Katelyn, annoyed, as she looked from Susan to Deveron with a creased brow.

"We will take this inside and talk about it in there, Katelyn," said Susan sternly.

"No… I want to know, right now. And stop treating me like a child, because I am a grown adult now," said Katelyn.

"Can I tell her?" said Deveron, looking at Susan.

Her nostrils flared, but she eventually nodded. "Yes."

"Katelyn… you have the outline of a butterfly tattoo showing on the back of your neck. Which means you are a Lepidoptera vampire. This only comes out at first when you are attracted to a male Lepidoptera," said Deveron.

"Is this true, Mom? Wait… don't answer that… you have known all along, haven't you, that I was a Lepidoptera vampire?" said Katelyn, heatedly.

"Yes. But I only wanted to protect you from this life. That is why I have never said anything to you," said Susan, with a creased brow.

"Sorry, Deveron… would you mind if I catch up with you tomorrow, sometime?" said Katelyn. "I need to go upstairs with my mom and have a chat about this first."

"Sure…" said Deveron, standing. "I will see you tomorrow, beautiful lady."

Susan helped Katelyn back into her wheelchair, and they headed upstairs to Katelyn's bedroom.

"I want the truth, Mom. Don't sugarcoat it. Am I really a Lepidoptera vampire?" asked Katelyn.

Sitting on the bed, Susan rubbed her hands over her face. Taking a deep breath, she said, "Yes, you are a Lepidoptera. And yes, I knew you were from the very first day I met you at the children's home."

"Why would you leave it until now to tell me?" asked Katelyn.

"Well… I think that is obvious. Don't you?" said Susan.

"You mean, Deveron?"

"Yes. But let me start at the beginning, when you were born. Come over here, my dear," said Susan, patting the bed.

Wheeling her chair over to the bed, Katelyn sat in front of Susan and listened with uncertainty, about how a Lepidoptera is born, from the queen, Talitha, and that she was given up at birth.

"But if that is true, then why did I end up in a children's home? And how did I end up being disabled? Something is not adding up here. What aren't you telling me, Mom?" said Katelyn, with her brow furrowed.

"I can answer that," said Queen Talitha, as she walked into the room.

Susan immediately stood up, and bowed her head.

"My queen."

"Sit down, my child," Talitha gestured to Susan to sit on the bed again.

Katelyn eyes widened. Mesmerised, she watched her take a seat on the bed in front of her. Gulping, she thought, *Wow… so beautiful. Regal.*

"Hello, my child. My name is Talitha. I am your birth mother."

Frowning, Katelyn took a moment to comprehend.

"Birth mother… was I born like this?" said Katelyn, indicating to her disabled body and the wheelchair.

"No, my child, you were not," said Talitha, taking her hand. "The night you left here with Sister Mongose, there was no indication that you wouldn't be able to walk and talk when you got older. The Debauched... well, they did this to you. Basically they ran the nun down and... well...you were in her arms... oh my... I shudder every time I think of this. Your injuries were so bad, that you became disabled. And it wasn't until Susan found you that we even knew you had survived."

Her breathing quickened, and she started to shake, as Katelyn tried to understand and take in everything the queen was telling her.

"If this is true, then why am I still disabled? I mean, I know Susan is a healer, so why can't she heal my injuries? Why am I stuck in this god-forsaken chair?" said Katelyn, trying to hold back the tears, that had now welled in her eyes.

"We are not sure, my child. Usually if one of us is injured, we heal fast. But you... well... I am not sure," said Talitha. "Maybe it might happen, now that you have found your life partner."

"Life partner... can you please explain what that is?" asked Katelyn, as she pulled her hand away from the queen's.

"I believe you have met Deveron," said Talitha.

"Yes, but what does he have to do with this?" asked Katelyn.

"Everything, my dear... tell me, did you feel an instant attraction towards him as soon as you met?" asked Talitha.

"Yes. He is the first man to show any interest in me," said Katelyn. Reality then hit her. "You mean Deveron is my life partner?"

"Yes," said Talitha. She then explained to Katelyn that she wouldn't turn into a Lepidoptera vampire unless she had sex with Deveron.

"Oh, right... well... I don't think that is going to happen," said Katelyn matter-of-factly.

Raising her eyebrows, Talitha said, "Never say never, dear... anyway, I must return to my home. You are welcome to come and see me anytime, my child." Standing, she placed her hand on Susan's shoulder. "Keep her safe, my child."

"Yes, my queen," said Susan.

"Good night," said Talitha, as she walked towards the doorway.

"Bye," said Katelyn. "It was nice meeting you."

"Good night, my queen," said Susan, watching her walk out the room.

"Are you Ok?" asked Susan to Katelyn.

"I think so... at least I now know how I became disabled. And I always wondered why you picked me out, over all the other disabled children at the home, and now I know why," said Katelyn.

"It wasn't the only reason I picked you out, over the other children. I felt a connection with you, Katelyn. And, well, I had always wanted a daughter of my own, and the more I spent time with you, the more I started to love you, and wanted to take care of you. Does that make sense?"

"Yeah, it does," said Katelyn, leaning forward to give Susan a hug.

"I was hoping that this wouldn't happen to you yet, Katelyn. Don't get me wrong; I am happy that you have found your life partner, Deveron. But it doesn't change the fact that I am so fearful for you," said Susan, hugging her back.

"Mom, I know you love me and only want what's best for me, but you need to let me live my own life and make my own decisions. I know being a Lepidoptera vampire is not what you want for me yet; but if it's meant to be then we should just let it. Life always has a way of sorting itself out eventually," said Katelyn, pulling away from their embrace slowly.

"Oh, Katelyn… how you have grown up into such a headstrong woman. I am sorry if I am holding you back from life, but I just don't want to lose you," said Susan.

"You won't lose me, Mom. I am always going to be here and I'm still your little girl," said Katelyn, hugging her.

"But how do you feel about becoming a Lepidoptera?" said Susan, pulling away from Katelyn and looking her in the eyes.

"Anxious… scared… worried… all of the above. I think as long as I have you to help me through it, Mom, then I will be all right. I don't know how I will feel about drinking blood though. Yuk. The thought of it grosses me out," said Katelyn, swallowing hard.

"You will be all right. And yes, I will be here to help you with anything at all. I love you so much, my dear daughter, and would do anything to see you happy," said Susan.

"Thanks, Mom… I am feeling a bit tired now, so I think I will go to bed, if that's all right," said Katelyn.

"Ok, my dear. As long as you are going to be all right?" said Susan, worried.

"Yeah, I will be Ok," said Katelyn.

"I will leave you to get dressed and see you in the morning then," said Susan, giving her a kiss good night on her forehead.

After Susan left, Katelyn sat on her bed in disbelief about what had happened that night and the tears spilled over onto her cheeks. Her life was about to be turned upside down and she wasn't sure she was ready for it. And what about her plans of finishing university and opening up her own business? Was that all to be put on the back burner now?

Putting on her pyjamas, she started to think about Deveron.

How can he even want me? I can't fathom why, even if I am meant to be his life partner, thought Katelyn.

Leaving her wheelchair next to the bed as she got in, she turned the bedside lamp on.

Is life playing a cruel joke on me? she thought.

Even though she was tired, Katelyn couldn't sleep. Her mind was going over and over everything that had happened that night.

Eventually she fell asleep sobbing, through sheer exhaustion.

Chapter Six

Daniel Fletcher

Woken from what seemed like a deep sleep, Daniel Fletcher's pupils were fully dilated when he opened his hazel eyes and tried to adjust to the darkened room. Looking around, the room was not familiar to him, but seemed comfortable as he noticed through the moonlit window, the lavish furnishings. Weak, he slowly sat up straight and rubbed his bandaged head to try and help soothe the throbbing.

Aww, God my head hurts. Where am I? thought Daniel, swinging his legs over the side of the bed.

Walking over to the window, Daniel looked down at his bare abdomen and noticed a white square bandage. Peeling back the edge of the bloodied bandage, he couldn't see any wounds, so he ripped it off quickly and discarded it on the floor.

Hmm, that's strange. There's blood on the bandage but no wound, thought Daniel, feeling his abdomen where the bandage had been.

As he glanced out the double-door windows to the back yard and pushed his brown hair out of his eyes, he happened to notice the shadow of a male in the distance walking towards the house, and then he saw what looked like more shadows, which were following him. He counted four in total.

Anxiously, he looked around the darkened room, but he couldn't see his clothing anywhere. He needed to get dressed and get out of the house before the shadows he saw returned.

"You won't be needing your clothes yet," said William, standing in the open doorway.

Startled by his deep voice, Daniel looked up to see a tall muscular man walking towards him.

"What... who are you?" asked Daniel, with clenched fists, standing with his feet apart, and his nostrils flaring.

"My name is William."

The room fell silent, as Daniel gulped back his saliva.

"I know who you are," said William, when Daniel didn't answer. "How are you feeling, boy?"

"How did I get here?" asked Daniel, watching William closely.

"My coven found you in some tunnels near here. You were injured so I brought you back here to get medical attention," said William, as he listened to the boy's thoughts.

"Coven... I see. So you are vampire?" said Daniel, matter-of-factly.

"Don't be coy... you know I am," said William, walking over to the bedside lamp and turning it on. "How's the head?"

"Fine... what do you want from me?" asked Daniel. *Fucking vampires... they are all the same.*

"Nothing... you are free to leave whenever you want. But a word to the wise: the Debauched will hunt you until you give in," said William, standing in front of him and looking him in the eyes.

"Right. Where can I get some clothes?" said Daniel, with his brow furrowed.

"Your jeans have been cleaned and are on the seat over there. I have also put a t-shirt there for you," said William, gesturing to the seat next to the wardrobe.

Daniel walked over to the where William was pointing. Climbing into his tight denim jeans and white t-shirt, he then headed for the doorway.

Before he could get to the doorway, William stood in front of him and said, "Boy, you are in no shape to leave here. How long since you have had blood?"

Daniel's eyes widened and his nostrils flared. "That's none of your concern."

Grabbing Daniel by the t-shirt, William lifted him off the ground and brought him up to eye level. "I don't particularly like ungrateful fucks like you, boy. So listen up... I am the leader of the Lepidoptera vampires here in France. If you would like to stay here for a few days until you sort yourself out, you are welcome to. But I won't tolerate your mouth, let alone your attitude towards me or my coven. Your choice, boy."

Daniel gulped, as William placed him back on the ground and listened to him explain in detail about his coven.

"I... I appreciate your kindness William, but I prefer to be on my own," said Daniel, anxiously.

"Your choice... just remember a meal and bed is always here for you. In this house we take care of our own kind," said William.

"Hmm, what do you mean by our own kind? I am not one of you," said Daniel, wondering how William even thought he was a vampire.

"You are seventeen... right?" asked William.

"Yes... but what does that have to do with anything?" asked Daniel, confused.

"When Lepidoptera males turn seventeen years old, they start the transformation."

"That doesn't mean I am a Lepidoptera," said Daniel. "Does it?"

William moved with vampire speed into the bathroom and returned with a small hand-held mirror. "Stand in front of that mirror over on the door there," said William, pointing to the wardrobe.

"What…why?" said Daniel.

"Just do as I say," said William, grabbing him by the arm and pulling him over to stand in front of the mirror. "Now… look into the mirror as I hold up this small one."

As William held the small mirror behind his neck, he saw the look of shock on Daniel's face.

Feeling the back of his neck, Daniel said, "Where did that come from?"

"As I said before: when a male Lepidoptera turns seventeen, his transformation from human to vampire starts. And when this butterfly outline appears on the back of the neck, then the transformation is already underway. So in answer to your doubt: yes you are a Lepidoptera vampire in transition."

"Fuck… oh, that's just terrific," said Daniel, as the heated tears formed in his eyes. He didn't want or need any other further complications in his life right now.

Placing a hand on his shoulder, William said, "You are safe here, Daniel. But it is your call if you still want to leave."

"Look… I appreciate your generosity, but I don't know what to think of all this," said Daniel, remembering back to how things used to be.

Daniel had originally grown up in Switzerland with his father, but he had never known or met his birth mother. His father had always refused to talk about her, let alone let Daniel meet her. Even his birth certificate didn't have anyone listed as the mother. So he never even knew where to start looking for her as he got older. Daniel's life had been pretty normal up until about two months before. But when his father had passed away, his life had taken him on a strange journey.

In his dad's will, he had left the upbringing of Daniel to his brother, who lived in Paris. But when Daniel moved in with his uncle, things started to get bizarre. His uncle introduced him to some vampires, which he now knew were Debauched, and they decided that Daniel was going to be their drug mule/toy boy for their customers. Eventually running from them, Daniel continued to live on the streets, until he had woken up today at the Gramaze residents.

"Knock, knock," said Violette, as she stood in the doorway.

Daniel jumped.

"Come in, Violette," gestured William.

Nodding, she walked straight over to Daniel, and held out her hand.

"Hello... my name is Violette. How you feeling, Daniel?"

Taking a deep breath as he watched Violette enter the room and stand in front of him with her hand extended, he said, "Hi."

Wow... she is beautiful, thought Daniel, as he shook her hand.

Violette raised her eyebrows when she heard his thoughts and then wondered what Michael would think of Daniel.

"So..." said Violette.

"Oh, yeah... I have had better days," said Daniel, trying to simulate bravado.

"What about now?" asked Violette, placing her hand on his shoulder.

"Umm... I feel good... wait, what just happened?" asked Daniel, frowning.

"I have healed you with my touch," said Violette, sensing how confused he was.

"Yeah, right," said Daniel, sarcastically. "No one can do that."

"Well, I can," said Violette, as she raised her eyebrows and smirked.

"Wow... really. How cool is that?" said Daniel, looking from Violette to William.

"Here," said Violette, holding a cup with a lid on it in front of her.

"What's that?" asked Daniel.

"Blood," said Violette, still holding the cup out in front of her.

"Nah... no thanks. I won't be drinking that shit," said Daniel, swallowing his saliva.

"Your choice. But pretty soon you are going to need it," said Violette.

"I don't think so," said Daniel, standing with his hands on his hips.

"Anxious yet, or feeling like your skin is crawling with insects?" asked Violette.

Gulping, Daniel frowned and then said, "What... how do you know?"

"I have been there too. Take a drink. You will feel better, believe me," said Violette, holding the cup out in front again.

"Nah, pass," said Daniel, as he backed away from Violette and William, towards the windows. *Got to be a way to open these windows...*

"You can't get off the property that way," said Violette, listening to his thoughts.

"Fuck... get out of my head, bitch," said Daniel.

"You will hold your tongue, boy. And bow to our princess," said William, heatedly, who was now standing in front of him.

"William... it's Ok. Sire..." said Violette, with a furrowed brow. "He is only a child."

William looked Daniel in the eyes with contempt. No one was going to speak to the princess like Daniel had, and he was there to make sure of it.

"Yes, you may be a child, but I warn you, speak to the princess like that again in my presence and you will pay," said William, his nostrils flaring. "I won't tolerate disrespect."

Nodding, Daniel swallowed hard.

"Now… drink this," said Violette, standing in front of him with the cup of blood held out front.

Taking the cup from her hand, Daniel put it up to his lips, and took a tiny sip.

"Ewe, God, that is disgusting," said Daniel, wiping his mouth with the back of his hand.

"Close your eyes and take another drink. Just try it," said Violette, as she placed her hand on his shoulder.

Daniel swallowed hard to try and stop the saliva and vomit coming out his mouth, as he put the cup to his lips once again. Closing his eyes, he took a big swig of the blood from the cup, and then continued to drink its entire contents.

"Well…" said Violette, as she watched him finish the drink.

Wiping his mouth with the back of his hand, and handing her the cup, Daniel said, "Hmm, not bad."

"You want more?" asked Violette.

He nodded.

"I will go and get some more," said William. "No funny business whilst I am gone, boy."

"Yes, sir," said Daniel.

"Still feeling like your skin is crawling with insects?" asked Violette.

"A bit… but I do feel somewhat better," said Daniel.

"If you don't feel totally better once you drink down the other blood William is bringing back, then we may need to hook you up to a blood drip. Don't worry, I am here to help you, and I won't let anyone hurt you," said Violette, listening to his thoughts on how scared he was feeling.

"Thank you, Violette," said Daniel, looking her in the eyes. But he still didn't entirely trust her yet.

"You're welcome. Take a seat on the bed," said Violette.

"Ok. So… you are a princess? said Daniel, sitting on the edge of the bed, frowning.

"Yeah. It's a long story. One for another day," said Violette, sitting next to Daniel and placing her hand on his arm.

"Oh, right. Actually, do you have any headache medication? My head is throbbing," said Daniel, touching the side of his head.

"Once we get some more blood into you the throbbing should subside. It's one of the side effects from not drinking enough blood. But if it doesn't go away, let me know and I will get you some medication. Ok?" said Violette.

"Ok. Thanks," said Daniel, remembering just how many headaches he had in the last couple of months and wondering why.

Huh, thought Violette, as a vision of Daniel's previous life flashed before her eyes. Shaking her head slightly, she took her hand away from Daniel's arm, and it stopped.

What was that?

"What are you?" asked Violette, as she watched his reaction to her question.

"What… why do you ask?" said Daniel, remembering that his father had always told him to never reveal their world to anyone.

"You are not just Lepidoptera. I can feel it," said Violette, listening to his thoughts. "Dream walker… what is that?"

"None of your business. Can you get out of my head?" snapped Daniel, as he stood up and walked over to the window.

Violette stood up and followed him to the window. "Sorry … I didn't mean to pry. Your secret is safe with me."

But Daniel didn't know who to trust these days.

Quickly smashing the double door windows open, Daniel decided to make a run for it. Jumping down from the balcony onto the grass below, he then ran as fast as his legs could carry him, only looking back once to see Violette still standing on the balcony watching him.

Why isn't she following me? thought Daniel, as he got to the gazebo.

Stopping in his tracks, he heard her voice in his mind.

Daniel… please… don't go. You are safe here.

"Get out of my head," said Daniel, clutching the side of his head.

Please, come back. I fear for your safety.

The words she spoke triggered a memory in his mind. It was one of the last things his father had spoken to him about before he died.

Daniel's father had always feared that one day his son would be left alone in the world to fend for himself. Even though he had left his brother to look after Daniel, he still feared for his safety and well-being. He knew that Daniel would be powerful and would be sought after by the supernatural world because he was half vampire and half dream walker. But he had always hoped that one day someone would take him in and treat him as family.

Daniel…

Can I trust you…? I am not sure, thought Daniel to Violette.

Within seconds, Violette was standing in front of him. As she placed her hand on his shoulder he flinched and then relaxed straight away.

"Yes, you can trust me. Listen… when my parents died last year, I too was left wondering if I would ever feel safe again," said Violette.

"And do you?" asked Daniel.

"Yes. The Gramaze coven are wonderful people. Well vampires, actually… they have made me and my sister feel so welcomed," said Violette.

"You have a sister?" asked Daniel.

"Yes. Please, Daniel. You just need to give it time. That's all I can say. It may be strict here, but you will have people here that will, how do you say… have your back," said Violette.

Daniel nodded.

Is everything Ok, Violette? thought William.

Yes. Just give us a minute, William, thought Violette, looking back at the house.

"William is asking if everything is all right," said Violette, looking at Daniel. "Come on, let's just go back into the house and get you some more blood. And after you are feeling better, if you still want to leave, then that is up to you. But I hope you stay."

"Humph… Ok. I will give it a go," said Daniel, looking back at the house, wondering who he could trust.

"Great," said Violette, as she placed her arm around his shoulder and walked towards the house with Daniel.

I see you have everything in control, Violette. I will leave Daniel in your capable hands to help him through the transformation. Please let me know how he is doing later on, thought William to Violette.

No problem, William. Daniel is starting to trust me, so I will keep going and try to gain his confidence, thought Violette to William.

Thank you, Violette, thought William.

So… he is part dream walker. I wonder how this happened? I might go and speak with our queen later and see what she has to say about this, thought William to himself, with his hand on his chin.

Chapter Seven

Opening her eyes, the memories of the night before came flooding back into her mind. Sickened by the thought of having to drink human blood, Katelyn sat up quickly and swung her heavy legs over the side of the bed. With her heart beating fast and her mind racing, she placed herself into the wheelchair, which was beside her bed, and pushed herself into the bathroom.

Looking into the mirror, Katelyn noticed the dark circles under eyes. Even if she had slept in until 10 o'clock, she still felt tired. Yawning and dismayed with how she looked, Katelyn decided to have a shower.

Placing her head under the hot water, Katelyn closed her eyes and tried to relax herself, by blocking the conversations of last night out of her head.

Why don't you want to become a Lepidoptera? It can't be that bad. Can it...? What about university? Am I ready for a life partner? thought Katelyn, washing herself.

Shaking her head, she turned off the water and wheeled herself out the shower, to dry herself off. She wrapped her hair up in a towel, pushed herself back into her bedroom and towards the wardrobe. Choosing a white pair of jeans, and a colourful top to suit, she dressed herself. Wheeling back into the bathroom, Katelyn dried her hair off and put it up into a ponytail.

With her stomach grumbling, she decided to go downstairs to the kitchen.

Mark... could you please come and collect me, so I can go downstairs? thought Katelyn.

Sure... be there in a minute, Kate, thought Mark.

Thanks, thought Katelyn.

"Knock, knock. Can I come in?" said Mark, as he stood in the doorway.

"Come in, Mark," said Katelyn.

"Good morning, Kate. How did you sleep?" asked Mark.

"Morning," said Katelyn.

"Are you Ok?" said Mark.

"Jury is still out on that one. I suppose you know what happened last night?" said Katelyn.

Nodding, he said, "Yes… now you have slept on it, how do you feel about becoming a Lepidoptera, eventually?"

"Not sure… I feel a bit ripped off, actually," said Katelyn, fidgeting with her hands and trying not to give him any eye contact.

Puzzled, Mark frowned and said, "Ripped off… how dare you think that…? To be a Lepidoptera vampire is one of prestige and don't you forget it."

Taken aback by his comments, she placed her hands on her hips and said, "Prestigious… I wouldn't exactly call a creature that needed human blood that, at all."

"What, and you think humans are any better than vampires…? You have a lot to learn, little girl. We are both looking for the same thing in life, and that is to be accepted and to live peacefully. In fact, if the Lepidopteras weren't around, then there probably wouldn't be a human race. The humans not only have to contend with the Debauched drinking from them, ripping them off and oh, did I forget to mention slavery? There are other kinds of supernatural folk out there as well that want to kill the human race and will do whatever they can to make that happen."

"What a load… just take me downstairs, Mark. I don't need you for anything else," said Katelyn, fighting back the tears and clenching her fists, frustrated.

"Find your own damn way downstairs," said Mark, walking off. He knew he needed to leave before he said something he might regret.

"Fine... go then... I don't need you," sobbed Katelyn, watching his back, as he walked out the door. When the door shut, she threw a pillow against it in anger. "All I wanted was someone to talk with about becoming a Lepidoptera. But what I got from him was a speech. How dare he?" Hopping out of her wheelchair, Katelyn threw herself onto the bed and sobbed into the pillow. She couldn't believe how bad this day had started out.

Walking up the stairs, Violette saw Mark storm out of Katelyn's room and run down the stairs. "Everything all right?"

He didn't answer, just kept running past her. But he looked furious.

Wonder what that is all about? thought Violette.

Walking past Katelyn's room, she heard her crying and decided to see if she was Ok.

Katelyn jumped when she heard a knock at her door.

"Can I come in?" said Violette.

"Please... just go away," sobbed Katelyn into the pillow.

Opening the door slowly, Violette said, "Are you all right?"

Katelyn didn't answer. Instead she sobbed into the pillow harder.

Sitting on the bed next to Katelyn, Violette stroked her hair and said, "Would you like a hug?"

Turning around to face Violette, Katelyn saw how sincere she was and sat up. With her tear-stained face she leaned into Violette and hugged her tight. Her whole body was heaving from sobbing, and as Katelyn continued to cry, Violette held her tight and patted her back. Within seconds, Katelyn relaxed and her mood shifted.

Pulling away from her embrace, Katelyn said, "Thank you, Violette."

"No problem at all. You Ok now? said Violette.

"I'm not sure. Violette… can I talk with you about the Lepidopteras?" said Katelyn.

"Sure. What would you like to know?" said Violette.

"Well… Susan and Deveron told me last night that I was becoming a Lepidoptera," said Katelyn, looking into Violette's eyes.

"Wow… how do you feel about that?" said Violette, remembering back to when she first found out she was a Lepidoptera.

"I feel ripped off," said Katelyn, watching Violette's reaction to her answer.

"Ripped off… why?" said Violette, puzzled.

"I had my life all planned out until I came here… first finish university, then start up my own practice. Now… well… I don't know… am I going to be able to do any of those things now? I don't even know if I am ready to be someone's life partner, let alone have sex with them. God, what am I going to do, Violette…?" said Katelyn, with tears spilling over onto her cheeks.

Wiping the tears from Katelyn's face, Violette said, "You are getting yourself all worked up over nothing. Of course you are going to be able to finish university and start your own practice. That won't change. And the life partner thing… well, only you can control that. No one else. So chin up, everything will be Ok."

"Really… you make it sound like nothing is going to change," said Katelyn, hopeful.

"Well, I wouldn't say nothing. Like I said, only you can control whether you want to become a Lepidoptera or not. But from what I have experienced since I met my life partner, you will know when it's the right time. Have you experienced any sort of attraction to Deveron yet?" said Violette.

"Um... I'm not sure. I do really like him though. You need to understand Violette, I have never had a boyfriend, ever, and for someone as good looking and wonderful as Deveron to like me, well, it just doesn't compute. We only met yesterday so I don't understand his attraction to me," said Katelyn.

Violette spent the next half hour explaining to Katelyn about being a life partner and how it worked. She also gave Katelyn some enlightenment into becoming a Lepidoptera vampire and what was expected of her.

"It's all starting to make sense now, Violette. Thank you for explaining it to me. I think I have some apologies to make though, to Mark. No wonder he got so upset with me. Would you mind taking me downstairs?" said Violette.

"Sure. Let's go," said Violette, picking up Katelyn and placing her in the wheelchair. "If there is anything else you want to know or if you need someone to chat with, come and see me. Ok?"

"Thanks, Violette. I appreciate it," said Katelyn.

"You are welcome," said Violette, placing the wheelchair on the ground at the bottom of the stairs.

"See you later on then," said Katelyn.

"Ciao," said Violette, walking back upstairs to check on the newest guest in the house, Daniel.

Wheeling herself in the direction of the kitchen, Katelyn spotted Mark in the front lounge room and made a bee-line for him. She knew she had to apologise for her outburst. When she entered the room, Mark was with Connor and as she approached Mark, he seemed agitated.

"Good morning," said Katelyn.

"Good morning. How are you this morning, Katelyn?" asked Connor.

"Don't even bother with that question," said Mark, his fists closed, giving Katelyn a contemptuous look. "Lepidopteras don't rank high on her list."

Frowning Connor said, "I think I will leave you both to talk. I don't want to get in the middle of this heated discussion."

He then walked off.

Wheeling over next to Mark, Katelyn said, "I am sorry for what I said to you earlier. After speaking with Violette, I now understand. Will you forgive me? Please...?"

Looking into her tear-filled eyes, Mark said angrily, "Still feeling ripped off, are we?"

Katelyn couldn't look at him, because she felt guilty. Instead she looked down at her hands and shook her head. "No."

"Good," said Mark, getting up out of his seat to walk away.

Katelyn grabbed his hand. "Please don't go. I know I have a lot to learn," said Katelyn, looking up at him with her tear-stained face.

Mark never had an argument or a bad word ever with Katelyn before, and when he saw her tears, his heart melted. Kneeling down in front of her, he wiped the tears from her cheeks. "I only want what is best for you, Kate. You know that. But what you said about the Lepidoptera... well... you didn't have the right to say such things," said Mark.

"I am sorry... it's just that my life has had so many ups and downs. When I found out I was going to become a Lepidoptera, I didn't want another change in my life that I couldn't be in control of. But I also didn't know that it was an honour to become a Lepidoptera either. Not the way Violette explained to me anyway. Please forgive me, Mark. I couldn't stand it if you were always mad with me," said Katelyn. Leaning forward, she gave him a hug.

"There is one thing that you need to realise about me Katelyn, and that is that I have been a Lepidoptera for many years, and I love and will do anything in my power to keep my family safe. But when someone bags them, well... I see red," said Mark, standing.

"I understand," said Katelyn.

"Can I see your butterfly?" asked Mark.

Lifting her hair, she said, "Sure."

Walking around the back of her wheelchair, Mark saw the outline of her tattoo. "Mmm, I wonder what colour you will be?"

"None, if I have my way. I am not ready yet," said Katelyn, stubbornly.

"That is your choice, of course. But don't be fooled. I have heard that once you find your life partner, then your attraction comes on really strong. Will surely be interesting to see how long you hold out for," teased Mark.

"We will see. So are we all good now?" asked Katelyn.

He nodded and said, "Yes... hey, was that your stomach I heard grumble?"

"Yep. I haven't had breakfast yet. I might go see what I can make for breakfast and catch up with you later, if you don't mind," said Katelyn.

"Ok. Will see you later on then," said Mark.

Entering the kitchen, Katelyn found Lamiae washing some pots. "Hello, Lamiae," said Katelyn.

"Good morning, sleepy-head. Would you like some breakfast?" said Lamiae, turning around.

"Yes, please," said Katelyn.

"What about pancakes, eggs and bacon? Does that sound Ok?" said Lamiae.

"Sounds great, Lamiae. Thank you," said Katelyn.

"There is some freshly squeezed orange juice in the fridge as well. Would you like some of that?" said Lamiae.

"Yes, please. Is there any coffee?" said Katelyn.

"Yes, there is some on the middle island bench there, my dear. The sugar and cream are there as well," said Lamiae, pointing to the bench.

"Thanks, Lamiae," said Katelyn, wheeling over to the island bench. "Where is everyone today?"

"They are either still sleeping or gone out for a while," said Lamiae.

"Have you seen Deveron this morning? I was wondering if he was still here," said Katelyn.

"Actually, I haven't seen Deveron this morning," said Lamiae.

"Someone mention my name?" said Deveron, walking into the kitchen, smiling.

"Good morning, Deveron. What would you like to eat this morning?" asked Lamiae.

"Eggs and bacon please, Lamiae," said Deveron. Pleased to see Katelyn, he said, "Good morning, Katelyn. Did you sleep well?"

Deveron knew she hadn't sleep well, as he had kept watch on her all night. But he was trying to be polite.

"Not really. I lay awake most of the night thinking, and that's why I am up late this morning. I am usually an early riser, but this morning I just couldn't wake up," said Katelyn.

"I'm sorry to hear that. Why don't you try to have a sleep this afternoon? It might just give you the energy you will need," said Deveron.

"Yeah, maybe. What are you doing for the rest of the day?" asked Katelyn.

"I am needed for patrol today," said Deveron, as he ate his breakfast.

"Oh, Ok," said Katelyn, disappointed.

"But I will see you later on this afternoon for the soccer game. You are still coming, aren't you?" said Deveron.

"You can't keep me away. Can you come and get me when it's time to leave?" said Katelyn.

"No problem. Well, I had better be off. See you later on," said Deveron, placing his dishes on the sink. "Thanks for the breakfast, Lamiae."

"You're welcome, my boy," said Lamiae.

Bending down in front of Katelyn, he leaned in and gave her a hug. Katelyn felt her stomach do somersaults and her body quivered from his touch. As he pulled away from their embrace, she remembered what Mark had said to her and blushed.

"Bye," said Deveron.

"Bye," said Katelyn, as she watched him walk away.

Mmm… cute ass in those jeans, thought Katelyn.

"I heard that, Katelyn," said Deveron out loud, from down the hallway.

Smiling, she blushed, but felt she couldn't help herself when Deveron was in her presence. She sure was attracted to him.

"He sure is a nice boy," said Lamiae, disturbing Katelyn from her thoughts.

Nodding she said, "Yes. He is." Hearing her phone beep, she reached into her pocket and pulled it out.

It was a text message from Susan. 'I will be out taking care of some business for the rest of the day sweetheart. Just make yourself at home and I will see you tonight at dinner.'

'Ok. Take care,' texted Katelyn.

The rest of the day seemed to go by slowly, and by 4pm Katelyn was glad when Annabelle came to get her and take her downstairs to the car. Waiting outside for her was Deveron.

"Hello. You ready to go?" asked Deveron.

"Yep," said Katelyn smiling. Picking her up in his arms, Deveron carried Katelyn into the back seat of the car, whilst Annabelle put her wheelchair in the boot and then hopped in the front seat of the limousine.

Pulling out the driveway, Deveron moved closer to Katelyn and held her hand tight. Knowing she was nervous, from the sound of her increased heartbeat, Deveron said, "It's Ok. Everything will be good; you will see."

Leaning in, he kissed her lips tenderly and felt her melt slowly into his arms. With her whole body tingling, and feeling the pull of attraction they had, she soaked up the flavors of his mouth. As he released his hold and she opened her eyes, Katelyn couldn't help but notice how good he smelled. Even his scent was turning her on.

How am I going to keep my hands off him? thought Katelyn.

Looking into his eyes she saw Deveron smile and she remembered that he could read her mind. Blushing, she didn't know where to look.

"You won't think I smell nice once I play a game of soccer," said Deveron, smirking at her.

"I don't think I would care. As long as I can have you, is all I care about," said Katelyn, leaning into kiss him.

As she pulled back from their kiss, she opened her eyes and said, "Sorry, I shouldn't say things like that, should I?"

"I feel the same way… but I don't know what is acceptable to you yet. I know we will have to be careful, though," said Deveron.

Thinking back to what Susan and Mark had told her, Katelyn knew Deveron was right. They did need to be careful. Nodding, she said, "Yes."

The car came to a stop next to an oval that had men warming up in front of the goals. Pushing the door open, Deveron got out and retrieved Katelyn's wheelchair from the boot. Climbing back into the car, Deveron put his arms under Katelyn and picked her up and carried her out the car and placed her into the wheelchair.

"I have to go now, but Annabelle will help you over to where you can watch me play soccer," said Deveron.

"Ok. Good luck," said Katelyn.

Leaning into her, he whispered into her ear, "By the way you smell absolutely delicious too."

Raising her eyebrows, she laughed and watched him walk onto the oval.

"You two seem to be getting on real good," said Annabelle, once Deveron was playing.

"Mmm... he is such a great guy, Annabelle. All I want to do is jump his bones," said Katelyn, with her hand to her mouth, as she realised what she had just said. "Sorry... did I just say that out loud?"

"You sure did, sweetie. Cat's out of the bag... I am not surprised that he has feelings for you too, Katelyn. You are such a great chick to be around," said Annabelle.

"Thanks, Annabelle. That's nice of you to say... truthfully though, I just don't know how I am going to keep my hands off him. I always feel so turned on when I am around him. I didn't know that I could have these types of feelings about anyone, let alone want to jump their bones. But there is one thing that I am sure of, and that is I don't think my mom would be too pleased if I turned into a vamp yet," said Katelyn, anxiously.

"Let's just watch the game, and maybe we can talk later about what you might be able to do about your predicament," said Annabelle, trying to sound positive.

"Thanks," said Katelyn.

Whilst watching the game, Katelyn got more and more turned on by Deveron and watching him play soccer. Observing the sweat pouring off him, she day-dreamed about licking the sweat off him and kissing him all over. Feeling her body temperature rising as she looked at his cute, tight ass, she envisaged touching it with her bare hands.

"Hey… I think we should go buy you an ice-cream or something to take your mind off him. Wow… you have it bad, don't you, Katelyn?" teased Annabelle.

"I sure do and when I am around him, that's all I think of is touching him and whoa, sizzle," said Katelyn, smirking.

Annabelle laughed as she pushed Katelyn's wheelchair over to the ice-cream van.

As they ate their ice-cream, Katelyn said, "I wish this niggling pain I have in the back of my neck would go away."

"Would you like me to get you some pain relief medication for your neck?" asked Annabelle.

"Yes, please," said Katelyn, rubbing her neck.

Pulling some medication out of her hand bag, Annabelle said, "Here you go."

"Thanks Annabelle," said Katelyn, placing her hand out in front of her.

By the time the soccer game had finished, Katelyn's neck and headache were gone. But her attraction to Deveron was still apparent.

Walking off the oval, all of the players were shaking hands and thanking each other for the game. When Deveron reached Katelyn and Annabelle he asked, "Are you both ready to go?"

Nodding, they both said, "Yes."

Driving out the car park, Deveron leaned into Katelyn and whispered in her ear, "You still want to lick the sweat off me?" Smirking, he waited for her reaction.

She nodded and smiled back at him.

"Naughty girl. I think we had better get you home," whispered Deveron, holding her hand.

As the car pulled up in front of the Gramaze house, Katelyn noticed that Susan was standing near the front door. She knew from reading her mom's thoughts that she was waiting to speak with her and Deveron.

"Hello Mom. How has your day been?" asked Katelyn, as Deveron placed her in the wheelchair.

"Good. Thank you. Could you both come into the sitting room for a chat?" asked Susan.

"Sure," said Katelyn.

Deveron nodded.

"I will see you all later," said Annabelle, walking towards the front door.

"Thanks for today, Annabelle. See you later," said Katelyn.

"See you later on Annabelle… actually, do you mind if I have a shower first, Susan? I don't smell the best because I have been playing soccer for the past two hours," said Deveron.

"Yes. Sorry Deveron, of course you can go have a shower. We can talk later," said Susan.

Once Deveron left Susan said to Katelyn, "Did you have a good time today?"

"Yeah, I had a great day, Mom. I went and watched Deveron play soccer. Wow… he is really good at it, too," said Katelyn, excited. "I also spoke with Annabelle, and she is going to help me through what I am going through with Deveron. So there is no need for you to do anything there."

"Katelyn, despite what you may think, I have been in love before, and I do know how you are feeling right now. In fact, what I really wanted to speak with you both about was that I don't want you taking any unnecessary risks when it comes to Deveron and the attraction you may be feeling for him," said Susan seriously, as she shut the front door behind them.

Katelyn felt her face heat up, as if it had turned beetroot red. "Mom, we are not children you know. I don't think either of us are planning on me becoming a Lepidoptera at this point of our lives, let alone having sex," stated Katelyn, annoyed that her mom had even brought this up.

As they chatted in the foyer, Deveron came down the stairs toward them and could hear what Susan had just said. "I think we may be best to take this conversation into the sitting room, if that's all right, ladies," said Deveron.

"Sure," said Susan.

Taking their seats on the couch, Deveron said, "In answer to your question or statement about unnecessary risks, you don't need to worry about that as yet. What Katelyn and I need to do is to sit down and decide if and when she wants to become a Lepidoptera. That is the most important question of all. Really, it's not up to you or me to decide on when Katelyn wants to have sex; it's actually up to Katelyn. She knows the consequences, and I think as long as she is informed on what is going to happen then we should be Ok," said Deveron matter-of-factly.

"Yes, I agree," said Susan.

As they were talking Lamiae entered the room. "Excuse me... dinner is ready in the dining room," said Lamiae.

"Thank you, Lamiae. We will be there in a minute," said Susan.

Once Lamiae left the sitting room, Susan said, "We will chat about this some more tomorrow, all right?"

They both nodded.

After dinner, Katelyn asked Mark to take her up to her room so she could have a shower and get ready. Deciding to wear her dark blue jeans and a nice floral, light blue blouse, she was excited about going sightseeing with Michael, Violette, Annabelle and Deveron. Putting the finishing touches on her make-up, Katelyn heard a knock at the door. When she turned around to see who was knocking, she found Deveron standing in her doorway.

"Are you ready to go?" asked Deveron.

"Yep. Just need to get my bag and a jacket and then I am good to go," said Katelyn, wheeling herself over to the bed.

Once she was ready, Deveron carried her in the wheelchair down to the car, which was waiting out the front for them already. Taking her out of her chair, he placed Katelyn into the car with Violette, Michael and Annabelle and then took his seat next to Katelyn. The driver then put the wheelchair in the boot of the car.

"Have a great night, all. See you when you get back," said Susan, popping her head in the door before it was shut.

"Thanks, Mom," said Katelyn.

Pulling out the gates, Deveron placed his hand on Katelyn's and they snuggled up together in the back seat. Kissing her cheek, he said, "Mmm... you smell really good. Good enough to eat, in fact."

"You smell good too," whispered Katelyn, looking into his adoring eyes. "Do you really want to go sightseeing tonight or do something else?"

"What do you have in mind?" whispered Deveron.

Violette heard their conversation and said, "Would you both like to go somewhere private without us, so that you can talk or...?"

"Where could we go?" asked Deveron.

"Well... my foster parents are out of town at the moment, and the house is empty. I am sure they wouldn't mind if you went there," said Violette, looking from Deveron to Michael.

"Are you sure about that?" said Deveron, frowning.

"Yes. I am sure it will be all right, and no one else has to know about this. We all can keep a secret," said Violette, looking from Michael to Annabelle.

Annabelle and Michael nodded once.

"Ok. That would be great," said Deveron.

"Thanks, Violette," said Katelyn.

"No problem," said Violette.

Annabelle then instructed the driver to drop Katelyn and Deveron off at Violette's old house.

"Don't forget, if you need us we are only a phone call away," said Annabelle.

"Thanks Annabelle. We appreciate it," said Deveron.

When they arrived at the house, Violette opened up the house for them and showed them to her old bedroom, the kitchen, and lounge room, whilst Annabelle and Michael stood guard outside. "Make yourselves at home here."

"Thanks, Violette," said Deveron.

But Katelyn was already having doubts and was starting to feel a bit worried that they were doing the wrong thing, going off on their own.

Standing at the front door, Violette said to Katelyn, "Don't worry, Katelyn. You will be Ok. Here is my phone number just in case you need someone to talk with about anything - and I mean anything. I have been in this situation previously and know how you are feeling at the moment. Just take it slowly. Ok?"

Hugging Violette, she said, "Thanks. You are a true friend and I do appreciate your help."

"My advice is to just go slow at first and see where it takes you," said Violette. "Just give us a ring when you want us to pick you back up."

"Ok. Thanks, Violette," said Deveron.

"Thanks, Violette," said Katelyn, giving her a hug again.

"There are already wards around this house bro, so you should be Ok. The Debauched won't detect you are in here, Katelyn," said Michael.

"Hmm… why would they be after us?" asked Katelyn.

"Well… when a female Lepidoptera is in transition, they omit a smell that not only Lepidoptera males can smell, but Debauched, too. The sweet fragrance you put off is so intoxicating and it seems to send the Debauched into a frenzied state. So when Danielle and I lived here, Adrian, my foster dad, put up some wards to keep us safe. So now the Debauched don't even know when any Lepidoptera are in this house," said Violette.

"Oh, right," said Katelyn, with raised eyebrows.

"Anyway, you are safe here. So we will see you all later," said Michael.

"Ok. Thanks, bro," said Deveron, watching them all walk out the front door.

Chapter Eight

Closing the door after Violette left, Deveron knew he had to take things slowly with Katelyn, unless she indicated otherwise. He had been warned by William earlier in the day about taking advantage of Katelyn and the consequences of his actions.

"Would you like to go and watch a movie in the lounge room?" asked Deveron, turning around.

"Sure. Hopefully they have some good movies to pick from," said Katelyn, smiling up at him.

"Yeah, I hope so. What about if we go and check out the kitchen first to see what we can get in the way of something to drink and eat?" said Deveron.

"Ok. Lead the way," said Katelyn.

Entering the kitchen, Deveron spotted the fridge. Opening the door, he said, "Looks like we have some water or coke in here to drink."

"Ok," said Katelyn.

"Let's check out the pantry," said Deveron closing the fridge door and walking over to the pantry.

Katelyn wheeled her chair over to the pantry doorway.

"Ok… we have some potato crisps, and popcorn in here to eat. What would you like?" said Deveron.

"I will have a coke and crisps, thanks," said Katelyn.

"Me too," said Deveron. Taking the crisps out the pantry, he threw them in Katelyn's direction. "Catch."

Excited by his mischievous attitude, she caught the crisps. "Would you like me to take the drinks too?" said Katelyn, with one eyebrow raised.

"Sure," said Deveron, walking over to the fridge. Opening the door, he grabbed two cokes and threw them her way, one by one.

Awkwardly, she caught one of the cokes, as the other crashed to the ground and splattered out its contents everywhere, including on Katelyn face and clothes.

"Shit... look at the mess this has made," said Katelyn, looking at herself and all around the kitchen.

"God... sorry, Katelyn. I thought you would catch them both," said Deveron, looking at the coke dripping down the cupboard doors and the pools on the floor.

"Did you now!" said Katelyn, mischievously shaking the can, and flipping the lid on the other can of coke, and pointing it in Deveron direction. Coke sprayed out all over him and the kitchen floor. Laughing, she said, "Pay back." She tried to wheel away from him quickly, but he pulled her back.

Kneeling in front of her, Deveron leaned in and kissed her lips passionately. As their lips parted, he kissed the side of her face, and with his tongue, he lapped up the coke she had dripping from her face.

"Mmm... tasty," teased Deveron, looking into her eyes. Sweeping her up in his muscular arms, he carried her over to the sink. Placing her down on the bench, he wet the sponge cloth and gently wiped the coke from her face and hands.

She did the same to him.

"All clean now," said Katelyn, looking into his warm eyes. "I suppose we had better clean up the rest of this mess."

"I'll do it. Give me a second, and I will clean up your wheelchair and then find a mop and bucket to clean the floor," said Deveron.

"Once you have finished my wheelchair, and put me back in it, I can help clean the cupboard doors. Many hands make light work," said Katelyn, smiling.

Wiping down her wheelchair, he listened to her thoughts. She was in a playful mood, so he thought he would run with it. Picking her up off the bench and holding her close to his chest, Deveron placed Katelyn back in the wheelchair; but lingered in front of her to steal another passionate kiss. When their lips parted, Deveron heard her heart beat quicken. Kneeling in front of her on the coke-stained floor, he leaned in and kissed her earlobe and sucked it slowly.

Closing her eyes, her mind became clouded, as she pushed her long hair away from her ear and enjoyed every minute of his torment. As his teeth grazed her earlobe, she felt her body quiver and her breathing increase.

Deveron couldn't get enough of her, and wanted to take it further, but something inside him said 'no'. Reluctantly, he slowly pulled away from their embrace, and watched Katelyn catch her breath.

"We had better clean this up," said Deveron, trying to gauge her reaction.

"Is something wrong?" said Katelyn, worried he didn't feel the same way about her as she did for him.

"Nothing is wrong," said Deveron, standing up and looking for the mop and bucket. He had to distract himself from her pull.

"You've changed your mind, haven't you? I knew it was too good to be true," said Katelyn, looking at her hands in her lap.

Kneeling in front of her, and pulling her chin up with his hand, so she could see his face, Deveron said, "Never think that... ever. I just think we should slow this down a bit, that's all."

"I suppose you are right. One thing usually leads to another, doesn't it? And I am not sure I am ready to become a Lepidoptera yet," said Katelyn. "Come on, I will help you clean up."

When they had finished cleaning up the mess, Deveron looked down at his clothes and then at hers and said, "Let's go upstairs and get cleaned up."

"Sounds like a good idea. I'm feeling a bit sticky from the coke. I wonder if Violette and Michael have any spare clothes in their wardrobe we can wear?" said Katelyn. "They look about the same size as us, so I am surmising their clothes will fit until we can get ours washed."

"Not sure. Let's go and check it out," said Deveron, picking the wheelchair up with Katelyn in it and walking towards the marble staircase.

Sitting Katelyn gently down on the vanity unit in Violette's bathroom, Deveron then retrieved a wash cloth from the shower recess. "Here we go," said Deveron, handing Katelyn the wash cloth and soap.

"Thanks... but I am going to need a hand to get out of these coke-stained clothes. Can you help me?" said Katelyn, cheekily watching his reaction.

"Umm... I don't think that is a good idea, Katelyn," said Deveron, seriously.

Smirking and watching him squirm, she said, "I'm only kidding. I can undress and dress myself, you know. I just wanted to see the look on your face."

"Really..." said Deveron, placing his arms around her waist and looking into her playful eyes, he pulled her in close. "You are such a beautiful lady... mischievous, but beautiful."

"Thank you. I have never had any man say that before," said Katelyn, feeling her cheeks redden.

Looking into her eyes, his eyebrows creased when he listened to her thoughts and realised why. "Unbelievable."

"Not really. Who would want to hook up with a girl in a wheelchair? Come on, let's be honest here, I am not what you would call the catch of the county," said Katelyn, trying to put things in prospective.

"Well it was their loss and my gain. I am so glad we have met," said Deveron.

"Me too... But I wanted to ask you a question," said Katelyn.

"What is it?" said Deveron.

Here goes, thought Katelyn.

"Well...umm... How would you feel if I don't want to become a Lepidoptera? And please be honest," said Katelyn, looking at Deveron for a reaction.

"I don't understand the question," said Deveron, confused.

"I will start at the beginning then... since I was a little girl, all I ever wanted was to be loved by a family that wanted me, and I have found that with Susan. But since I have been able to do most things for myself and have achieved great results at school, I have wanted to go to university and then start up my own psychiatrist practice. I only have one more year left a university, and then my dreams of opening and owning my own practice will come true. That is until I came to Bagnolet and met you. From what I understand about the Gramaze Lepidopteras, if I become one of you, well, then I would have to live here too. I am not sure I am ready for that yet. Let alone becoming a Lepidoptera. It's just all happening a bit too fast for me. That's all I am saying, Deveron," said Katelyn.

"Whether you are a full Lepidoptera or not, it just doesn't matter to me. I will live wherever you want to live. Look... all I want to do now is get to know you better and we can take it from there. I don't and won't pressure you, Katelyn. I am willing to wait for sex and all that comes along with it," said Deveron.

Could this guy get any more adorable? Wow, I am so fortunate, thought Katelyn.

"It is I who is fortunate, Katelyn. I have waited hundreds of years to meet you and now I have finally met you, my world has changed for the better," said Deveron, brushing his hand down the side of her face. Leaning in, he kissed her soft lips fervently and captured the flavors of her mouth.

I love the way his lips are warm and tender and so inviting. Oh boy, his muscular body awakens every inch of me, thought Katelyn.

Hearing her thoughts, Deveron was torn. He knew the consequences. His heart was saying *go for it*, but his mind was saying *go slow*.

With nothing but the sweet taste of each other on their minds, they surrendered. As their hunger for each other grew, Deveron picked Katelyn up off the vanity and carried her through the doorway to Violette's bed. Gently, he lay her down on the bed and positioned himself next to her. Through the material of her blouse he cupped her breast and felt her nipple harden. Impatient, Deveron undid the buttons on her blouse and lapped at her cleavage. Her skin was smooth and supple. "So lovely," he whispered whilst his fingers undid the front clip of her blue lace bra. He couldn't remember ever feeling this deprived.

Her moan was one of unmistakable pleasure, as Katelyn arched her back off the bed and pressed her nipple into his warm mouth. Feeling the scrape of his rough tongue, she wanted him to be greedy. With her blood racing throughout her veins and her heart pounding, she felt, for the first time, alive. Abandoning her fears, she needed him to take her here and now.

Taking her hand in his, he placed it on his hardened penis through his denim jeans. Desire fluttered in the pit of her stomach as he looked down on her with his carnal eyes, watching her reaction. Without speaking he moved her hand up and down his shaft, whilst he took a brief taste of her lips.

"Undress me," whispered Katelyn, breathlessly.

"No need to rush," said Deveron, as he ripped at her control with a lingering kiss, whilst his fingers roamed to trace her body.

In a daze, she let him lead her. Anticipation shivered along her skin as Deveron unzipped the fly on her jeans and pulled them down, along with her matching lace panties, and discarded them to the floor. With her blouse now off as well, she lay on the bed naked, watching and waiting for what he would do next.

Standing up, his breathing was ragged when he removed his shirt and then his denim jeans. Deveron wasn't even aware of his control slipping away. Kneeling on the carpet in front of her, he opened her legs and kissed her inner thigh, and then lapped at her clitoris.

With emotions high, she moaned and trembled in delight of the pleasure he was inflicting on her. "Please..." said Katelyn. "Please... I want you."

Ignoring her pleas, but listening to her thoughts, he realised she was eager to please him in many ways. Taking her hand once again, he directed her toward his hardened penis as he continued to suck her nub. She knew what he desired. Placing her hand down his briefs, she sprang his cock free for the first time. Moving her hand up and down his shaft in rapid movements, she offered him a pleasure he had long forgotten. Moaning from the enjoyment of every stroke, he finally put his hand over hers and said, "Would you like to take this further?"

She nodded. But was she willing to take a chance knowing she would become a Lepidoptera vampire? Her mind was all over the place.

Pleasure or destiny, she thought.

Hovering above her on the bed, Deveron listened to her thoughts, whilst he pulled her legs up on either side. "Are you sure?" asked Deveron.

"Yes," she said impatiently. She was ready.

"I will take it easy. If it hurts, just let me know," said Deveron, with a furrowed brow, kissing her forehead.

She nodded knowing she was about to lose her virginity.

Katelyn watched in anticipation as he rolled the condom on his shaft, and wondered if his huge penis would fit into her pouch. Easing into her wet vagina, Deveron pulled his cock in and out slowly, so she could adjust to the size of him. Feeling her becoming comfortable, as he took her innocence, his mouth consumed hers.

She felt a tight pinch at first as his shaft entered her vagina. Trying to adjust to his size, Katelyn soon recognised the pleasures he had generously awakened, when she felt every nerve ending in her body tingling. As he fucked her faster and hard, she panted in anticipation of an orgasm.

Stilling over her, breathless, but sated, Deveron lay next to her on the bed. Contented, Katelyn shuddered, then moved closer to Deveron.

"You cold?" asked Deveron, drawing her in closer to him, until her head rested on the curve of his shoulder.

"Just a bit," said Katelyn, looking around for a blanket. Naked, she felt vulnerable.

Reading her thoughts, Deveron pulled his arm out from under her head and retrieved a blanket from the foot of the bed and placed it over them both.

"Thanks," said Katelyn, looking into his eyes, as she snuggled back into the curve of his shoulder again.

Kissing her forehead, he asked, "What are you thinking?"

"I never thought sex would be as awesome as that was,

and I was wondering if sex would be like this all the time for us?" said Katelyn.

"It will only get better for us. Especially when you transform into a Lepidoptera. Vampires give intense pleasure to each other when they are life partners. Something to remember," said Deveron.

"Oh. Ok... so much for getting cleaned up," said Katelyn, smirking.

Chuckling, Deveron said, "Yeah. Would you like to have a quick shower?"

"Yes please," said Katelyn.

Getting up off the bed, Deveron watched the blanket fall to the ground, only to reveal her beautiful, pale, naked skin. He stood there for a few moments taking in the vision of her, until she grabbed the blanket and placed it back over her body.

"You shouldn't be ashamed of your body, Katelyn. God, you are so beautiful and you have an awesome looking body."

She was glad there was no real light coming into the room, because her face felt red from embarrassment.

"Thanks," said Katelyn, not knowing what else to say.

"Come on, let's get you in the shower." said Deveron, standing next to the bed.

"Umm, Ok," said Katelyn. She couldn't help but feel awkward, as she wondered how they would have a shower together, considering she couldn't stand by herself.

Why was I born with this useless body? thought Katelyn.

"Actually, would you mind getting me a drink of water from the kitchen," said Katelyn.

"Sure," said Deveron. Placing his briefs and jeans back on, he ran with vampire speed to the kitchen and back.

By the time Deveron came back with two waters for them to drink, Katelyn was dressed in her clothes and sitting on the bed waiting for him.

"Changed your mind, have you?" asked Deveron, handing her the bottle of water.

"Well, it's not as though I could actually have a shower with you, Deveron. Considering I can't stand unaided," said Katelyn, matter-of-factly, placing the bottle on the carpet.

Taken back by her comment, Deveron said, "But isn't that what a life partner is for, to help? Anyhow, they have a ledge in their shower here. I already checked it out. But if you don't want to, then I understand. There is no pressure."

But you will see my body. God... I hate this body, it's useless, thought Katelyn.

Turning his head sideways, he listened to her thoughts. "Why do you hate your body so much?" said Deveron.

Frowning, Katelyn realised that he could still hear her thoughts. "Please don't do that," said Katelyn.

"Why... being that you are my life partner, why wouldn't you want me to listen to your thoughts? I don't get you, Katelyn," said Deveron, running his hand through his hair in frustration.

"Because my thoughts are sometimes mine to know and private," said Katelyn, getting agitated.

"I understand... but these thoughts you have about your body... well they are... how do I say... just ridiculous," said Deveron, sitting next to her and taking her hand in his.

"Easy for you to say. You are not the one in a wheelchair and not able to walk," said Katelyn.

"I suppose you are right. It is easy for me to say, as I'm not in that predicament. But I want you to understand one thing... no matter if you are in a wheelchair and can't walk for the rest of your life, I will still think you are beautiful and want to spend my life with you. There are so many other things that I like about you as well," said Deveron, looking into her eyes.

"Really... like what?" said Katelyn, holding his hand tight.

"Besides all the attractive qualities you have, Katelyn, and believe me, your body is very attractive, you are also easy to talk with, intelligent, caring, and you think of others first. Believe me when I say, I am your number one fan," said Deveron, letting her into his thoughts, so she could see he was telling her the truth.

Leaning on his shoulder, she said, "I believe you." But she was still feeling vulnerable about being naked in front of him.

"Would you like me to call Violette and ask her to come and take us home?" asked Deveron.

"Not yet," said Katelyn, looking into his eyes. Leaning into him, she kissed him with soft, parted lips, soaking up the flavors of his mouth with her tongue. She didn't want their night to end just yet.

"How are you feeling, anyway? Do you feel any different since we have had sex?" asked Deveron.

"I don't think so. I just feel the same... except... I am feeling a tingling sensation in my legs and feet at the moment," shrugged Katelyn.

"I wonder..." said Deveron, with his hand on his chin.

"What..." said Katelyn.

"So... were you able to walk at all, prior to tonight?" asked Deveron.

"Yes, but I still need assistance," said Katelyn.

Standing in front of her, Deveron put his arms out in front of him. "Can we see if you can walk now? Did you want to?" asked Deveron.

"Hmm, I don't know... not really sure I want to," said Katelyn.

"Come on. There is no harm in trying hey," said Deveron.

"Hmm...Ok... sure," said Katelyn, excited at the prospect. But in the back of her mind she wasn't getting her hopes up. She'd had too many years of disappointing results already.

Pulling her up to stand next to the bed, he put his arm around her waist to hold her up whilst she took the first step. "Don't worry... I won't drop you, my love. I will be holding you every step of the way," said Deveron, holding her firm.

Katelyn's first couple of steps were a bit painful and she faltered a few times before coming to a stop. "This is useless," said Katelyn, frustrated.

"Come on. Try again," said Deveron.

"Ok," she sighed and held onto his arms firmly.

Keeping her upright, Deveron continued to help walk further.

"This is the furthest I have walked in years. I actually feel like I have more sensation in both my legs and feet," said Katelyn, with a grin from ear to ear.

"Unbelievable, Katelyn," said Deveron, excited. "Let's try the stairs and see how you go. Don't worry, I will be right by your side."

Swallowing hard, Katelyn held onto the marble side railing that ran down the stair case. With Deveron by her side, she felt she could achieve anything. Taking one step at a time down the stairs, she turned to Deveron and smiled. "I am doing it."

"Keep going. You are nearly at the bottom," said Deveron, watching her achieve the impossible.

Breathless as she reached the bottom landing, Katelyn had sweat beading on her upper lip as she crumbled into Deveron's arms, smiling. "Now that was hard work. And you know what? I don't have pain anymore."

"I am really happy for you, Katelyn," said Deveron, kissing her forehead.

"God, I am exhausted. Can we sit down somewhere?" said Katelyn, sweat beading on her top lip.

Deveron scooped her up in his muscular arms and carried her up the stairs and into Violette's bedroom. Placing her down on the bed, he said, "You get undressed and I will run a bath for you."

"Thank you, Deveron," said Katelyn, who was now feeling a bit more comfortable about being naked in front of Deveron.

As she waited for Deveron to fill the bath, Katelyn could smell a peach perfume coming from the bathroom.

Being that peach is a healing herb, Deveron knew it would help to settle her nerves and anxiety.

"That smells divine. What is it?" asked Katelyn, with raised eye brows.

"It's peach bubble bath. I believe peach is good for your wellness," said Deveron, as he walked through the doorway from the bathroom.

"Thank you. You are so sweet for running the bath for me. I think I will enjoy this," said Katelyn.

Placing her on the edge of the bath, Deveron stood beside her so she could use him to lean on as took off her final piece of clothing. With her collared shirt now discarded to the floor, she stepped into the bath, aided by Deveron. She took her time to slowly sitting down in the water as it was still really hot. Finally, lying back in the bath, the bubbles engulfed her and made her feel calm. Opening one eye, she noticed Deveron still standing half-clothed, watching her.

"Would you like to get in with me?" asked Katelyn, hoping he would say yes.

"I would love to," smiled Deveron, discarding his jeans and boxers quickly. Stepping in behind her, he rested his back up against the end of the bath, and then pulled her into him, so she could lie back against his chest.

"Mmm, this sure is nice. Thank you…" said Katelyn, with her eyes closed.

"You are welcome," said Deveron, kissing the side of her head as he enveloped her with his arms.

"I can feel my toes," said Katelyn, pulling her foot out the water and wriggling her toes. "I have never been able to do that, ever." She smiled when she realised just how different her life was about to be. No longer wheelchair bound or solely dependent on anyone. But she was also frightened it wasn't going to last.

"That's great. Can you lean forward for a minute because I want to have a look at your butterfly tattoo to see what colour you are?" asked Deveron.

Leaning forward and pulling her hair up out the way, she waited for Deveron to tell her what colour she was. But he went quiet.

"Well… what colour is it, Deveron?" said Katelyn, excited to find out what her ability would be.

"It hasn't changed colour, Katelyn. In fact, it only has the black outline still. This is not usually what is meant to happen after we make love. It should have turned a colour straight away," said Deveron, worried.

"Well maybe I won't be a full Lepidoptera vampire. We can ask Susan or Renee when we get back," said Katelyn.

"I don't want to ask them Katelyn, because then they will know what we have been up to tonight," said Deveron. "I am sure that they will not be too happy about this."

"We are going to have to tell them just in case this is a delayed reaction. Because if I do turn into a Lepidoptera then I will need some A+ blood straight away and I don't want to chance anything going wrong," said Katelyn, remembering the lecture she got from Susan.

"Yes, you are right. What was I thinking?" said Deveron, wondering what William and Susan would say to them both. "For the moment, can we just lie here for a while and soak up the connection we have?"

"Sure. I am enjoying the peach anyway. I feel nice and relaxed lying in your arms," said Katelyn.

After they lay there for another thirty minutes, the water started to go cold. "Let's get our clothes on and then we can ring Violette, Michael and Annabelle and ask them to come and collect us," said Deveron.

Chapter Nine

As Deveron was waiting for Katelyn to get dressed, he decided to ring William. Taking his phone out of his pocket, he dialled the number.

"Yes," answered William.

"Sire... I have some news. I don't think you will be happy with us," said Deveron.

"What do you mean us?"

"Katelyn and I... it just happened... we couldn't control ourselves, and well..."

"Stop... how did this happen when you are with the others?" asked William, heatedly.

"We separated from them," said Deveron, not wanting to give him the full details, for fear of getting Violette in trouble.

"What the fuck were you thinking, Deveron?" said William.

"We were overwhelmed with passion, sire. We can't help what we feel for each other. You of all people should know this," said Deveron.

"Fuck... Susan is not going to be too happy about this, Deveron. Why couldn't you just keep your dick in your pants?" stated William. "I want you and Katelyn to come home now."

"Yes, sire," said Deveron. Hanging up his mobile, he watched Katelyn walk out the bathroom.

Katelyn eyes widened and she gulped as she overhead the conversation. She wasn't looking forward to getting a talking to by Susan.

"Sorry, Katelyn, but while you were getting dressed I rang William and let him know what has happened tonight. He was not too happy, but he did say to me that he would let Susan know, and hopefully by the time we get there she will be a bit calmer," said Deveron.

"Yeah, I know. I overheard the conversation. I understand you telling, William. But I am not looking forward to the reaming I am going to get from Susan when we get back to your house," said Katelyn.

"Yeah, me neither," said Deveron. "But we can deal with them together."

I am an adult, I can do what I want, thought Katelyn.

When the limousine pulled up outside Violette's old house, Katelyn and Deveron were waiting at the front doors. As Deveron helped Katelyn into the car, they noticed that Michael, Violette and Annabelle weren't inside.

"Where are the others?" asked Deveron to the driver.

"I dropped them off at the Fire and Ice night club, sir, and I don't need to pick them up until 2am," said the driver, looking through the rear view mirror. "I have strict instructions from William to take you and Katelyn home. So sit back and enjoy the ride."

Katelyn and Deveron looked at each other and gulped. Snuggling into each other in the back seat, their thoughts raced, as they pulled away from Violette's house.

"I don't know whether or not I am wishing for this to happen, but I am starting to feel my legs and feet, more so than before," said Katelyn, feeling a tingling sensation in her legs and feet.

"Really…" said Deveron, excited for her. "Driver, please stop the car."

"Yes, sir," said the driver, pulling the car over to the sidewalk.

"What are we doing?" asked Katelyn.

"You'll see," said Deveron, opening the door and then scooping Katelyn up in his arms. "Are you ready?"

"For what?" asked Katelyn, as she looked around at the houses that lined the street.

"For this," said Deveron, placing her feet firmly on the ground and standing her up straight, as he held onto her body.

"Deveron…"

But before Katelyn could get another word out of her mouth, she felt the hard concrete ground under her feet. Gulping, she turned to Deveron and smiled.

"Don't worry, I won't let you go," said Deveron, watching her reaction.

Nodding, Katelyn moved her left foot along the ground, and then her right, as Deveron held onto her firmly and listened to her thoughts. Faltering a few times, from lack of muscle strength, Katelyn took it slowly.

"I'm doing it… I can walk," said Katelyn, with a smile from ear to ear. "Let me try by myself?"

"You sure?" asked Deveron, with a creased brow.

"Yep."

Her first step was shaky, but Katelyn was determined to keep going. With Deveron by her side to catch her if she fell, she continued to take more steps.

"You're doing great, Katelyn. Well done…" said Deveron, taking every step alongside her. He was in awe of her determination and patience. "Wait until Susan and everyone else sees this, Katelyn, they won't believe it."

"I can't believe it myself, Deveron," said Katelyn as she came to a stop. "I think that may be enough for now. I am feeling a bit light headed."

"Sure… that's understandable. Let's get you back in the car," said Deveron, as he scooped her up in his muscular arms.

Snuggling into his neck and shoulder, Katelyn's tears welled in her eyes. She had only ever been this happy once previously, and that was when Susan fostered her.

"I have never been able to walk unaided all my life, and I never thought that it would happen, either. To be able to walk a few steps and to just feel the ground under my feet, is so incredible. I still don't believe it," said Katelyn, as the tears of happiness rolled down her cheeks.

"I am so proud of you," said Deveron, as he placed her in the car and shut the door. Holding her in his arms, he kissed the side of her head. "Congratulations, my love, you have done it". He then kissed her tenderly. "Let's go, so you can show everyone... driver, take us home."

With the car slowly driving through the front gates, and along the driveway, towards the house, Katelyn and Deveron spotted William and Susan waiting for them at the front doors.

"They don't look too happy, Deveron," said Katelyn, holding his hand tight.

"Don't worry, my love. I am here and I won't let them yell at you. Everything will be all right," said Deveron. "Let me carry you in and then you can show them."

"Ok, that sounds good. Thank you, Deveron, you are such a gentle, loving person and I don't know what I would do without you in my life at the moment." She then leaned in and gave him a passionate kiss.

Deveron carried Katelyn inside, and as William shut the front door, Deveron placed Katelyn in a standing position, in clear view of Susan.

"What is going on?" asked Susan, with her eyebrows raised.

They both didn't say a word.

Katelyn smiled up at Deveron, and he at her, as his arms slowly let go of her. She then took a few steps towards Susan.

Taking a deep breath in, Susan placed her hand over her mouth. "How did this happen?"

"We are not sure, Mom. It seems that after we… well… made love tonight, that I was able to feel my legs and feet more and more, as the night went on," said Katelyn, smiling.

The tears welled in Susan eyes, as the realisation hit her. Placing her arms around Katelyn, she hugged her tight. "Oh, my darling daughter. How I have wished this for you over the years. I am so happy for you, my dear."

"Me too. It just doesn't seem real," said Katelyn, slowly pulling away from their embrace. "I just hope my transformation is not something that comes and goes."

"Don't worry, my dear, I will ask the physiotherapist to come and see you tomorrow. Hopefully they should be able to help you improve your muscle tone and strength," said Susan.

Nodding, with excitement, Katelyn's legs began to feel heavy and tremble. Taking a step closer to the wall, she held herself up.

Deveron was at her side quickly, to catch her before she fell. "I have you, my love. Would you like to sit down now?"

"Yes, please. Thanks, Deveron," said Katelyn, looking up into his loving eyes.

Susan watched as Deveron carried Katelyn into the sitting room, and how his affection for her was totally transparent.

"Let me have a look at your tattoo, Katelyn," said William, sitting next to her on the sofa.

Shooting a glance at Deveron, who was kneeling beside her, Katelyn lifted her hair up off her neck and gulped.

When Susan and William had a look at Katelyn's neck, their eyes widened in disbelief, as the tattoo had no colour. With their eyebrows furrowed as they looked at each other and then back at the tattoo outline, intrigue set in.

"Have you ever come across this in your life time, William?" said Susan.

"No, I haven't. Usually by now the colour of the tattoo is starting to form at least," said William, scratching his head. "Katelyn, we are going to take you down stairs to our queen and see what she has to say. I don't want to take any chances with anything happening to you when we are not expecting or ready for it."

Katelyn nodded, and looked at Deveron.

"It will be all right," said Deveron, holding her hand.

"Wait…" said Susan. "I want to try something first."

Susan placed her healing hands on Katelyn's neck to see if she could force the tattoo colour to appear.

As William, Deveron and Katelyn waited, for what seemed like forever, Katelyn said, "Ouch… my neck is really hurting now."

"I'm sorry, my dear," said Susan, lifting her hands from Katelyn's neck.

Susan gasped when she saw the colour starting to appear on Katelyn's neck.

"Well… what can you see?" asked Katelyn, impatiently. "Don't keep me in the dark."

"It's green," said Deveron, looking at her tattoo.

"Green. What does that mean?" asked Katelyn, excited.

"That means you have the healing power, like Susan," said Deveron.

Katelyn looked up at Susan, and smiled.

With tears welling up in her eyes, she said, "How ironic is this that I had healing powers, all along?"

Susan smiled at Katelyn and placed her hand on her shoulder.

"Fate..." said Susan.

Renee then walked into the room with a cup in her hand.

"Here, my dear, you are going to need to drink this," said Renee, handing her the A+ blood.

Katelyn took one look at the contents of the cup, swallowed hard and felt her stomach churn.

"I don't know if I can drink that. It's making me feel sick just looking at it," said Katelyn, looking at Renee.

"That's Ok, Katelyn. Maybe we can try again later. In the meantime, I have called the doctor and he is going to come and put in drip, as well. He should be here in about ten minutes," said Renee.

"Oh, right...," said Katelyn, with her brow creased. *I wonder what the drip is for? Not looking forward to that at all!*

"Thank you, Renee," said Deveron.

"Yes, thank you, Renee," said Susan. "Well... best we get you sorted and ready for the doctor."

Deveron picked Katelyn up in his arms and she cuddled into his chest.

"I will take Katelyn up to her room, so she can get ready," said Deveron.

"I'm sure Susan can do that," said William, flaring his nostrils at Deveron.

Susan nodded in agreeance. *Life partner or not, what does he think he is doing? I am her mother.*

"That's Ok. I don't mind," said Deveron, totally ignoring the mind talk, and walking towards the doorway.

Susan looked at William, raised her eyebrows, and took in a deep breath through her flared nostrils.

Hmm… I don't think you are gonna stop that, thought Renee, as she looked at Susan with raised eyebrows.

Walking over to the double doors, which lead out into the backyard, Susan's brow furrowed as she pondered over if it was just a coincidence that Katelyn was a healer too. Remembering back to when she first met Katelyn at the children's home, teaching her to eat, taking her home, and adopting her, she wondered if it had all been by chance that they had been brought together or whether it was because she was a healer Lepidoptera.

"You comfortable?" said Deveron, pulling the quilt up on Katelyn's bed.

"Yep. Don't fuss… it's all good," said Katelyn, leaning back against the pillows.

"So… how you feeling?" said Deveron.

"I feel a bit agitated, which is not like me," said Katelyn, as she hastily itched her arm.

"Hmm… feel like you want to rip my head off yet? asked Deveron.

She nodded. "I don't think that it is a good idea you being in here with me," said Katelyn, trying to remain calm as she twitched. "Where is this doctor?"

"He will be here soon," said Annabelle, as she walked into Katelyn's room.

Sitting on the bed next to Katelyn, Annabelle placed her hand on Katelyn's forearm. "I am here to help."

Frowning, Katelyn said, "How…"

"My touch can calm you," interrupted Annabelle, as she looked into her eyes.

"Right..." said Katelyn, as her body felt the release and her breathing became steady. "Hmm... thank you, Annabelle."

"You're welcome," said Annabelle, listening to her thoughts and watching her body relax.

"I might lie down," said Katelyn, as she yawned, and pulled the pillows out from behind her.

"Thank you, Annabelle," said Deveron, with his hand on her shoulder.

"Anytime, bro. She should be Ok until the doctor gets here," said Annabelle, as she stood up and walked to the doorway. "See you later."

"Bye. And thank you again, Annabelle," said Katelyn, looking up from the pillow.

Katelyn woke to find her room was partially lit by the moonlight shining in through the window and onto her face. Feeling a pinch on her arm, she looked down and realised that a cannula had been inserted into her vein, with a bag of blood hanging from a stand. Remembering the events of the previous night, Katelyn sat up in bed, and placed her legs over the side of the bed.

"You Ok?" asked a familiar voice at the foot of her bed.

Startled, she jumped. "God, you frightened the crap out of me. What are you doing sitting in the dark?" asked Katelyn, with her hand on her chest.

"Besides keeping guard... well... I was admiring you whilst you slept," said Deveron, walking over to her.

"Oh... right," said Katelyn with a raised eyebrow. *Creepy...*

"Sorry... I didn't mean to be... anyway, how are you feeling?" said Deveron, sitting on the bed.

"Good, I think. Have you slept at all while I have been sleeping?" said Katelyn.

"No. I am not tired. I don't need much sleep, you know, vampire and all," said Deveron.

"Oh, right," said Katelyn, wiping the sleep from her eyes. "I don't feel any different, Deveron. Is that normal to feel like this?"

"I am not sure, but I would just take it as it comes. No need to worry about anything yet," said Deveron.

"Ok. Umm… could you take me to the bathroom, Deveron. I need to go to the toilet," said Katelyn.

"Why don't you see if you can walk there yourself, my love? If you have trouble I will be there to stop you from falling. But I think you will probably find you can now walk without me holding onto you," said Deveron, standing and unhooking the drip.

Katelyn removed the cannula from her arm and placed both feet flat on the ground and felt the floor beneath her. Pushing herself upwards with her hands and legs, she stood tall by herself. Taking the first couple of steps towards the bathroom, she looked back at Deveron, to see him smiling from ear to ear.

"Keep going, my love. You are doing really well," said Deveron trying to give her confidence.

She smiled at him, briefly.

As she approached the bathroom door, Katelyn grabbed hold of the doorway, and then walked slowly in, closing the door as she went.

As the minutes passed by, Deveron became worried when Katelyn didn't return from the bathroom. He hadn't heard any noise that resembled her falling, so knew she was all right, but as the minutes ticked away, he became anxious and headed for the door.

"Knock, knock," said Deveron, turning the door handle.

"Come in," said Katelyn, turning from the mirror to see him coming through the door.

"You Ok?" asked Deveron. His eyes lit up when he saw her standing there naked, in front of the mirror. "What are you doing?"

Katelyn face turned beetroot red. "Umm…"

"It's Ok," said Deveron.

"I feel a bit embarrassed, actually," said Katelyn, trying to pick up her clothes from the floor.

"Don't be… the view is awesome from where I stand," said Deveron, smirking.

She smiled and tried to get dressed.

Oh, how embarrassing that I was looking at my body. He probably thinks I am shallow. I wonder if he will understand that I have never been able to see my full body in the mirror before, thought Katelyn. Her cheeks felt heated.

"Of course I understand," said Deveron, after he read her thoughts. "It's only natural that you would want to do that."

Screwing her lips together, she sighed. "I wish you wouldn't do that."

He looked at her dumbfounded.

"You know, read my thoughts. It's invading my privacy," said Katelyn, with her hands on her hips.

"Oh… sorry. I keep forgetting. It's a force of habit," said Deveron, as he watched her struggle to put her clothing on. "You don't have to hide yourself from me, you know."

Raising her eyebrows, she let her clothes fall back to the tiled floor, and said, "Come over here."

The wind shifted her hair as Deveron moved, with vampire speed, in front of Katelyn and enveloped her in his arms. Breathing in her intoxicating peach scent, he kissed and lapped at her neck. Reaching her left ear, she moaned as he nibbled it erotically, stimulating her every nerve ending.

With her head leaning back, enjoying his every move, she said, "I want you… take your clothes off."

Deveron pulled away from her quickly, and took in a deep breath. With his eyes widening, he took off his t-shirt and discarded it to the floor, then his jeans. Drawing her naked body closer to his, he kissed her lips tenderly.

His muscular body felt warm and carnal to her as Katelyn breathed in his alluring peach scent.

"Take these off," said Katelyn, feeling his hardened penis through his briefs.

Hastily discarding them to the floor, Deveron swiftly picked her up and carried her back to the bed.

Laying her down on the bed, he hovered above her, and continued to pleasure her body with his tongue.

"Would you like to try something a bit different?" asked Deveron, looking up from her belly button.

"Mmm… sounds interesting," said Katelyn, with a raised eyebrow, looking into his eyes.

Deveron hoped off the bed and headed for her wardrobe. Retrieving a scarf from the first drawer, he returned to the bed. As he stood at the side of the bed, he showed her the scarf and then tied her hands behind her head, to the headboard.

"Hmm… kinky hey? You like it like that?" said Katelyn, watching him tie her hands back.

"Sometimes… I hope you like it too," said Deveron, watching her reaction. "That feel Ok?"

She nodded and glanced back at her hands tied to the headboard.

Lying next to Katelyn, Deveron kissed her lips passionately as he cupped and caressed her left breast. With his mouth lapping at her ear, then her neck, he continued down to her left nipple and teased it slowly with his tongue, and pulled at it gently with his teeth.

Pressing her head back into the pillow, she moaned with pleasure and pushed her breast further into his mouth, as he relentlessly tortured her some more.

Deveron did the same to her right nipple and as his warm mouth sucked and nipped at her breast, she felt her body tingle all over, when her wet patch screamed of an orgasm.

Kissing her lips once again, he continued down her belly, kissing and nipping at it gently as he went. Katelyn moaned loudly when he reached her inner leg and then sucked the bulb on her clitoris.

"Oh... Deveron... don't stop," said Katelyn, her breathing heavy.

Mmm... she smells good, thought Deveron, as he took a deep breath, and placed his tongue into her vagina. *Peach*. As his breathing became rapid, the blood rushed to his pulsating penis and his immediate response was to drink from her. Pulling away quickly, he dared not look up at her, for fear she may see the blood lust in his red eyes. Instead, he turned her over onto her stomach. Deveron sat on her bottom and then pulled the hair away from her neck. Kissing from her neck, and down her back, to her bottom, he listened to her pleasurable moan.

"Deveron... please... no more. Fuck me... please," said Katelyn, as her body's inner core tingled from excitement.

"Not yet, my love," said Deveron, as he pulled her bottom into the air and placed his finger into her vagina, just teasing her a bit more. "Mmm... so wet."

"Oh... Deveron... I can't take much more of this. My body feels like it's a hot molten rock and is about to explode," said Katelyn, breathlessly.

Untying her hands, he said, "Stay still."

With her knees pressing into the mattress and her bottom in the air, he slipped his elongated, hardened penis into her wet pulsating vagina. Holding onto her hips, he pounded her hard and fast, and moaned pleasurably. His thoughts were scrambled, and he knew he had to get his lust under control, but he couldn't help himself. He just wanted to feel every inch of her beautiful body. Even her scent was intoxicating, sending him crazy.

With her head down and resting firm on the mattress, Katelyn said, "It's coming… I feel that I was about to orgasm."

"Try to hold off and the effect will be more pleasurable," said Deveron, as he grabbed hold of her hair and pulled her up towards him. He continued to fuck her harder and harder and just when he thought he couldn't fuck her anymore, he came, and she orgasmed at the same time.

Finally, his blood lust disappeared.

Sated, and cuddled into the nook of his neck, Katelyn said, "That was too good."

"It's a lot better doing it that way, isn't it?" said Deveron.

"Mmm… where did you learn how to do this?"

"Well, you are not the only one who reads books, Katelyn," said Deveron.

"Is it always going to be this good, Deveron?"

"If you want it to be, my love. I am only too happy to please you. I can't seem to get enough of your beautiful body."

"I feel the same way about you too, Deveron."

He kissed her forehead and cuddled her tightly.

"Would you like to have a soapy hot bath? I have a huge bath tub in my bedroom," said Deveron.

"Sure. Sound good. Let's go," said Katelyn, sitting up.

Once Deveron filled the white, claw foot bath tub, he said, "Ladies first," as he pointed to the bath.

Stepping into the bath, Katelyn's body adjusted quickly to the hot water as she sat down amongst the bubbles. Deveron then stepped in behind her, and lay back onto the bath. His arms opened wide and gestured for her to cuddle into him.

Smiling, Katelyn noticed that his hardened penis was peeking through the top of the bubbles, so she bent down and kissed the head. Looking up at him, she sat up straight and raised her eyebrows up and down.

Knowing she was in a playful mood, he lifted his penis out the water and smirked.

Leaning towards him, she kissed his lips quickly and then latched onto his penis. As she sucked it hard, and pulled it in and out of her mouth, she tormented him by twirling her tongue around the head.

Deveron moaned in pleasure and his breathing became rapid as he lay back in the bath with his head pointed towards the ceiling and his eyes closed.

"Oh, God. Please... don't stop. I love what you are doing," said Deveron gyrating his penis in and out of her mouth.

Turned on by his scent, and feeling his pleasure, Katelyn felt her inner body tingle. Knowing he was about to come, she decided to give him pleasure another way. Sitting on his cock, she watched his eyes open as she pulled herself up and down his shaft, and the water swirled around them.

Exhausted and breathing heavily from their love making, they lay in each other's arms cuddling, whilst the hot water enveloped their bodies, making them feel relaxed.

Noticing her breathing had quietened and there was no chatter coming from her mind, Deveron soon realised she had fallen asleep. Picking her up in his arms, Deveron carried Katelyn out of the bath and put her into his bed naked. Katelyn was so tired that she didn't even wake when he put the blanket on her to keep her warm. As he stood there admiring her beauty, his body and mind ached to be near her when she slept. So he quietly slipped into bed and cuddled up next to her.

Chapter Ten

Katelyn woke to find her naked body intertwined into Deveron's. Smiling, and feeling happy about the past day's events, she lay there watching him sleep peacefully and etched every detail of his face into her memory.

With her bladder calling for a break, she tried to ease her way out of the bed, but felt a hand pulling her back.

"Good morning, my lovely lady. How are you feeling this morning?" said Deveron, wiping the sleep from his eyes.

"Good… can you give me a minute?" said Katelyn, pulling away from him.

Before he could answer, she jumped out of bed and ran, with vampire speed, to the bathroom.

Within minutes, Katelyn was back next to him in bed and cuddling into his chest. "That was quick! Looks like your legs are working fine this morning," said Deveron, wrapping his arm around her.

"Yeah, I can't believe how good I feel this morning. My whole body feels alive," said Katelyn.

"That's good. Are you hungry yet?" asked Deveron.

"A little bit," said Katelyn.

"Let's get dressed and go get some breakfast," said Deveron, slowly pulling away from their embrace.

"Sure," said Katelyn, sitting up and watching him walk towards his wardrobe naked. *Oh my… look at that. It's all mine. How lucky am I?* She took a deep breath in and out to calm herself as she drooled over his muscular, v-shaped physique.

Deveron smirked when he heard her thoughts. He turned to her and said, "It is I who is lucky, Katelyn. I have been waiting for you for hundreds of years and now I have found you, I won't ever let you go."

With vampire speed, she ran to stand in front of him. As her soft lips touched his, he breathed in her peach scent. She was intoxicating to his heightened senses in every way. Placing his broad arms around her waist, he pulled her in even closer, and enjoyed the flavors of her mouth.

Katelyn felt his penis harden as he pressed up against her. Her vagina switched, sending her into a frenzy. Pushing him with her new-found strength up against the wall next to his wardrobe, she felt something move in her mouth.

Pulling away quickly, Deveron realised Katelyn's fangs were descending from her gums. He recognised that look all too well. Her eyes were crimson-red and the pupils fully dilated; she was in need of blood and he knew she would need to feed.

"Katelyn," said Deveron, trying to keep her at arm's length. Shaking her, he watched as her eyes looked straight through him. "Katelyn."

"Hmm... what's happening?" said Katelyn, dazed.

"Let's get you some blood," said Deveron, steering her over to the bag of blood hanging from the machine. Luckily, he had brought the machine and the bags of blood into his room the previous night.

Sitting on the edge of the bed, Katelyn took the bag from Deveron, tore it open with her teeth and gulped down the contents.

Deveron realised that she needed more as he watched her only take seconds to drink the half-full bag. Rushing over to his small bar fridge, he retrieved a full bag of blood. As he stood up straight and turned around, Katelyn was standing behind him. With blood dripping from her fangs and smeared around her mouth, she appeared breathless.

"Give me that," said Katelyn, with flared nostrils, snatching the bag of blood out of his hands. Tearing the bag open, she grunted continually when the blood hit her taste buds and she enjoyed its flavor. Quickly finishing the bag, she sat back down on the bed, and wiped away any remnants of blood from her mouth with the back of her hand. With her breathing once again returning to normal, she looked up at Deveron, who was standing in front her. "Sorry... I don't know what come over me."

"I do... you nearly hit blood lust. Fuck, Katelyn, I don't want to ever go through that again... you Ok now?"

"Shit. Really. Thank you, Deveron, for helping me through that. I am feeling a bit more at ease now though," said Katelyn. She didn't want to believe how enraged she had felt. Guilt-ridden, she placed her hands over her face, as the tears heated up in her eyes and she began to sob. "I can't believe how irresponsible and totally out of control I became."

Deveron sat next to her on the bed and placed his arm around her shoulder. "Shhh... come on... everything is Ok now. Let's just forget it," said Deveron, as he kissed the side of her temple. "Let's get dressed and go and have some breakfast."

She nodded and wiped her runny nose with the back of her hand.

Deveron and Katelyn walked hand in hand down the marble stairs, and as they reached the bottom, they could hear voices coming from the dining room, and realised everyone was in there having breakfast, so they joined them.

"Good morning to you both," said William, looking over his shoulder. "How are you feeling today, Katelyn?"

"I feel good," said Katelyn, looking to Deveron for support.

"Well, at least you can walk by yourself now. Oh, and run at vampire speed," joked Deveron.

"That's good, my dear," said Renee, smiling.

"Why don't you both get something to eat, and take a seat. I have something I want to discuss with you," said William, gesturing to the breakfast bain-maries.

Placing their plates on the table, and taking their seats across from Renee and William, Katelyn said, "What did you need to speak with us about, William?"

William took an envelope from his jacket pocket and handed it to Katelyn. "Susan asked me to give you this letter," said William.

"Oh, Ok," said Katelyn, taking the letter out of the envelope.

It read,

> *My dear darling Katelyn, I have had to go to Germany to help out with some healing on one of my oldest and dearest friends. I shouldn't be gone any more than a week. You will be in good hands with William and Renee, oh, and Deveron. So please be good and enjoy yourself, my dear. If you need me for anything please don't hesitate to ring. Talk to you soon. Luv you heaps. Love Mom. xx*

Folding the letter back up and placing it in the envelope, Katelyn sighed.

"Everything all right, my love?" asked Deveron, placing his hand on hers.

"Yeah. I think so... Susan has gone away to heal someone for a week. That's all. It's not the first time this has happened since I have been with Susan. But... I really would have liked for her to be here whilst I transition. It's... well, a bit scary for me, you know," said Katelyn.

"We are all here for you, Katelyn," said Annabelle, as she stood behind Katelyn with her hand on her shoulder.

"Thank you," said Katelyn, placing her hand on Annabelle's and looking around the room at everyone who was seated at the table.

"What about if after breakfast we take you down to the combat room and teach you how to fight?" said Deveron. "Sometimes keeping busy helps."

"Ok. Maybe then I will be able to help you patrol for some Debauched," said Katelyn, matter-of-factly.

Deveron swallowed hard, and shook his head. "I will teach you to protect yourself Kate, but I won't be taking you on patrol."

"Why not? said Katelyn frowning, as she looked to Deveron for answers.

"Because you are not ready for patrol Katelyn, and it's not something you take on lightly. It's a very dangerous job and you can get killed," said William, answering for Deveron.

"You mean when you all go out on patrol at night, that maybe you might not return? Oh my god... I didn't know that." said Katelyn, looking to William and placing her hand over her mouth.

"Don't worry," said Deveron, placing his hand on Katelyn's. "We are all highly skilled and truthfully, it's unlikely to happen. We are better equipped and have more combat experience than the Debauched."

"When are you due to go out next, Deveron?" asked Katelyn. Even though she had listened to what he had just said, she still was worried for his safety.

"Deveron is not going out on patrol for a while, Katelyn. Instead he will be looking after you and making sure that whilst you are transitioning to a Lepidoptera, you don't get taken by the Debauched vampires. If they get their hands on you

Katelyn, it won't end good. They will turn you into one of them. Do you understand me?" said William authoritatively.

"Perfectly clear sir, and I do know how dangerous it is out there," said Katelyn.

"Good," said William, taking a gulp of his coffee.

You know what is expected of you, Deveron. So keep an eye on Katelyn. She is not to leave this house without you. Are we clear? thought William to Deveron.

Yes, sire, thought Deveron.

Katelyn sighed as she pushed her food around the plate with her fork, and for a split second wished she had never come to Bagnolet. The only good things that had come from this holiday was meeting Deveron, her life partner, and being able to walk. She wasn't sure she wanted to be a Lepidoptera, and now realised why Susan had kept it a secret all these years.

Deveron placed his hand in her lap and whispered in Katelyn's ear, "What would you like to do today, besides have hot sex again?"

She didn't answer. Instead, Katelyn intertwined her fingers into his and grinned at him for a second. She wasn't sure how much longer she could hold back the tears she felt looming in the back-ground.

Reading her mind, Deveron knew she was upset. "Eat some breakfast and then we can go for a walk and maybe cuddle up somewhere. How does that sound?"

"Sounds good," said Katelyn. As she ate her breakfast, she couldn't help but think about all that had happened to her in the last couple of days.

In my haste to become a Lepidoptera vampire and to be with Deveron I never really thought about any of the consequences of actually being a Lepidoptera and what they had to do to survive. My life has been sheltered by Susan up till now and it was pretty normal. But these people who are sitting at the table around me are fighting to keep their race alive. Even though I have only been here for a couple of days, I feel like these people are my family and god forbid anything should happen to any of them as I would be devastated to say the least, because I love them all so much, thought Katelyn, as she looked around the table.

Katelyn glanced over at William and watched him nod in her direction. She wondered if he had been listening to her thoughts.

"Yes, he heard you; we all heard you. Family is very important to this coven, and we do feel the same way about you," said Deveron sincerely.

Katelyn then heard everyone at the table, through mind talk, welcoming her.

Thank you, thought Katelyn as she looked each of them in the eyes.

"Deveron, can we go for a walk around the grounds outside?" asked Katelyn, placing her fork down on the plate.

"Sure," said Deveron, standing. "Come on."

The warmth of the early morning sun through the clouds greeted them as Katelyn and Deveron walked out into the manicured gardens and took a seat under the gazebo.

"What seems to be the matter, my love?" said Deveron, placing his arm around Katelyn's shoulder and pulling her in close.

"I'm not sure... I... I feel like my world is crumbling. Too many changes...my transition... Mom leaving... it's all too much, I suppose," said Katelyn, staring out into the sky as she cuddled into Deveron's shoulder.

"Don't worry, everything will sort itself out, you'll see. And in the meantime, I am here to help you," said Deveron, rubbing her arms up and down for comfort.

"I'm glad I at least have you here with me, Deveron," said Katelyn, watching Renee walked out into the gardens from the house and straight towards them.

"Renee," said Deveron, as he read her mind.

"Deveron... Katelyn. You Ok dear?" asked Renee.

Katelyn sat up straight and sighed. "Just don't feel myself, that's all."

"You may need this," said Renee, handing Katelyn a cup of A+ blood. "It should make you feel a whole lot better."

Gulping as she took the cup from Renee and looked inside, Katelyn shivered and tried to hold back the saliva that was pushing its way upwards.

"I'm not sure I can," said Katelyn, looking from Renee to Deveron. Even though she had drunk blood from the drip bags, through her blood lust moment in Deveron's room that morning, Katelyn's mind was still in denial over whether she could partake in something so revolting, like drinking blood.

"Just try," said Renee.

The first sip took Katelyn by surprise as it washed over her tongue and down her throat. As she drank it down, the blood seemed to comfort her in ways she couldn't understand.

"Mmm... it's sweet, yet tangy. I feel it calming me," said Katelyn, her eyes dilating.

"Until your butterfly is fully coloured in green you will have difficulties in dealing with some situations and may feel out of sorts. So until it does form, you need to drink blood at least three times a day, more if needed," said Renee, sensing Katelyn relaxing. "Also, if you are still feeling any type of anxiety after you have drunk the blood you need to go and see Annabelle. Her touch can help calm you and this will help you through until we get you more blood."

"Thank you, Renee. You are so kind to me. I don't know what I would do without your help."

"You are welcome, my dear. As you are now family, we do take care of our own you know. How are you feeling now?" said Renee, placing her hand on Katelyn's shoulder.

"A lot better, thanks," said Katelyn.

"Good. Well, I need to go and organise what we are having for lunch with the cook. I shall see you both later," said Renee.

"Thanks Renee," said Deveron.

"Ok. Thanks again, Renee," said Katelyn, watching her walk inside.

"So... what would you like to do for the rest of the day?" asked Deveron.

"I don't know... what about you? What would you like to do?" said Katelyn.

"Umm... would you like to go for a swim?"

"That sounds like fun. Just what the doctor ordered," said Katelyn. "Let me just go and put my bikini on."

"Ok," said Deveron, watching her walk back inside. He still couldn't believe that she didn't need her wheelchair any longer.

Mmm... doesn't he look good enough to eat, in those tight board shorts and oh... sizzle... that gorgeous body, thought Katelyn, standing in the doorway watching the way Deveron's muscular back flexed, as he cleaned the pool. *Wouldn't I love to kiss that body all over? Perfection...*

Deveron turned around to see Katelyn taking off the towel she had wrapped around her body and place it on the chair.

Beautiful. As she stood next to the pool in her bikini, he hung the pool scoop net back up, and then joined her.

"Mmm don't you look good enough to eat. I just want to take you now," said Deveron, with a raised eyebrow, as he stood in front of her and placed his arms around her waist.

Katelyn smiled and Deveron laughed. The attraction they felt for each other was overwhelmingly apparent.

The heated opal blue pool looked inviting, when the sun shone down upon the body of water and rainbow colours fanned its way across it. But as they stepped into the pool, Katelyn sensed something was amiss with Deveron. Instead of his calm demeanour, she felt sadness and longing. She tried to listen to his thoughts, but for some reason he was blocking her.

"What's wrong?" asked Katelyn, looking into his eyes and running her hand down the side of his face.

"Nothing."

Deveron didn't want to answer. Instead he pulled her up onto his waist, wrapping her legs around him, leaned in and kissed her lips passionately.

As the water swirled all around them from the jets, Deveron came up for a breath, only to inhale in her intoxicating peach scent. Aroused, he started to kiss and nip at her earlobe and neck.

Katelyn tilted her head to one side and moaned quietly, as she welcomed Deveron's sensual touch.

"Don't go," said Deveron, as he kissed her neck.

"Hmm… what…?" said Katelyn. Her eyes widening.

"Don't go back to Switzerland," said Deveron, pulling away from their embrace and looking her in the eyes. "We have only known each other for a few days, but I feel like I have known you for longer. I am dreading when you have to leave."

"I knew something was wrong," said Katelyn, her brow furrowed. "Deveron, I feel the same way, but you have to realise I have a life back there."

"I know... I know. But we have only just found each other," said Deveron.

"I don't know what to say," said Katelyn, feeling his sadness.

"Say yes to staying with me," said Deveron. "Listen, I know you want to graduate from university and open your own practice, but am I being selfish for asking you to come and live with me and my family instead?"

"Deveron, I can't even think that far ahead yet. And I don't want to leave you either. Maybe we can come up with some solution so that we can stay together. One thing I know for sure is that I do want to graduate and open my own practice," said Katelyn, placing her arms around his shoulders. She sighed. "Can we just enjoy the time we have together now, as I don't want to have to think about it yet?"

He nodded, pulled her in close and kissed her again.

Chapter Eleven

It was lunch time at the Gramaze house and Deveron could hear Lamiae calling him and Katelyn into the dining room.

When they approached the dining room there seemed to be a lot of chatter and commotion going on.

Walking into the room, with Katelyn by his side, Deveron said to William, "What going on?"

"Katelyn, I need you to take a seat so we can have a chat," said William, gesturing to the table.

"What's wrong...? I know something is wrong, as I can feel it and see it in your face," said Katelyn, sitting next William. Her anxiety levels had risen.

"Susan has been taken by the Debauched vampires and we don't know where they have taken her," said William.

"What... how did that happen? She was only going to Germany to help heal someone," said Katelyn, frowning and flopping down on the seat next to William in dismay.

"The house she was staying at was compromised and when the Debauched vamps found out she was a healer, they kidnapped her. You see, when you are a healer, you are a very valuable resource to the Debauched vampires. I don't think they would hurt her, but you can never tell with these bastards," said William.

"Oh, shit... what can I do to help find her?" said Katelyn, with a creased brow.

"There is not a lot you can do at this stage, Katelyn. After lunch, some of us are going over to Germany to help look for your mom. Susan is one of my oldest and dearest friend and I don't want anything happening to her. I will leave instructions and information about where we are staying and our mission with Brock," said William.

"Oh, right. Can I come?" said Katelyn, searching his face.

"No... I need you to stay here, Katelyn," said William.

"Did you need me to come on the mission, sire?" asked Deveron, standing next to William.

"No, Deveron... I think you will be needed here to help Renee and Brock out with anything we may need," said William.

Deveron put his hand on William's shoulder, and said, "Thank you William, but are you sure you don't need me to come? I will be of no use here."

"I will be all right here, William. Renee will help me if I need anything, and you need every man you can get to find my mom. So if you need more men, please take Deveron," said Katelyn, sincerely.

"Thank you, Katelyn," said William, placing his hand on his chin and looking from Katelyn to Deveron. He needed to think about what was best for his mission and his coven. "Hmm... Ok. We are leaving in about one hour so be ready to go, Deveron."

Katelyn sat on the bed in Deveron room and watched him pack his combat gear into a long black, vinyl bag. With tears welling in her eyes, she thought, *I hope Mom is going to be all right. If those Debauched fuckers hurt her, they will have me to deal with... who am I kidding? What can I do? God, I can't believe this is happening.* Tears spilled over onto her cheeks.

"Hey..." said Deveron, as he sat next to Katelyn on the bed. "Everything will be all right."

"You don't know that, Deveron," said Katelyn, with a furrowed brow, as she placed her arms around his shoulders and cuddled into him. "Just… please promise me you will come back to me too."

"Don't worry, my love. I will come back for you and we will have Susan with us. You'll see," said Deveron, holding her firmly.

Smiling briefly, she pulled away from their embrace. "Oh Deveron, I have only just found you and to lose you would end my world. Please come back to me safe. I love you so much, much more than you know," said Katelyn, brushing her hand down the side of his face.

"I'll be careful, my love. I always am," said Deveron. As he was trying to console her, there was a knock at his door.

"It's time to go," said William, opening the door. "Don't worry, I will bring Susan and Deveron back safely to you. This is my promise to you, Katelyn."

"Thank you, William. Please make sure you come back safe, too," said Katelyn, looking over to the doorway.

He nodded.

"Meet you downstairs, Deveron," said William.

As the SUV drove away, Katelyn's heart was in her mouth. She then remembered the last words she had spoken to Deveron.

I will never leave you if you just come back to me.

Renee placed her arm around Katelyn's shoulder. "It's best to keep busy, dear. That way you don't worry too much."

"What can I do to help, Renee?" said Katelyn, wiping the tears from her cheeks and sniffing.

"Do you have any computer skills, my dear?" asked Renee.

"Yes. I have really good computer skills…why do you ask?" said Katelyn.

"I need you to go to our operations room and help Brock with the intel," said Renee.

"Right… I can do that," said Katelyn, happy to be helping.

As she stood in the doorway to the operations room, Katelyn could see that Brock was busy trying to find her mom through satellite tracking.

"Are you here to help me?" asked Brock, registering she was standing behind him, he turned around.

"Yes… just show me what you want done and I am good to go," said Katelyn, walking over to the computer and taking a seat next to Brock.

"Right… I will get you set up on this computer here. What I am trying to do at the moment is to find the place and time where your mom was taken by following the satellite tracking images from the street cams, to track where she is now. But for some reason I always seem to lose track of the car she is in," he said, pointing to the computer screen.

"Let me have a look as I might see something you are not seeing, Brock," said Katelyn, sitting next to him.

"Yeah, two sets of eyes are better than one. That's for sure," said Brock, moving to the side.

As she closely scanned through the images of where Brock lost track of Susan, she pointed to the screen and said, "Here… I have found the car again. It looks like what the Debauched vampires did was switch cars where there was no street cam footage. But what they never counted on was that the shop front window reflection showed us what type of car they transferred to."

"You are a genius, Katelyn. From here we can track it to where she has been taken to," said Brock, giving her a high five. "I will relay this to William."

Katelyn smiled.

On the way to the airport, William sat in the back of the SUV and gave instructions to his coven about their mission plan for the night, when his mobile phone rang.

"Yes."

William listened carefully to Brock.

"Tell Katelyn I said well done and thank you. Keep up the good work, Brock," said William.

Deveron watched William hang up his phone and place it back in his jacket pocket and look in his direction.

"That is one clever woman you have there, Deveron. She actually worked out from looking at the satellite images that there was a switch of car and all they had to do was follow that car. They have found out where Susan is being held captive," said William.

Deveron smiled and felt proud of Katelyn. "Excellent... William, when we get back from this mission, I would like to speak with you about what will happen with Katelyn and me," said Deveron.

"No problem, Deveron. I am sure we can sort something out. But for now, we have more important things to worry about," said William, taking his phone out of his pocket to ring the Germany Lepidoptera leader.

"Thank you, sire." Deveron nodded.

Annabelle leaned into Deveron and said, "Don't worry bro, everything will work out." She had previously been listening in on Deveron's thoughts about Katelyn.

"Thanks, Annabelle," said Deveron.

Once William had spoken and hung up from his call with Braxon, the leader of the Germany Lepidoptera vampires, he said to his coven, "Listen up everyone... when we arrive in Berlin we will be collected at the airport by some of Braxon's men, who will take us to where the Debauched are holding

Susan captive. Once we are there, we will kill these mother-fuckers and get Susan out safely," said William, looking at each of his coven's faces. "Braxon and I will give you more instructions on our plan when we arrive. I don't want anyone thinking they are indestructible tonight, as I promised Renee and Katelyn I would bring each and every one of you home safe with me. Are we clear on this?"

"Yes, sire," they all said loudly together.

When they arrived at the Debauched house, Braxon was there to greet them with a few more of his men. Jumping out the SUV first, followed by the rest of his coven, William introduced his family to the Berlin leader.

Both William and Braxon gave the orders on where each of their coven soldiers would be positioned.

As the first grenade was thrown into the large front yard of the house, which held a few cars and motorbikes situated near the door, some of the Debauched came running out the front door to see what was happening. But before they could ascertain what was going on outside, Jonas and Leon, two of Braxon's soldiers, charged for them and cut the Debauched vamps' heads off with their long machetes. Their bodies disintegrated before they hit the ground.

Simultaneously, Annabelle and Grayson approached the back of the house, and watched as five Debauched vamps tried to escape. But they didn't get far as Annabelle fired up her blow torch and burnt them where they stood, whilst Grayson cut their heads off. With their bodies disintegrating, Grayson high-fived Annabelle.

"Mmm... we do work well together," said Grayson, smirking as he wiped the blood from his blade on his pants.

Annabelle smiled.

It's all clear out the back, sire, thought Annabelle to William.

With the back door unlocked and no Debauched in sight, Deveron and William walked inside. Just as they got to what looked like the laundry room, they were ambushed by two more Debauched vamps, who jumped William and Deveron from the back. But these Debauched were no match for William, let alone Deveron. It wasn't long before they were beheaded.

Continuing to walk throughout the house, William and Deveron were once again set upon by four more Debauched vamps. When the fight was finally over, and William picked himself up off the floor, he realised he was covered in blood, but not his own blood, it was the Debauched vamps' blood.

Looking around the room for Deveron, William noticed him on the floor, under an unconscious Debauched. But he was not moving. He ran over to Deveron and quickly moved the Debauched off Deveron's body and cut off his head.

"Deveron, are you Ok, my friend?" asked William, grabbing him by the shoulders and shaking him.

There was no answer.

When William couldn't rouse Deveron, he then noticed his bloodied clothing. Ripping his shirt open, he ascertained Deveron had been stabbed in the chest and was bleeding badly. For some reason, which William couldn't comprehend, Deveron's body wasn't healing itself.

Grayson… get inside now. Deveron has been hurt badly, and I need you and Annabelle to take him safely out of here, thought William.

Within seconds, Annabelle and Grayson were by William's side.

Quickly looking around the house for something to stop the bleeding, William noticing a red-hot poker resting in the fireplace, and decided to use this on Deveron's wound.

"Sorry, Deveron," said William, as he placed the hot metal poker on his wound.

"Arrr, fuck…" screamed Deveron and passed out again.

As Grayson and Annabelle carried Deveron out to the medic's car, he woke briefly and muttered, "Tell Katelyn… I love her."

"You can tell her that yourself, bro. Don't think you are leaving us just yet," stated Grayson, with a creased brow.

But Deveron fell unconscious again. He had lost too much blood.

William stood at the entrance to the medic's car and watched them insert a cannula into Deveron's arm and hook up a bag of blood. "Annabelle, when you have finished here, come find me. I will need your help with Susan once I find her."

"Yes, sire," said Annabelle.

Not knowing where Susan had been kept captive in the house, William searched, at vampire speed, throughout the house for her. Once he was upstairs, he came upon a closed door that was locked. As he placed his shoulder on the door to force it open, he heard Annabelle shouting at him from behind.

"William! Don't open that."

"What… why?" asked William, turning around to see Annabelle coming towards him.

"Because it's rigged with explosives," said Annabelle.

"How do you know this, Annabelle?" asked William, frowning.

"I can't answer that, William. I just have this strange feeling that something is not right," said Annabelle, placing her hand on his shoulder.

Nodding, William took his phone out of his pocket and rang Braxon.

"Braxon… can you have one of your men scale up the outside of the building, to the second floor, and get in via the window to have a look around. We think that there may be explosives rigged to the door handle."

"On it, now," said Braxson.

As William and Annabelle waited in front of the doorway, they then heard Jonas scream out.

"Don't open that door! It's rigged to go off!"

William looked at Annabelle and nodded. "Thank you. You have just saved mine and Susan's life. I will never forget that."

"You are welcome, sire," said Annabelle, bowing her head to him.

Maybe it was intuition, William wasn't sure, but he was glad that Annabelle figured out that there were explosives on the other side of the door.

It seemed like a long time to William and Annabelle as they waited patiently at the door, but it was only thirty minutes later that Jonas opened the door, carrying Susan in his arms. She was unconscious and from the needle marks in her forearms, she looked like she had been drugged. With her face and body bruised all over, William knew she would need blood to heal, so he opened up his vein on his forearm with his teeth and held it to Susan's mouth.

Within seconds, she came around. Growling, her eyes widened, as she sucked the delicious blood from William's arm with vigour.

He knew the signs of blood lust only too well, as he pulled his arm away quickly from her mouth.

"How do you feel?" asked William, looking into her eyes.

"Better, thank you... but why did you give me your blood, William?" asked Susan. Her breathing was ragged as she tried to contain her lust.

"You needed blood and fast. And I needed to repay our debt, my friend," said William, referring to how Susan had healed him previously.

Susan smiled and said, "Thank you."

Taking Susan from Jonas' arms, William carried her out to the medic's car to get checked over and to have a top up of blood.

"How's she going?" asked Braxon, standing next to William.

"Much better, my friend. Thank you for all you have done for my coven here tonight," said William, turning to Braxon, and shaking his hand.

"Anytime... anything for an old friend," said Braxon, shaking William's hand. "We have just done a final inspection of the place and it seems all the Debauched have been exterminated. Good riddance to them... are you and your coven ready to go?"

"We will be in a few minutes. The medics are just making sure Deveron is good to travel," said William.

"Right... I will have my men take you back to the airport, once Deveron has been sorted," said Braxon. "Well, I must be off. It was good to see you, William. We must do this again and soon, but under better circumstances."

"Yes... that would be good, my friend," said William, cupping his shoulder in friendship.

As the SUV, which had the Gramaze coven inside, sped away from the Debauched house, they watched the building explode into a huge fireball. Watching the debris scatter over the property and burn brightly, William said, "Good job everyone."

Chapter Twelve

William watched on as the medics loaded an unconscious Deveron, who was still hooked up to a blood drip, into the plane on a stretcher. He knew it was only a matter of time before Deveron would eventually heal from his wounds, but he still wasn't sure why Deveron's vampire body wasn't healing itself.

Sitting next to Susan on the journey home, William watched her vampire body heal super-fast, as she rested. By the time they had arrived at the Gramaze house, Susan only had bruising that would heal in a matter of days.

One day... thought William, with his nostrils flared, and lips thinned. *One day we will be rid of these fuckers, and then there would be no more Debauched to ruin our plans of keeping mankind safe.*

Katelyn watched her own reflection appear in the blacked out windows, as the limousine pulled up beside her. Opening the door, she watched William step out first.

Nodding once, she looked over his shoulder to see Susan sitting in the car. Stepping around him, Katelyn placed her hand out front to help Susan slowly ease out the car. As she placed her arm firmly around Susan's waist, Susan winced from the vicious beating she had taken over the past twenty-four hours. Seeing that her mother was still in pain, she loosened her grip.

With tears slowly rolling down her cheeks, Katelyn said, "Sorry, Mom."

"It's all right," said Susan, looking into her tear filled eyes. "Don't cry."

Susan turned and placed both arms around her daughter's waist. She was glad William and his coven had found her, as she thought she was never going to see Katelyn ever again.

"I'm so glad you are Ok, Mom. I was so worried... I love you," said Katelyn as she hugged Susan and her tears flowed freely.

"I love you too, sweet heart," said Susan.

"How are you feeling, Susan?" said Renee, coming to stand beside them.

"I feel like I am healing, but still very sore from the brutal beating I got from those Debauched bastards," said Susan, leaning on Katelyn.

"Bloody low-life scum... we had best get you inside to rest so you can heal quicker," said Renee. Placing her arm around Susan's shoulder, both Katelyn and Renee helped her inside.

"You go see how Deveron is going, dear. Don't worry about me, I will be all right and anyway I have Renee here to look after me," said Susan to Katelyn, as they stepped inside the doorway.

"Are you sure?" asked Katelyn.

"Yes... go," said Susan, shooing her away.

Katelyn waited at the front door entrance to the house for the car to pull up with Deveron inside. Feeling his presence coming towards her, Katelyn's stomach contents churned over and over, for fear of what she might see.

She knew he was still unconscious and what had happened because William had rung her from the plane and informed her of his condition. But she was worried, because it wasn't normal for a vampire to not be able to heal themselves.

When the medic's car drove up to the house, she held her breath. With her hand over her mouth, she watched an unconscious, bare-chested Deveron being pulled out the back of the car on a stretcher by two medics. As they walked on by Katelyn, carrying Deveron into the house, she realised just how badly he was hurt.

He needs some serious healing time, thought Katelyn, looking at the bruising all over his face. She then noticed the bloodied bandaging around his chest, which was covering the stab wound he endured from the Debauched fight.

A lump formed in her throat and tears welled in her eyes, as she watched the medics carry him inside.

"He will be Ok. Deveron just needs time to heal," said William, coming to stand beside her and place his arm around Katelyn's shoulder.

"Can I heal him, William?" asked Katelyn, looking up at his face. "I don't know if I have all my healing power yet, but can I try.

"Hmm… that's right, I forgot about your healing power. Give it a try," said William, positively. But he knew that even if she couldn't heal Deveron that Violette had acquired her healing ability now and she would be able to help.

Katelyn watched from the doorway of Deveron's bed-room, as the medics placed him into his queen size bed, and then hooked up another bag of blood. Once they dressed his wound again and took a sample of his blood for testing, she was able to sit with him.

As she ran her fingers through his hair, and kissed his temple, she was interrupted by Susan clearing her throat.

Turning her head, Katelyn said, "How are you?"

"Don't worry about me… I will be Ok. More importantly, we need to heal Deveron," said Susan, looking from Katelyn to Deveron. "Do you know how to heal him?"

"No I don't… could you show me how, Mom?"

"All you need to do is touch him on his wound with both hands and think to yourself, *heal this wound.* It's as easy as that," said Susan, coming to stand next Katelyn.

Placing both hands over Deveron's wound, Katelyn chanted to herself over and over.

Heal this wound.

Nothing seemed to be happening. He still lay there unconscious.

"Give it time, Katelyn. It doesn't always happen straight away," said Susan, placing her hand on Katelyn's shoulder.

Katelyn looked up at Susan and nodded and tried once more to heal Deveron.

As the minutes ticked by, with her hands held on top of Deveron's body, Katelyn said, "All of a sudden I feel drained. Is that normal?"

"Yes, it's quite normal, dear. Plus don't forget, you are still transitioning at the moment," said Susan, sitting on the bed.

"Hmm. You Ok, Mom? You look pale," said Katelyn, worried.

"I'm tired. That's all," said Susan, rubbing her forehead. "I might leave you now, and get some rest."

"Oh, Ok. Thank you for your help, Mom. I will come and see you later on," said Katelyn, standing and giving Susan a hug.

As the door shut, Katelyn lay down on the bed next to Deveron and placed her whole body up against him, hoping that this may help.

Heal…heal… heal, thought Katelyn, closing her eyes.

She lay there for hours doing this until she fell asleep from exhaustion.

The next morning, Katelyn woke to find Deveron lying beside her with his eyes open. Smiling, she wondered how long he had been awake.

"Good morning," said Katelyn.

"Hello, my love," said Deveron.

"How are you feeling? Can I get you anything?" said Katelyn.

Deveron smiled. "I'm Ok. Maybe a nice passionate kiss would be good."

Leaning into him, she kissed Deveron's lips fervently. As she placed her arm around his torso, she felt him wince in pain.

"Sorry," said Katelyn, pulling away from their embrace.

"That's Ok... actually, I wanted to ask you a favor, Katelyn," said Deveron, drinking in her scent. "But you don't have to say 'yes'; just think about it, Ok?"

"What is it, Deveron?" asked Katelyn.

"Do you think that you would be able to feed me some of your blood?" asked Deveron, watching her reaction. "It's just that because you are my life partner, if I drink your blood I will heal faster."

"I don't even have to think about that, Deveron. Just take what you need from me" said Katelyn, not knowing the ins and outs of giving her life partner her blood.

"The only thing is... you need to be aware that once I drink your blood, if I can't stop... well, I could suck you dry, which could kill you," said Deveron.

"Deveron, I don't think you will hurt me," said Katelyn, running her hand through his hair. "I know you love me. So where do you want to drink from me?"

"Your inner thigh is the best place to drink blood from," said Deveron.

Katelyn sat up on the side of the mattress and pulled her denim jeans off. Laying back down on the bed, with her head resting on the pillow, she teasingly said, "Take your time down there. You know I love it when you touch me there."

Deveron smirked at her and positioned himself in between her thighs.

With his fangs extended, he quickly drew down on her thigh, and started to suck the blood from her body vigorously.

At first, Katelyn winced from his sharp fangs piercing her skin, but a few seconds later, she felt pleasure from him. Moaning from the enjoyment he was inflicting on her, Katelyn also quickly realised that she felt light-headed and was beginning to feel weak.

Deveron growled with every gulp he took from her thigh.

As she looked into his eyes, Katelyn noticed his eyes were turning crimson red and the look of pure hunger. She soon realised that Deveron was not going to stop.

"Deveron, you need to stop," said Katelyn, as she sat up quickly and placed her hands on his shoulders to push him away.

But he didn't acknowledge her. Instead he kept drinking.

"Deveron…" screamed Katelyn out loud, as she tried to push him away.

He growled at her and tore at her supple skin.

Annabelle… Grayson, please… help me, thought Katelyn.

When they burst through the door, Annabelle and Grayson were shocked to see Deveron drinking madly from Katelyn's thigh. They knew he had hit blood lust.

Quickly pulling Deveron off Katelyn's inner thigh, Grayson slapped Deveron's face and threw him up against a wall.

"Deveron… pull yourself together," said Grayson, as he held him at arm's length by the throat up again the wall.

Deveron growled and tried to wriggle free from Grayson's hold, but Grayson was much stronger than him.

"Get a fucking hold of yourself man," said Grayson with his nostrils flared, as he increased the pressure on Deveron's throat.

As he looked from Grayson to Katelyn, Deveron realised what he had done. *Fuck… blood lust…what have I done. Katelyn…* thought Deveron.

Finally breaking free from Grayson's hold, Deveron ran off at vampire speed out of the bedroom.

I'm sorry, Katelyn, thought Deveron to his life partner.

"You Ok, Katelyn?" asked Grayson.

"Yes, I'm fine," said Katelyn, pulling her denim jeans back on and sitting on the side of the bed.

"Annabelle… let's go. We need to find Deveron," said Grayson.

"Right… Ok. Renee will be here in a minute to help you, Katelyn," said Annabelle walking over to Grayson.

"Ok… please don't hurt him," pleaded Katelyn as the tears stung her eyes.

"I can't promise that, Katelyn. He has hit blood lust and God knows what he will do when we catch up with him," said Grayson matter-of-factly. "Let's go Annabelle."

Katelyn watched them run off after Deveron.

"Knock, knock," said Renee, walking into the bedroom. "How you feeling, dear?"

"Weak," said Katelyn, sitting on the side of the bed with rounded shoulders.

"Here you go," said Renee, handing Katelyn a cup of blood. "Should make you feel a lot better."

"Thank you… but how did you know? Oh, never mind… you read my thoughts," said Katelyn with a raised eyebrow, as she took the cup from Renee.

"Yes, dear."

Gulping down the cup contents, Katelyn immediately started to gain her strength.

"Could I have some more, Renee?"

"Sure," said Renee. "I will be back in a moment."

Annabelle and Grayson searched, with vampire speed, the entire house for Deveron, but he was nowhere to be seen. Taking the limestone stairs down to the back shed area, they split up and listened carefully for Deveron's thoughts.

Within minutes Grayson had found him.

"Come out, Deveron," demanded Grayson, with his hand on his sheath, as he continued to search.

"Fuck off," grunted Deveron, his breathing rapid and his eyes darting from side to side.

"You will do as I bid, soldier," shouted Grayson, as he stood three feet in front of Deveron.

Deveron's lips thinned and his nostrils flared, as his piercing crimson red eyes watched Grayson walk towards him.

"Get the fuck away from me, asshole," grunted Deveron, as he tried to run past Grayson.

Grabbing hold of his arm and swinging him up against the concrete shed wall, Grayson said, "Where the fuck do you think you are going?"

"Just… piss off," said Deveron, wrestling free from Grayson's hold.

But as he got to the doorway, Annabelle was waiting for him, and knocked him to the ground with her fist.

She pushed him face first into the ground and held him down with his hands behind his back. As he tried to wriggle free from Annabelle's strong hold, Grayson took control and darted Deveron with a sedative.

Within seconds Deveron was unconscious.

When Annabelle and Grayson, who was carrying Deveron over his shoulder, walked back up to the house, they were greeted by William, who was waiting for them on the back steps.

"Put him in the padded cells below," said William to Grayson.

"Yes, sire," said Grayson, walking inside.

Katelyn waited with Renee in Deveron's room, and calmly drank down a few more cups of blood.

"Feeling better?" asked Renee, placing her arm around Katelyn's shoulders.

"Yes, thank you. Much better... I still can't believe Deveron turned on me, and just like that... there was no warning," said Katelyn, shaking her head.

"That's what blood lust can do to some of us," said Renee.

"In fact, this is what has happened to Deveron. He has hit blood lust," said William, walking into Deveron's bedroom and overhearing the conversation. "When our kind are badly hurt like Deveron was, it takes a lot of healing to get back to normal again. He may be like this for weeks. We just have to take this day by day, Katelyn."

"Oh, right. So... he will eventually go back to the person I know?" asked Katelyn.

"Yes, eventually, dear," said Renee.

"But in the mean time we have had to lock Deveron up in a padded cell down below the house. It's for his own safety, of course," said William, standing in front of Katelyn and Renee.

Taking a deep breath inwards, Katelyn placed a hand over her mouth. She couldn't believe what William had just told her.

"What... no... you can't do that. I don't care if it's for his protection or anyone else's for that matter of fact. This is barbaric... Deveron is my life partner and I won't hear of this," stated Katelyn, as she stood up straight with her hands on her hips.

William's nostrils flared with heated rage and his jaw was rigid as he stood in front of a defiant Katelyn. But before he could say a word, Susan walked into the room and cut the conversation short.

"Katelyn... how dare you speak to William like that. You will apologise NOW!" said Susan, angrily.

"I won't apologise. That is barbaric," said Katelyn, defiantly.

"You will know your place in this coven, woman. I am the leader here and I won't tolerate your defiance, let alone your childish outbursts," said William heatedly. "Susan... you will get her under control or leave. I think my generosity is over."

"I apologise, William. It won't happen again," said Susan, bowing her head to William slowly.

"It had better not, Susan. Otherwise heads will roll. Am I making myself clear Katelyn?" said William, coming to stand directly in front of Katelyn and dominating her space.

"Yes, sir," said Katelyn, as she gulped back her saliva.

"Now that we have this sorted, I will return to our coven business," said William, holding out his hand to Renee, for her to stand and go with him.

"Thank you, William," said Susan, as she watched him and Renee walk towards the doorway.

Between the blood lust Deveron was going through and the chastising she received from William, Katelyn felt overwhelmed by it all. Slumping down onto the bed she wept blindly into her own hands.

"Shh... it will be Ok," said Susan, sitting next to Katelyn and rubbing her back.

"Oh Mom, I wish we had never come here," said Katelyn, leaning into Susan for a comforting hug. "I have never been so scared in all my life… and to think that my own life partner tried to suck me dry. I just can't believe any of this."

"Why don't we go back to your room and you can have a shower? It should make you feel a whole lot better," said Susan, sitting up straight and pushing Katelyn's hair away from her face.

Wiping the tears from her eyes, Katelyn nodded and sniffed back her runny nose.

As Katelyn was drying herself off with the soft white fluffy towel, she heard a familiar voice in her head.

Katelyn.

Yes, thought Katelyn.

I am sorry, thought Deveron.

She could feel his pain, but didn't know what to say to him.

Quickly dressing herself, she glanced at her reflection in the mirror.

Hmm… puffy eyes. Not a good look, thought Katelyn.

Positive that she wanted to speak with Deveron to get some answers, Katelyn decided to go downstairs to the padded cells where he was locked up. As she approached the metal doorway, she heard screaming and then what sounded like punching of the walls. Frightened, she took a deep staggered breath. With her tears welling in her eyes and her hand held over her mouth, Katelyn ran towards the stairs. She couldn't bear to hear or feel Deveron's pain.

"Are you going to be all right, Katelyn?" said Grayson, who was standing at the top of the stairs.

"Oh God, you frightened me," said Katelyn, coming to a halt and wiping the tears from her cheeks.

"Sorry. I forgot that you are still getting used to your vampire abilities and would not have realised that I was here," said Grayson.

"That's Ok. I am just a bit jumpy. To be honest with you, Grayson, I don't know how to feel. I have never seen Deveron like this before and at the moment I am really concerned for my safety, let alone Deveron coming through the blood lust. What I heard down there really frightens me."

"Don't judge him, Katelyn. Eventually Deveron will heal and he will be the same again," said Grayson.

"Have you ever been like this, Grayson?"

"Yes, I have. It took me weeks to get back to some sort of normalcy again," said Grayson, remembering the time he almost killed one of his coven.

"Really…" said Katelyn.

"Listen… why don't we go for a walk and I can explain to you how this all works and then maybe you can understand a bit more. It may make you feel better," said Grayson.

"Hmm… Ok," she said.

Grayson placed his arm around Katelyn's shoulder as they walked slowly throughout the back garden area. He tried his best to make Katelyn understand what it felt like to be in blood lust once you are wounded from battle.

"The cravings… they don't seem to go away. They haunt you in your dreams and whilst you are awake. Hallucinations… God, they seem real. But then… one day, you wake up and it seems to get better all of a sudden," said Grayson.

"Is there anything I can do for him? Maybe a healing?" asked Katelyn, sounding hopeful.

"Probably the best thing you could do right now, is to go back home. You see, it is your blood that he would crave the most, because you are his life partner. So if he can't track your blood, and we don't give him anymore blood than what is required of a... what we call an addict, then his body will start to heal and work through the blood lust," said Grayson.

"But I don't want to leave Deveron while he needs help, Grayson. It just wouldn't seem right. It's not Deveron's fault he is like this," said Katelyn, as they sat on the back steps.

"I know that, Katelyn. But by you just being in the same house, he can feel you and your blood and it would be driving him crazy. You must have realised that when you were outside the cell and could hear him screaming and punching things, that he felt your presence," said Grayson.

"No, I didn't realise. Otherwise I would have kept away," said Katelyn. "Is there no way of healing him quicker?"

Shaking his head, Grayson said, "No."

Susan stood in the back patio doorway and listened to the conversation between Grayson and Katelyn.

"I think it's best we go home for a few weeks, Katelyn," said Susan, walking over to steps. "It will only be whilst Deveron is healing."

Looking in Susan's direction, Katelyn said, "I can't leave him like this, Mom... it's just not fair."

"What is not fair, my dear, is that you have to see him like this every day until he heals. It will kill you, Katelyn, to see him like this all day and night. And William has told me that he will give me daily updates on Deveron's healing if we do decide to go home," said Susan.

Saddened at the thought of leaving her life partner, but knowing it was the right thing to do, Katelyn said, "Ok, Mom. I know you are right, but I want to say good bye first. I love him so much."

"Yes, you can say goodbye. But I warn you, do not open the door to his cell," said Susan, with her hands on her hips.

"Yes, Mom."

Katelyn leaned against the doorway to Deveron's cell.

"Deveron… it's me… Katelyn."

There was no answer, just silence, but she could feel he was listening.

"I am going to go back to Zurich until you have healed. I don't want to leave, but I have been told that I am driving you crazy with my blood. I love you so much, Deveron… please don't forget me. You will be in my thoughts every minute of the day."

But again there was just silence.

As she was about to leave, Katelyn heard him mind talk to her.

I love you Katelyn. I won't ever forget you. Please don't be afraid of me.

Then Deveron started to scream in pain again.

Katelyn ran up the stairs sobbing and into Susan's waiting arms.

Chapter Thirteen

The flight from Paris to Zurich seemed to last forever, as a forlorn Katelyn stared into the white fluffy clouds. Her world had changed immensely since arriving in Bagnolet. She had gone from being wheelchair bound, to being able to walk, and in the process had found out she was a Lepidoptera vampire with healing abilities. But most importantly, she had found that someone special to share the rest of her life with. Well, she thought she had, until Deveron hit blood lust.

"Katelyn... Katelyn," said Susan, standing in the aisle.

"Hmm?" said Katelyn, looking around to see Susan waiting.

"We've landed, dear," said Susan, handing her a carry-on bag.

"Oh, Ok," said Katelyn, looking around at everyone else on the plane standing in the aisle waiting for the plane doors to open.

As Wynton pulled the car to a stop near the front doors of their house, Katelyn impatiently jumped out the car, and ran at vampire speed up to her room.

"Katelyn..." called Susan after her from the car, as she watched her heart broken daughter burst through the front doors of their house.

Katelyn... are you Ok? thought Susan as she entered the house.

Please mom, I just want to be left alone, thought Katelyn.

With her face embedded into the mattress of her bed, Katelyn wept uncontrollably in fear of what she may lose and how she felt about Deveron.

Eventually exhausting herself, she fell asleep.

With her head throbbing and the feeling of exhaustion as she woke the next morning, Katelyn picked up her mobile phone to see if there were any messages from the Gramaze coven. But there was nothing. Wondering what time it was, she glanced at the time on her phone.

Hmm, ten o'clock. I suppose I had better get up, thought Katelyn, sitting up straight in bed.

"Knock, knock," said Mark. "Can I come in?"

Startled, Katelyn looked at the doorway and said, "Come in, Mark."

"Here you go," said Mark, as he walked towards her with a cup of blood.

"Thank you, Mark. What would I do without you? You're so caring," said Katelyn, as she took the cup from his hands. When the taste of blood hit her tongue, she gulped it down fast, and within seconds her head had stopped throbbing and she began to feel alive again.

"How do you feel now?" asked Mark, as he sat on the side of the bed.

"A lot better, thank you," said Katelyn.

"That's good," said Mark. He leaned in and gave her a comforting hug. "I am glad to have you back home, Katelyn."

"Yeah, it's nice to be back home. I have missed you, Mark," said Katelyn.

"Yeah, I have missed you too kiddo," said Mark, pulling away from their embrace. "It was a bit of a shame we didn't get to spend much time together in Bagnolet. Bloody Debauched were causing trouble back here so Connor and I had to come back to help sort them out."

"Well, I am glad you are both all right anyway," said Katelyn.

"Susan tells me that you are now able to walk unassisted," said Mark, smiling.

"Yeah," she said, remembering how it all happened. Her heart was still heavy and she couldn't seem to put two words together as she started to think about Deveron.

"Why don't you have a shower, Katelyn, and come down for breakfast?" said Mark, reading her thoughts.

"I don't feel hungry, Mark. Thank you anyway," said Katelyn.

"I know you are sad, but I won't allow you to be like this, Katelyn, so get your act together now and get into the shower," said Mark, matter-of-factly.

She was so shocked by his tone that she said, "Yes, sir," Then jumped out of bed quickly, retrieved some clothes from her suitcase and headed for the bathroom.

When she eventually came out of the bathroom, wet hair wrapped in a towel, she noticed Mark was still waiting for her. "I will back in five minutes to collect you for breakfast."

"Ok," said Katelyn. She knew not to argue with Mark.

Plugging her hair dryer into the power point in the bathroom, Katelyn tipped her head upside down and dried off her hair and then put it up in a ponytail.

The last thing on my mind is to have breakfast. I am really not that hungry, thought Katelyn, as she plonked herself face down in the pillow on her bed. *I wonder how Deveron is going?* With the tears spilling over onto her cheeks and onto the pillow, she crawled into a ball and wiped her runny nose. As she sobbed into her pillow, she felt someone's hand touch on her arm. Turning around she noticed Mark standing next to the bed.

"Come on," said Mark, looking at her tear-stained, blotchy face. "Let's get you out of here." Quickly, he scooped her up into his arms and carried her down the stairs to the back garden's gazebo, where he had asked Zoe to bring Katelyn out some pancakes and a coffee.

As he placed her down on the wooden chair, next to the table, Mark gestured to the food and said, "For you... eat..."

Nodding, Katelyn sighed and picked up the first pancake and spread some creamy butter on it. Placing her knife down, she took the first bite, her chewing motion slow as she stared aimlessly out at the blue morning sky.

Mark pulled his chair closer to Katelyn's and placed his arm around her shoulder and they sat silently, as she rested her head on his shoulder and chewed on her pancake. He was like her best friend and a big brother all wrapped into one, and being very close, he always seemed to know how to help her.

"Don't worry, he will be all right," said Mark.

"How do you know that he will be Ok, Mark?" asked Katelyn.

"Because I too have been through blood lust. I can't promise you that he won't suffer Katelyn, but I can promise you that he will be all right in a few weeks," said Mark.

"Oh, really... you have been through blood lust? I would never have known," said Katelyn.

"Yes. I remember it well. The hallucinations, the thirst for as much blood as I could get, even the torment. This is not something you forget overnight," said Mark, as his body quivered, cold, thinking about when it had happened to him a few hundred years back.

"I'm sorry you have had to endure that type of pain, Mark. But thank you for being honest with me... I have missed you whilst I was away," said Katelyn, sitting up straight and looking into his face.

"I have missed you as well, kiddo. You are like my little sister and I hate to see you upset like this. But... you know... one of the good things that has happened to you is, you can now walk. Wow... how exciting! And now I can chase you around the house and we can go horse riding, oh... so many things we can do together," he said, excitedly.

She smiled, knowing that he was right. She had a world of things to try, now she could walk.

Katelyn was glad Mark had pulled her out of the gloomy cloud she was under, because she knew she never would have survived otherwise. He was such a great friend to her, and she didn't know what she would do without him around.

Each day without Deveron seemed to last a week for Katelyn. She continued to receive updates on Deveron from the Gramaze coven that he was getting better day by day, and today, William was going to let him out of the padded cell to go back to his own bedroom. He would still need constant supervision, but was healing just the same.

Soon enough, Katelyn knew she would have to tackle another issue that was about to rise, and that was going back to university to finish her degree. Not only would she have to contend with being around humans and not wanting to suck them dry, but also she would have to explain how she could now walk. But most of all she didn't know how she was going to be able to concentrate on her studies, when Deveron and being a Lepidoptera vampire was on her mind 24/7.

Chapter Fourteen

With Katelyn returning to university, and things seemingly returning to some sort of normalcy for her, the transition from human to vampire was going well. Even her best friend, Fiona, didn't question the answer Katelyn gave her on how she was now able to walk, when she told her that she had gone to Paris for treatment and that it had worked.

As the weeks turned into months since Katelyn and Susan had returned home from Bagnolet, Katelyn had not heard from Deveron, so she assumed that he was not interested in her anymore, even if they were life partners. She wasn't sure why, but she did know that he had recovered from the blood lust, because William had constantly given Susan updates on his condition.

Katelyn watched Wynton punch the code into the keypad as usual, and then watched the iron gate slide open. As he pulled the car up closer to their house, she noticed a black car parked in front of the house. Katelyn didn't recognise the car and wondered who had come to visit Susan, whilst she was out at her hairdresser appointment.

Walking in through the front doors of the house, Katelyn said, "I'm home."

"Hello, sweetheart," said Susan, as she walked towards Katelyn. "Oh, wow… your hair looks nice."

"Thanks. I got them to add some highlights today," said Katelyn, fiddling with her hair.

"They did a good job. So… what do you have planned for the rest of the day?" asked Susan.

"Not sure. Might do some study," said Katelyn. "And you?"

"I have some business dealing to contend with at the moment, and I have some friends coming over later this afternoon, but otherwise, I was just going to see Zoe and plan dinner," said Susan.

"Oh, Ok. Well, I might head up to my room. See you later on then," said Katelyn.

"Ok, dear. See you later. Oh and by the way, there is a surprise for you waiting on your bed," said Susan, smirking.

"What is it?"

"You will have to go and see," said Susan, with a raised eyebrow and smiling.

But before Susan could get another word out, Katelyn had run with vampire speed up the stairs to see what was waiting for her in her bedroom.

When she neared her bedroom doorway, she sensed someone was in her room. Turning her head sideways, she felt his presence.

Deveron.

Nervous, she hesitated for a minute in front of the door and then eventually turned the door handle.

When the door opened, Deveron turned to see his life partner standing in the doorway. Reading her mind, he knew her anxiety levels were high.

"Hello," said Deveron, sitting on the bed.

For the first time since she had met Deveron, Katelyn didn't know what to say to him. She knew she still had feelings for Deveron as soon as she saw him again, but she wasn't sure what their next step would be.

"Hi," said Katelyn, walking into the room towards him.

"How are you?" asked Deveron, his brow furrowed.

"I'm fine," said Katelyn, as she sat on the bed next to him. "Obviously you are over the blood lust, otherwise you wouldn't be here."

"Yes. I am much better now. I… I want to apologise for the way I treated you … and well… I will do anything for your forgiveness, Katelyn," said Deveron, looking into her eyes.

With her lips creased in a thin line, Katelyn took a deep breath in and out, as she looked into his eyes and listened to his thoughts. Looking away from him, she stood up and walked over to the double-door window.

Looking out over the back yard, with her arms crossed over her chest, she wondered to herself if she would ever forgive him.

"If you don't want me here, I will understand, but I am here today to tell you that I love you and never want to leave you again," said Deveron, now standing behind her.

"It's not that I don't love you or want to be with you, Deveron. I do still feel our life partner connection more so than ever, now you are here. But I am concerned that if you hit blood lust again, that you will kill me or at least try to and that scares me," said Katelyn, as she continued to stare out the window.

Turning her around to face him, Deveron said, "Please… I am ashamed of my actions. I won't let that happen again. I promise you."

As she watched a single tear streak down Deveron's cheek, she realised he was sincere and meant every word he was saying. Leaning in, she wiped his tear away with her fingers. As Katelyn listened to his heartfelt thoughts she placed her arms around his waist and cuddled into his shoulder.

"Oh, Deveron… I love you."

"I love you too, my sweet lady," said Deveron, cuddling her back. "I have missed you. I really didn't think you would even want to talk with me today, but I had to try."

"I'm glad you did," said Katelyn, tracing every inch of his face that she had missed since they had been apart.

Deveron smiled and leaned into Katelyn, only to pull her chin up to his face and kiss her sweet lips tenderly.

As her lips warmed to his intoxicating touch, they tasted each other for the first time in months.

Katelyn pried herself away from his alluring lips slowly. "So… how is your blood lust?"

"It has disappeared completely. God, I hope I never have to go through that again. The hallucinations and the thirst I had for blood, was painful," said Deveron, remembering the torment he went through.

"Must have been awful," said Katelyn with a creased brow and shaking her head slowly. "I knew you were getting better as I was ringing every day to find out about your progress, but William never told me that you were completely healed."

"That's because I told him not to tell you. By then I had become so ashamed at what I did to you, Katelyn, that I couldn't face you."

"But you are here now, so something must have changed?" said Katelyn.

"Yeah, it did. As my thoughts became clearer, I realised that I couldn't live my life without you. I spoke with Susan and she told me to come here and find out for myself if you would take me back," said Deveron.

"Oh, right… I am glad you are back to the Deveron I know and love. You have been on my mind ever since I returned home," said Katelyn, her heart melting as she caressed the side of his face with her hand. "It's been hard, you know."

"So how are you coping with Lepidoptera life?" asked Deveron.

"Good... I think," said Katelyn, as she paused to remember the last couple of months.

"Can I have a look at your butterfly tattoo?" said Deveron.

As she turned around and lifted her hair off the back of her neck, Deveron said, "Wow... that has fully formed and it's so beautiful; just like the owner." Sensually, he kissed her tattoo and breathed in her peach scent, which always calmed him.

Katelyn felt her stomach do somersaults. Catching her breath, she turned around and said, "I have missed you, Deveron... your smile, your touch, your caring nature. I was starting to think that we would never see each other, ever again."

Picking her up with his muscular arms, he carried her over to the bed and sat her down gently. Stroking her hair, as he sat next to Katelyn, he said, "My world wouldn't be the same without you in it." Leaning in, he placed his arms around Katelyn's waist and kissed her ruby lips passionately.

As he pulled away from her, Deveron said, "I wanted to ask you something, Katelyn."

She looked at him perplexed.

"You don't have to answer me right away, but... I was wondering... well, I was wondering how you would feel about living with me?" said Deveron, watching her reaction.

"Umm... honestly... I'm not sure. As we haven't been a couple very long, it's not something I have thought about. And I am not sure I am ready to move away from my Mom and this house yet," said Katelyn, with a furrowed brow.

"I understand. But where would you prefer to live, here or at the Gramaze house, Katelyn?" asked Deveron.

"Can we live at both for a while until we decide what we want to do?" asked Katelyn.

"Sure... sounds like a plan," said Deveron.

"Knock, knock. You decent?" asked Michael, who was standing on the other side of the doorway with Violette.

"Come in, bro," said Deveron, looking over towards the door.

"Hello Katelyn. Nice to see you again. How's it going in here? You love birds all sorted yet?" asked Violette, as she walked into the room with Michael.

"Yeah, we are all good," said Katelyn, standing and walking over to Michael and Violette.

"Nice to see you again, Katelyn," said Michael, as he leaned in and gave her a hug.

"Nice to see you both too," said Katelyn, giving Michael a hug first and then Violette. "What are you both doing here?"

"We came with Deveron for support. Plus we wanted to see how you were doing with the transformation," said Michael.

"That's all going good. I just have to learn how to use my abilities a bit better. I haven't had the time since I have been back home. Been busy with university and all," said Katelyn. "How long are you both here for?"

"Not sure yet. So, what are you up to tonight, Katelyn?" asked Violette.

"I don't have anything planned. And you?" asked Katelyn.

"Well, why don't we four do something together... I don't know, maybe a movie, or sight-seeing. I haven't been to Switzerland before. What is there to do here anyway?" asked Violette.

"Umm... what about the Bolero Club and Lounge in Winterthur? It's very much like a night club and is only about a thirty minute drive from here," said Katelyn. She had been there previously with her best friend Fiona once or twice.

"Sounds good," said Violette, looking to Michael for approval.

"Hmm... not sure. I will check with Susan first and have to let you all know. If Susan can provide some soldiers to guard you, Violette, whilst we are out, then it should be Ok," said Michael. "Because Violette is a multi-coloured female Lepidoptera, we need to be careful that she is not taken. The Debauched would have a field day if they knew you were here."

"Oh, right. Well, there's probably not a lot we can do outside the house then. We could always go swimming and have a dinner out in the back gardens. Maybe listen to some music. The weather here at the moment is really nice at night," said Katelyn.

"Let me check it out with Susan and I will get back to you. In the meantime, Violette and I will go and unpack and get settled into our room, and leave you love birds to chat some more," said Michael.

"Ok. See you later on then," said Katelyn, as she watched them walk towards the door.

"See you later, guys," said Deveron.

Chapter Fifteen

"Knock, knock," said Susan, as she stood in the doorway to the room Violette and Michael were staying in.

"Come in, Susan," said Michael, looking back at the doorway from the wardrobe.

"You both settled in now?" asked Susan, walking into the bedroom.

"Yeah... how did you go with William?" asked Michael.

"Well... he said, no, to going to the night club. But he said if I could spare some soldiers to guard you, Violette, then he would permit you to go sight-seeing at least. But there was one condition. And that was that you have to sight-see from the car only. You are not allowed to leave the car at all. He just didn't want you putting your life in any danger," said Susan.

"That's a fair call," said Michael looking from Susan to Violette.

"Hmm, I suppose," said Violette.

"Also, William is flying over Danielle, Christian and Daniel to help with guarding you. They should be here within the hour," said Susan.

"Oh, Ok," said Violette, looking forward to spending some time with her sister and the others. "So what time will we leave tonight?"

"Maybe, say around eight? That way we can all have dinner together and then you can go out," said Susan.

"That sounds like a good plan," said Deveron, overhearing the conversation and walking into the bedroom with Katelyn.

"Well, now that this has been sorted out, I will go and organise some cars for tonight's adventure," said Susan, smiling.

"Thanks Susan. Appreciate you doing this for us," said Violette.

"That's no problem, at all. I will see you all later then, at dinner," said Susan, walking towards the doorway.

They all nodded.

The three cars, one limousine and two SUVs, were waiting for them outside the front door entrance, as they stepped onto the porch.

"Have a good time, guys," said Susan, as she watched them walk over to the vehicles.

They all said goodbye at the same time.

"Bye, Mom. We shouldn't be too late," said Katelyn, smiling.

"Take your time, dear," said Susan. She waved them all off, as the vehicles pulled away from the house and drove towards the front wrought iron gates.

Connor and Mark were in the first SUV up front. Katelyn, Deveron, Violette, and Michael were in the limousine, and Danielle, Christian and Daniel were in the SUV behind them.

"So... where we off to first?" asked Violette, excited.

"I have organised for a tour of the city first. The lights are just magnificent at night," said Katelyn. "Then we are going up to the cliffs. The view up there of the city is perfect."

"Sound good," said Violette, as she snuggled into Michael's arm and sat back to enjoy the ride.

The cars pulled up next to the curb on the south side of the Limmat river, and Katelyn explained about each building and their contents in detail. She was proud to call Zurich her home and it showed in the way she knew every intricate detail about each place and its history.

"Wow… this is beautiful. Look at all the city lights… looks like lots of jewels shining brightly all at once. And I can't believe how awesome the architecture is," said Violette, mesmerised by what the city had to offer.

Beautiful… just like you, Violette, thought Michael to Violette.

Violette smiled as she looked into Michael's eyes.

"Yeah, I never grow tired of this beautiful city. I feel blessed to have grown up here, that's for sure," said Katelyn, as she held Deveron's hand.

As they drove from one end of the city to the other, Deveron listened in wonderment to Katelyn's voice and was astonished at how much she loved the city she had grown up in.

Anyone feel like a drink or a snack before we continue out of the city? thought Katelyn to everyone in all three cars.

She heard them all say 'yes'.

"Could you please give me a hand to carry the drinks and food?" said Katelyn to Deveron, as the driver stopped across the road from one of her favourite cafés.

"Sure," said Deveron, pushing open the car door and hopping out with Katelyn.

As Katelyn and Deveron waited at the counter for their order to be prepared, Connor and Mark stood guard outside the café.

"You feel that?" asked Connor, looking around.

"Yeah, Debauched. They are near," said Mark.

Time to go Katelyn. Debauched are close, thought Mark.

Ok. Just waiting for the coffees to be made, thought Katelyn, as she watched the barista put the cups into a cup holder tray.

Within seconds Christian and Daniel had joined Connor and Mark at the café entrance.

Let's go, Katelyn. The Debauched are now eyeballing us across the road, said Mark, his fists clenched and his jaw rigid.

Keep your pants on. We are coming, thought Katelyn.

"You're cutting it close, Katelyn," said Connor, as he watched the door swing open and Deveron and Katelyn walk out with the drinks and food in their hands.

With vampire speed, they ran back to their cars and sped away, all the while watching the Debauched through the back windows of their cars.

We won't be stopping again, for anything. That was way too close. I read one of the Debauched's minds and they know Violette is here. So once we are done with the cliff tour, I think we will be heading back home, thought Mark to everyone.

Fucking bastards. They never give up, thought Michael, as he held Violette's hand.

Why do they want Violette so badly? thought Katelyn. This was all new to her.

Because if they can drain a multi-coloured female of her blood, then they will be able to reproduce the perfect Debauched. But it's not only Violette that they wanted. They also will take any female Lepidoptera, thought Michael to Katelyn.

Jesus, I didn't realise until now just how valuable we women are to the Debauched, thought Katelyn.

Don't worry ladies, I am here to protect you; no matter what, thought Daniel, who was the newest coven member of the Gramaze household.

Violette, Danielle and Katelyn all smiled at the same time, and thought, 'thank you.' They all welcomed his allegiance.

Thank you, Daniel. I am glad we brought you with us today and that you are part of our coven. I feel you will be a great asset to our team, whilst we are here, thought Michael to Daniel.

Thank you, Michael. I would give my life for any of the Gramaze coven, especially Violette. She made me feel like family as soon as I met her, and family means the world to me. So I am indebted to her, thought Daniel to Michael.

I appreciate your candour, Daniel, thought Michael, remembering when Daniel decided to join the Gramaze coven only months earlier. Since then, he had become a great asset and was fitting in nicely.

Secretly, William had sent him on this mission to not only guard Violette, but to test his loyalty to the Gramaze coven.

With the three cars driving around the winding roads of the Uetliberg mountainous cliff sides, the panoramic view of the entire city of Zurich and Lake Zurich was breathtaking.

Nearing the top of the mountain, Michael heard a screeching of tyres and looked behind him through the back window to see what was happening. He noticed that a SUV had joined the drive up to the Uetliberg and was way too close to the back of the Danielle, Christian and Daniel's SUV.

"What's going on?" asked Violette, as she looked out the back window.

"Debauched. Fuckers are toying with Danielle, Christian and Daniel's car," said Michael.

Christian… be careful. Debauched are behind you, thought Michael to Christian.

Yeah, we know bro… fuck… they just rammed our car, said Christian, stomping on the brakes and looking in his side mirrors.

But before Michael could get another word out, he watched the Debauched soldier drive around to the left hand side of Christian, and side swipe his car. Again and again the Debauched rammed their car sideways into Christian, Danielle, and Daniel's car.

As Christian tried to steer his car into the Debauched van, he hit the wooden barrier at the side of the road. Stomping on the brakes hard, he watched the Debauched black SUV hit their car again and again. Eventually the force of the bull bar on the SUV pushed them through the barrier and Christian, Danielle and Daniel's car went soaring into the air and off the side of the mountain.

"No... Danielle..." shouted Violette, as she watched her sister's car, through the back window, become airborne off the side of the mountain and burst into flames when it hit the ground.

Wynton... you go up ahead with Violette and Katelyn, and we will drop back and protect you from behind, thought Connor.

Yes, sire, thought Wynton, as he drove past Connor and Mark.

"No... stop! Wynton... my sister...!" screamed Violette, when she realised what was happening.

When Katelyn, Deveron and Michael looked over at Violette, she had her hand held out front of her and as she curled her fingers into her palm, they noticed Wynton started to choke. With her abilities, she had cut off his airways.

All of a sudden their car came to a screeching holt, and with Connor and Mark's SUV behind them, Connor quickly swerved sideways to miss ploughing into the back of them.

"Violette... stop... you're killing him," said Katelyn, as she watched Wynton choking.

Violette pushed past Michael, and jumped out the car. As she saw the Debauched SUV coming towards her, she stood firm, and held both her hands out front and used her abilities once more, to make the Debauched driver steer off the side of the mountain. Running over to the side of the road, she watched the Debauched van explode into a fire ball as it hit the ground.

With the tears streaming down her cheeks, Violette placed her hand over her mouth as she watched her sister's car burn below.

"Danielle!" she screamed.

"Violette…" said Michael, as he reached her and enveloped her in his arms.

She cried uncontrollably into his chest.

Sickened and outraged by what the Debauched vampires had caused, Katelyn stood near the cliff side and watched both cars burn below. As she looked out into the horizon, she saw a vision of Daniel's bloodied body in her mind's eye.

"Guys… I think Daniel is still alive," said Katelyn, turning around to them.

"What… that's impossible. We saw the explosion," said Mark.

"I am telling you, he is down there and alive," said Katelyn, matter-of-factly.

Running over to the side of the roadway, Mark used his vampire vision to look down side of the mountain. Within seconds, he had spotted Daniel's body, which wasn't far from the top.

Daniel had his arm stretched out into the air and was waving for Mark to come and get him.

"He's alive… I see him," said Mark. Climbing down the side of the mountain, and holding onto anything he could, Mark reached Daniel within seconds.

"Are you OK, boy? asked Mark, as he knelt down beside Daniel and looked at his bloodied head and torn clothing.

"Yes," said Daniel weakly. "I hit my head." Before he could get anything else out he fainted.

Mark called up to Connor, who was standing on the road side. "Can you throw down some rope, Connor?"

"Sure. I think there is some in the van," said Connor, running back to the van.

As Mark placed Daniel's unconscious body into the van, Katelyn asked, "Is he going to be Ok?"

Looking back at Katelyn, Mark said, "He should be Ok. He just has a bad cut on his forehead."

Katelyn looked at Daniel, and again another vision appeared in her mind's eye.

This time it was of Daniel as a newborn baby, being taken by Talitha to a hotel. The name on the front of the building she saw was 'Crestwell'.

Frowning as she looked at Daniel and continued to see the visions, and watched on as Talitha gave Daniel to the brown haired man, and listened to their conversation.

Thank you, Talitha. I am grateful that you have at least given me one of my children. I was devastated when you fostered out our daughter years ago. I still don't understand your reasoning. I could have taken care of her. You know that, said Talon, heatedly.

Yes, I am aware... I will not be darkening your doorstep again, Talon. This was a mistake for a Lepidoptera and a Dream Walker to have children. I don't want you ever to speak of this to anyone. Are you understanding me? said Talitha, handing over the boy.

Yes. You have my word, said Talon.

Shaking her head, Katelyn's eyes widened as she took in a deep breath.

"You Ok?" asked Mark to Katelyn.

"Hmm... yeah... I think so," said Katelyn, frowning and wondering if this was one of the abilities she had been given, now that she was a Lepidoptera.

"Help!"

They all heard it.

"Help! We are here!" screamed Danielle.

Looking over the side of the mountain, Violette pointed and said, "There… there they are."

Michael rushed with vampire speed down to where Danielle and Christian were hanging from a thick branch that was protruding out of the mountain side.

As he neared Danielle and Christian, he said, "Hold tight, guys. I will get a rope and we can help you back up."

"Hurry, Michael. I don't know if this branch can hold us both for much longer," said Christian. They were both hanging freely, with no foothold, over a gully.

Reading Michael's mind, Connor and Deveron retrieved two coils of rope, one for Danielle and one for Christian. As Connor and Deveron attached the rope to their waists and threw it over the mountain side, Michael grabbed hold of both ends of the coils.

"Here… can you reach it?" said Michael, as he tried to direct the rope into Danielle and Christian's hands.

"Got it," said Danielle.

"Yep, me too," said Christian.

"Now let go of the branch. Connor and Deveron will pull you both up," said Michael, with a furrowed brow.

With tears of happiness, Violette hugged Danielle when she got to the top of the cliff, and sobbed. "Oh, sis, I thought you were dead."

"Shhh… it's gonna be all right, Violette. Anyway, you can't get rid of me that easily," joked Danielle, hugging her tight.

Violette giggled. Plying herself away from her sister, she turned around to Christian and said, "Are you Ok?"

"Yeah, I will be fine. Nothing a good hot shower and some clean clothes won't fix," said Christian, as he leaned in and gave Violette a hug.

"I am so glad you are both all right," said Violette.

"Guys, let's get the fuck out of here. We don't want to be here when the police arrive," said Connor, hearing the sirens in the distance.

"Would it be Ok if I ride with Daniel? I would like heal his wounds," said Katelyn.

"No problem. Deveron, you riding along with us too?" asked Connor.

"Nah, I think I am better off riding with the princess," said Deveron, watching Violette and Michael get back into their car.

"Right. Good thinking," said Connor, walking back to the SUV.

"See you back at Susan's, my girl," said Deveron, giving Katelyn a quick hug.

"Bye," said Katelyn.

Sitting in the back of the SUV with Daniel still uncon-scious, whilst Connor drove and Mark sat next to him in the front, Katelyn placed her hands on Daniel's chest to help heal him faster as they drove along. She was still learning how to use her abilities, but she had faith in herself that she could heal him.

But that wasn't the only reason she wanted to be near him. Katelyn was also curious as to how she was having the visions. And they only seemed to be happening when she was near Daniel. Was it because he was a dream walker that Katelyn was able to see his memories, or was it something else? She needed to know.

Placing her hand over his head wound, she watched as his wound completely vanished. Smiling, she looked down at his unconscious body and wondered what it had been like for Daniel growing up with his dad.

As Daniel's hazel eyes opened, and he sat up quickly, Katelyn said, "Hello... it's Ok."

"Is everyone all right? asked Daniel.

"Yes, we are all Ok," said Katelyn. "You, on the other hand, had a nasty fall from the car when it drove off the cliff. You had a cut on your head, which I have healed. But otherwise, you are all right. Nothing some rest won't fix."

"Where are we?" asked Daniel.

"We are on our way back home," said Connor.

"Good to see you awake," said Mark, turning around.

"How long was I out?" asked Daniel.

"Oh, not long. We think the bump to your head may have rendered you unconscious. Actually, if it wasn't for Katelyn, we would never have known you were alive. She spotted you," said Mark.

"Really... thank you, Katelyn," said Daniel, placing his hand on her shoulder.

"You are welcome," said Katelyn.

"What happened to the Debauched?" asked Daniel.

"Them fuckers are dead. Disintegrated on impact when their car exploded, I would say," said Connor, his fingers gripping the steering wheel tight.

"Good," said Daniel, raising his eyebrows up and then down.

So... what is the Crestwell Hotel? thought Katelyn to Daniel.

Daniel frowned at Katelyn, and wondered why she was asking.

I don't know, lied Daniel. *Why do you ask?*

Oh, it doesn't matter. I just saw it in one of my visions, thought Katelyn.

Visions... ah. What else did you see in these visions? thought Daniel.

You as a baby... your mother and a man who I think was your father. By the way, we have the same mother," thought Katelyn.

I sort of figured that out already, thought Daniel. *I have met Talitha, but haven't had much to do with her yet.*

She is beautiful. Some say regal. Lovely to speak with, thought Katelyn.

Yeah she is nice.... so what else have you seen in your visions? thought Daniel.

Not much else. Mainly things about you. And that's how I found you... I saw a vision in my mind's eye of you lying where we found you, thought Katelyn.

"You two are quiet. What's going on?" asked Mark, turning around in his seat again.

"Nothing, Mark. Just chatting," said Katelyn.

"Right. Everything Ok? asked Mark.

"Yeah, it's all good, bro," said Katelyn, looking sheepishly from Daniel to Mark.

Why is she having visions about me? thought Daniel to himself.

Chapter Sixteen

With her arms crossed over her chest, Susan waited anxiously for the two cars to pull up safely at her front door. Since she had taken Katelyn home fifteen years before, Susan had never had to worry about Katelyn's safety or if the Debauched knew she existed, because she was still human. But now that Katelyn was a Lepidoptera, and would be well sought after by the Debauched, Susan didn't like how it made her feel vulnerable as a mother.

When the SUV pulled up beside her, and the sliding door opened, Susan's face lit up when she saw her daughter's appearance.

"I am so glad you are all right, Katelyn," said Susan, as she pulled her quickly out of the van and hugged her tight.

"I'm Ok, Mom," said Katelyn, welcoming her hug. "In fact, we are all Ok. I can't say the same for the other SUV though. Sorry Mom."

"Oh, don't worry about the SUV. I am just glad you are all safe," said Susan, now looking around at everyone else who was standing in front of her.

"Yeah, I think we dodged a bullet there," said Michael. "I think it's time we head off home to Bagnolet, don't you?"

Susan nodded. "I have rung William to let him know what has happened and he is of the same opinion. He has ordered you all to come home. I have organised for the plane to be refuelled and it's now ready."

"Thank you, Susan," said Michael. "And thank you for having us too. If only it could have been under better circumstances."

"My pleasure," said Susan. "Are you going back to Bagnolet too, Deveron?"

Looking from Katelyn to Susan, and then to Michael for approval, Deveron hesitated and then said, "If it's all right with you, I would prefer to stay here."

"Yes, you are welcome to stay for as long as you can," said Susan, looking from Deveron to Michael for support.

"I think that would be a good idea, bro. You are fully recovered now, and I think Katelyn will need someone else, besides Mark and Connor, to guard her anyway. You know what the Debauched will do if they detect Katelyn's scent."

"I sure do," said Deveron, taking Katelyn's hand in his.

Katelyn smiled, as she gripped his hand tight.

"I will speak with William and let him know that you are staying here to protect Katelyn, Deveron," said Susan.

"Great, thank you," said Deveron.

"Well, we had better get upstairs and pack up our bags," said Violette.

"That has already been done for you, dear. Your bags are waiting in the foyer," said Susan, indicating to the doorway. "Mark, Connor, I want you both to go with the Gramazes to the airport. Wynton, you can drive them in the limousine."

"Yes ma'am," said Wynton.

Mark and Connor nodded once.

"Thank you for having us, Susan," said Violette.

"You are welcome. In fact you are all welcome to come for a visit anytime. It's a pity it had to end like this, this time around," said Susan, looking around at them all.

They all smiled and nodded in agreeance.

Katelyn watched on as the limousine drove out the front gates. *It was so good seeing them all again. I'm gonna miss them.*

"I am sure you will see them all again, soon," said Deveron, as he placed his arm around her waist and watched the car pull out onto the roadway.

"But most of all, I am glad you are sticking around for a while, Deveron. Life hasn't been the same without you," said Katelyn, placing her arm around Deveron's waist and placing her head in the nook of his shoulder.

The warm night air blew into Violette's face and jostled her hair about as she alighted from the limousine with Michael onto the tarmac. Climbing the metal stairs she took one last look of Zurich in the distance and then continued on into the plane to take her seat.

"Beautiful place, isn't it?" said Michael, as she sat next to Violette.

"Yeah... it's a pity we didn't get to stay longer. I would have liked to see more of this city," said Violette.

"Yeah, me too," said Danielle, overhearing their conversation, as she sat next to Christian.

"Maybe we can ask William if we can come again one day," said Violette.

"I doubt that. You know how protective he is of you, Violette," said Christian, matter-of-factly.

"Well, she is the princess, after all," said Daniel. "And we do need to remember that she needs to be kept safe, at all times."

"Yes, you are correct," said Michael.

Rolling her eyes, Violette sighed and placed her seat belt on and then looked out the plane's small round window. Violette loved being a Lepidoptera, but she was not thrilled about being the Gramaze princess and how restrictive it was. The Debauched always seemed to be after her and her valuable blood.

"That's quick. We are moving already," said Violette to Michael.

"The sooner we get out of here and back home, the better. I am sure the captain knows this," stated Michael.

As the plane started its taxi down the runway, Violette leaned into Michael and said, "I think something is wrong. We haven't heard from the captain yet... and usually by now, he is telling us to place our seat belts on."

With a furrowed brow, Michael thought for a second. "Hmm, you could be right..."

But before he could finish his sentence, his speech slurred and he became unconscious, along with everyone else on the plane.

Up front in the cockpit with gas masks on were two Debauched soldiers, who had killed the pilot and co-pilot and taken over the plane. They had pumped a gas throughout the cabin to make everyone fall unconscious.

As the wheels lifted from the tarmac, and the plane's motor roared, the oldest of the two Debauched took a mobile phone from his jacket pocket. "Master... we have her and also as a bonus, four others as well," said the soldier.

"You have done well. I will see you shortly when you arrive in Berne," said Fredrik.

"Yes, sire," said the soldier. Closing the cover to his mobile phone, and placing it back in his black leather jacket, his grin widened as he remembered the words of his master, that he would be sizably rewarded if he returned with the princess.

With the Gramaze coven still unconscious and slumped over in their seats, the small jet plane came to a halt on the tarmac roadway which was at the back of Fredrik's property on the outskirts of the city.

When the plane's door extended opened, and it dawned on Fredrik that his dream of becoming a powerful Debauched leader was going to eventuate, the expression of amusement was apparent on his face.

"Sire," said the soldier, as he watched his master board the plane, and walk over to the princess's seat.

Fredrik yanked Michael out of his seat and threw his limp body to the carpet covered floor. As he sat next to Violette and pushed her head back in the seat, he sneered as he gazed upon her beauty.

"It's a shame we will have to eventually kill you, princess. Your beauty is not one I have seen for a few thousand years," said Fredrik, as he ran his hand down the side of her face. Turning around to his soldier, he said, "Take her inside. The rest of them - chain them up in the tunnels below the house. Then I want them all drained."

"Yes, sire," said the youngest soldier.

"What would you like me to do with the plane, sire?" said the oldest soldier.

"Burn it," said Fredrik, as he stood up.

"Yes, sire."

"Well... what are you waiting for? Load these fucking Lepidopteras into the van, NOW!" shouted Fredrik.

The two soldiers anxiously nodded and started to load the Gramaze coven into the waiting van.

"Aww," said Daniel, opening his eyes and raising his head from his chest. Looking towards the ceiling he tried to work his hands free from the chains that were hooked over a wide metal beam from the ceiling holding him in place, as his feet barely touched the ground. *Where the fuck am I?*

"Ah, you're awake," said the Debauched soldier, walking over to Daniel.

"Release me, you moron," said Daniel, trying to wriggle free.

"Moron? We will see who is a moron, Lepidoptera," said the soldier, as he produced a cattle prod from his jacket and pushed it into Daniel's chest.

Daniel's body convulsed violently as the current ran throughout his body.

As the Debauched pulled the cattle prod off Daniel's chest, he said, "Now Lepidoptera, you will tell me where your master lives. Otherwise, I will press this into your chest again."

As the sweat beaded on Daniel's brow and across his top lip, he said, "Do what you need to, Debauched. I will never tell you."

"Your wish is my command," said the Debauched soldier pressing the cattle prod into Daniel's chest again.

"Aww... fuck... stop," said Daniel, feeling like his head was going to explode.

"Had enough yet?" said the Debauched soldier, as he stood in front of Daniel with a smirk on his face and the cattle prod still primed.

"Go to hell, Debauched," said Daniel, as he lifted his legs into the air and placed the guard into a head lock with his inner thighs.

As the soldier tried to forcibly wriggle free from Daniel's hold, he dropped the cattle prod and it smashed onto the concrete flooring.

Holding the Debauched firmly in place, whilst twisting his inner leg muscles back and forth, Daniel finally felt the soldier's body go limp. Releasing his hold, he watched on as the soldier's body hit the ground hard below him. Wondering how long it would be before someone else would come, Daniel looked around the brick lined tunnel and spotted some keys on the belt of the Debauched on the floor. He placed his foot on the Debauched's belt and tried to unhook the keys with his toes.

With every move he made, the pad locked chains ripped into the flesh of Daniel's wrists, and the blood started to drip down his arms.

Finally releasing the keys from the Debauched's belt, Daniel swung his leg up towards his chest and grabbed hold of the key ring. Once he had undone the locks on his injured wrists, his body crumpled to the ground.

"Aww... fuck," said Daniel, rubbing his bloodied wrists as he looked around the tunnels and noticed the other Gramaze coven members, chained to the walls.

Shit... where is Violette? thought Daniel, as reality hit him like a ton of bricks, when he couldn't see her anywhere.

As he reached each Gramaze coven member he tried to rouse them, but to no avail. Releasing each one and lying them flat on the ground in the foetal position, he tried to ascertain their injuries and figure out why they were unconscious. Searching each of their bodies, he soon realised that each one of them had been drugged, from the puncture marks on each of their arms. It also looked like each of them had had some blood drained from them as well, from the tell-tale track marks.

Fuck... I need help. But how am I going to let William know? Think Daniel, think.

Katelyn woke suddenly from what seemed like a dream and tried to steady her breathing. Sitting up quickly in bed, she felt her heart beating fast and wiped the sweat away from her top lip.

"Deveron," said Katelyn, rocking him gently.

But he didn't wake.

"Deveron," said Katelyn, louder.

"Hmm... yes, my sweet lady," said Deveron, in a sleepy voice, with his eyes closed.

"Wake up. Something is wrong. I..."

Deveron sat up quickly. "What... what is it?" asked Deveron as he looked into her worried eyes.

"I think Violette has been taken by the Debauched. In fact, I don't think they made it home from here... I don't know... I just woke from a dream. But it felt real, you know?" said Katelyn, panicking.

"Calm down, Katelyn," said Deveron, placing his hand in hers. "It was only a dream... right?"

"I don't know," said Katelyn, her eyes wide and her breathing rapid. She knew the Gramazes had been dropped off at the airport, because Mark, Connor and Wynton had returned to the house safely. But she couldn't help the feeling of dread in her bones. "I need to give the Gramaze house a call."

Reaching over to his mobile phone which was on the bedside table, Deveron said, "Give me a minute and I will ring William. Are you sure...? It's just... I don't want to upset William."

"Upset him? Fuck, give me that phone. I would rather be safe than sorry, wouldn't you?" said Katelyn, taking the phone from his hands and dialling the number.

"What can I do for you, Deveron?" said William, as he answered the phone.

"William, it's Katelyn."

"What is wrong?" asked William, in a serious tone.

"Have the others returned yet?" asked Katelyn.

"Not yet. I just assumed they left Zurich late. But why do you ask?" said William, with a furrowed brow.

"I dreamt it, William... I could be wrong, but I think something has happened to them," said Katelyn.

"You dreamt it...humph," said William.

"Please, William. Just check it out. Don't dismiss this. I have a strong feeling about this," said Katelyn.

"Hand the phone to Deveron," said William.

"Here… William wants to speak with you," said Katelyn, passing the phone to Deveron.

"Yes, sire."

"What is going on there?" asked William.

"She… well… she woke from a dream and needed to find out if it is true," said Deveron.

"Yes, yes. I know this already. Have you asked her any details about the dream?" asked William, as he watched Grayson enter the combat room and walk towards him.

But before Deveron could answer William, he overheard the conversation William was having with Grayson.

"Fuck… she could be right, Deveron. Grayson has just informed me that the plane has gone missing. The flight responder has been turned off too," said William. "Put Katelyn back on."

Deveron handed the phone to Katelyn. "William wants to ask you some questions."

"Yes, William."

"What did you see in this dream?" asked William.

"Not much. Besides Michael, Danielle, Christian laying on a concrete floor, in what looked like bricked tunnels. I didn't see Daniel or Violette though. But the others looked like they were sleeping. Besides that… that is all I saw. What is going on, William?" said Katelyn.

"I don't know… I suspect that what you saw was from Daniel's eyes. You know he is half dream walker?" said William.

"No, I didn't know he is a dream walker… hmm, that would make sense. For some reason he and I have seem to have a connection. It happened here too when the Debauched tried to run us off the road. I saw Daniel on the side of the cliff in my mind's eye. I never thought much about it at the time, but now… well… maybe he is trying to warn me so we can help them. What do you think?"

"I think you may be right," said William. "Do you think you may be able to go back to sleep, Katelyn? It might be the only possible way we are going to be able to find them."

"I can try," said Katelyn, with a raised eyebrow.

Handing the phone to Deveron, she laid down on her pillow, closed her eyes and tried to calm herself.

"Leave it with us, William," said Susan, entering the bedroom.

"Did you hear that?" asked Deveron, watching Susan walk in.

"Give the phone to Susan," said William.

"Yes, sire," said Deveron, handing it over to Susan.

"I have some sedatives here for Katelyn to take. They should be able to make her sleep. We will ring you back," said Susan.

"Right… in the meantime I will see what we can find out from our sources here," said William. He then hung up the phone.

"Here Katelyn, take these," said Susan, sitting on the bed.

Katelyn sat up in the bed and gulped down the sedative with some water and then lay back down on the pillow. As she closed her eyes, Deveron and Susan waited patiently to see what would happen.

Good, you're back… thank God, thought Daniel.

Daniel… how am I seeing this? thought Katelyn.

Through our dreams. For some reason, we're able to connect with each other through our dreams, said Daniel.

Frowning, Katelyn thought, *So where are you? And why can't I see you? This is all just a bit too weird for me.*

Yeah, yeah, I know. What you are seeing is through my eyes, this is why you can't see me. And I don't know where we are. All I know is that I can't find Violette yet. God knows what they are doing to her. Michael, Danielle and Christian are all still knocked out, thought Daniel.

Then why aren't you unconscious too? thought Katelyn.

I don't know. All I know is we need to find Violette and fast, thought Daniel.

Ok, Ok. Keep your shirt on. First, we need to find out where you are. Are there any windows or something like a landmark you can see from where you are situated? thought Katelyn.

Daniel walked towards a small window with bars on it and looked outside.

I see something. Looks like an old historical building that is lit up with blue and purple colours.

Historical building… what is lit up like this at night? questioned Katelyn. *I should know this. It seems familiar. Wait… it's the Bundesplatz. Ok, this gives us a starting point. So now let's go find Violette.*

Don't worry, I will find Violette. You just need to get some back up coming my way, Katelyn. Just wake up, hurry, thought Daniel.

Ok. We will be there soon to get you, thought Katelyn.

Thrashing in her sleep, Katelyn woke suddenly to find Deveron, Susan, William, Grayson and Annabelle all standing next to the bed watching her.

Sitting up and shaking her head, she wondered how William and the others were already there. *How long have I been asleep for?*

"They are near the Bundesplatz," blurted Katelyn.

"Right… this gives us a starting point. Katelyn, get dressed. You are coming with us. We will meet you downstairs in five minutes," said William, authoritatively.

"Yes, sir," said Katelyn, jumping out of bed and heading for her wardrobe.

Wynton drove the limousine onto the tarmac and pulled up next to the Gramaze aeroplane. Waiting for them at the bottom of the stairs were Nicky, Sherrie, Temperance, Stephen and Brock, all dressed in battle gear and ready to protect not only their leader but also their princess and the Gramaze family.

As Katelyn, Deveron, Grayson, and Annabelle jumped out of the car, they all boarded the plane and took their seats ready for take-off.

"Sire, we are ready," said Brock, standing at the bottom of the stairs.

"Good… let's get the fuck out of here and rescue our family," said William, standing in front of Brock.

Brock and William boarded the plane and took their seats.

Whilst in flight, William stood at the front of plane and gave instructions to his coven on what the plan of attack was: to not only rescue their princess but also the rest of their coven from the Debauched.

But first they needed to actually find them. And that wasn't going to be easy from the description that Katelyn had given them.

Chapter Seventeen

Their SUVs parked near the Bundesplatz, a government plaza in Berne, Switzerland. With vampire speed, Katelyn exited the van and leaped up to the roof with William to get a better view of the area, whilst everyone else stayed in the vans and awaited instructions.

"Anything look familiar?" asked William, scanning the area.

"Not sure. Give me a minute," said Katelyn, distracted by the water fountains squirting up from the floor in front of the building. Quickly looking left then right over the tree tops and buildings, she remembered from her dream with Daniel that there was a white bridge in the distance.

"There," said Katelyn, pointing in the direction of the river. "I remember seeing that white bridge. But it was in the distance, so I would say it's in that direction that we must travel."

"Anything else?" asked William, his brow furrowed.

"Only that there were a lot of trees lining the property. Sorry, William. That's all I remember," said Katelyn, worried they wouldn't find the house.

Placing his hand on her shoulder, William said, "You did good. Now let's go."

Jumping down onto the pavement, and back into the van, William took his seat next to Brock, with Katelyn on the other side.

"Brock, can you bring up an aerial shot of Berne in the direction of that white bridge," said William, pointing in the direction of the bridge.

"Sure. Give me a minute," said Brock, as he retrieved his laptop from his bag and opened the lid.

Bringing up his search engine on the laptop, he then proceeded to search for aerial shots of Berne and its surrounding areas.

"Any of these look familiar, Katelyn?" asked Brock, as he pointed to the laptop screen.

Katelyn scanned the pictures quickly and spotted another thing that was of importance.

"I remember seeing that," said Katelyn, pointing to what looked like an octagonal cupola that was on top of a roof. "It wasn't far from the place where they are being held either."

"Way to go, Katelyn. Talk about attention to detail. That should be able to get us closer," said Brock, manipulating the screen to bring them closer to the cupola.

"Good work, Katelyn," said Deveron, feeling proud of his life partner.

"Stephen, start driving east and I will give you some more instructions as we get closer," said Brock, looking into the rear-view mirror at Stephen's face.

"Right," said Stephen, starting the van and placing it in drive.

Katelyn watched out the window of the van as it neared the building with the cupola.

"There… that's got to be the house," said Katelyn, pointing towards a lonely house, behind a limestone fence, covered with moss.

Excellent… now let's get our family and go home, thought William to each of his coven.

The Gramaze coven quietly glided with vampire ease over the painted limestone wall and silently landed on the other side.

As William scanned the front lawn and garden areas, he quickly realised that the Debauched house had cameras mounted throughout the front property. He signalled to his coven to stay out of the line of each camera until they could be destroyed, which was his first plan of attack.

With no Debauched in sight and the cameras destroyed, William instructed his coven to search the entire property and the house, via mind talk, whilst he continued around to the left of the house with Grayson, Nicky and Sherrie, to check out the back of the property.

As William, Grayson, Nicky and Sherrie crept past the three black SUVs that were parked near the side of the house, they were soon set upon by four of Fredrik's soldiers, who were guarding the back verandah area.

With his finger on the trigger of the blow torch in his hand, Grayson ignited the flame and ran forward to stop the soldiers in their tracks. As two of their bodies burst into flames, and the soldiers screamed in pain, fell to the ground, and William beheaded them. These young soldiers were no match for two of the oldest Gramaze coven men.

Watching their comrades' bodies disintegrate, the two remaining soldiers realised that they were outnumbered. But before they could get away, Nicky and Sherrie drew their swords from their sheaths and beheaded them. With their bodies turning to ash, Nicky and Sherrie high fived each other and smiled, knowing that their combat training was paying off. Ever since both of their life partners had died at the hands of the Debauched in the poppy fields, they were only too happy to kill each and every one of them for destroying the happiness they missed and also to repay William for taking them in and looking after them.

With their swords drawn, Temperance, Stephen and Brock walked around the right-hand side of the house in search of any Debauched. Noticing an unlatched gate, Brock pushed it open with the tip of his sword and continued to walk down the side of the house with Stephen and Temperance.

All of a sudden, they were blinded by a massive spotlight in front of them. Then out of the darkness an automatic machine gun fired its bullets into each of their bodies continuously. None of them could see who was firing the machine gun or how many Debauched were in front of them as they battled to stand. It wasn't long before they all hit the ground.

William... we need help around here, thought Brock as he tried to crawl along the ground towards the machine gun.

Within seconds, William, Grayson, Nicky and Sherrie arrived and scanned the area for Debauched. But there was not one in sight. Watching as their family was being slaughtered, Sherrie took her knife out of her belt and threw it towards the spot light. As the light smashed into pieces, the automatic machine gun fire stopped.

Running over to Temperance, Stephen and Brock to ascertain their injuries, Grayson turned over Brock to find his chest full of bullet holes. Then looking at Temperance and Stephen, he realised they too were full of bullet wounds. But as he watched their unconscious bodies, he saw the bullets extruding themselves from their bodies one by one.

"They are alive, but unconscious, sire," said Grayson, with a furrowed brow. "Fucking Debauched... they will pay for what they have done to our family."

"Bastards... we can't leave them here unguarded whilst we search for the rest of our coven," said William, looking around the property. "Sherrie, I want you to go back and get one of the cars. It will be your job to load these three into the van and then keep them guarded until we can return."

"Yes, sire," said Sherrie, nodding once and running off to get the van.

"Nicky, I want you to stay here and guard these three," said William, pointing to his coven members. "When Sherrie gets back, you can then join us."

"Yes, sire," said Nicky, bowing her head slightly.

"Let's get these fuckers, Grayson. They will pay for what has happened here tonight," said William, his sword gripped firmly in his hand.

Grayson nodded.

Annabelle, and Deveron entered the house through the open front screen door with their swords drawn, and Katelyn followed behind them, ready for any Debauched that might attack.

"Stay behind us, Katelyn. You don't have any combat experience, and we don't want you getting hurt," said Deveron.

"Ok," said Katelyn, nodding.

Quickly scanning the front living room, then the rest of the house, top and bottom, they ascertained the house was empty.

"Let's see if this joint has a basement, or tunnels," said Annabelle, as she come across a doorway which when opened, led down to some stairs.

Katelyn and Deveron nodded and followed her every instruction as they headed down the wooden stair case to the basement.

Noticing a cord for a light hanging from the ceiling, Annabelle pulled it slowly. As the light shone down in the basement and they reached the bottom of the stairs, it became clear that their coven members were nowhere to be seen.

"Fuck... where are they?" said Deveron, as he tried to locate them with his vampire abilities.

"Look…" pointed Katelyn, noticing a half moon scrape mark on the floor. Running over to wall, she slid her hand across the wall to see if there was a handle or any sort of opening. As she pressed hard against the wall, it opened outwards, revealing some more stairs. "Let's go."

"Wait… it could be a trap," said Deveron, pushing past Katelyn. "Let me go first."

Katelyn stopped quickly in her tracks and waited for Deveron to pass.

Hoping he was wrong, Deveron slowly descended the stairs. When he reached the bottom, he couldn't believe what he was seeing. Michael, Christian and Danielle, were lying unconscious on the concrete floor.

"Annabelle… Katelyn… down here," said Deveron, as he rushed towards Michael, Christian and Danielle.

As Annabelle reached Michael, Christian and Danielle, and placed her hand on their chests, she realised they were still alive, but barely. "Go for help, Katelyn. They are in need of some blood. But be careful," said Annabelle.

"Ok," said Katelyn, taking the stairs two at a time.

"I wonder where Daniel and Violette are?" said Annabelle.

"That's a good question," said Deveron, looking around the tunnels for a fridge with some blood. But all he found were some dead rats.

As William and Grayson walked towards the back of the property, they saw a lake in the distance that was lined with pine trees, and a long, narrow jetty near the shore. But they weren't prepared for what was at the end of the jetty.

William and Grayson looked at each other in dismay, as they watched the leader of the Switzerland Debauched, Fredrik, carry a limp, unconscious Violette towards a shimmering portal, which was at the end of the long jetty, that had been created by a Debauched-employed warlock. Knowing they didn't have much time before the lightening blue coloured portal closed, they ran towards the lake.

"Stop…" yelled Grayson, as he and William ran towards Fredrik.

Turning to see William and Grayson running towards them, Fredrik hurriedly continued on through the portal with Violette in his arms, and his two dark skinned soldiers followed.

"Close the portal, Beyer… NOW!" shouted Fredrik, watching William and Grayson closing in on them.

With one wave of his hand, before he finally stepped through the portal, Beyer did as instructed.

When the portal doorway closed abruptly, William and Grayson came to a grinding halt.

"Fuck… sire… we are too late," said Grayson, staring out over the lake.

Saddened, and wondering if he would ever see his princess again, William breathed a heavy sigh. "I can't believe she is gone."

Placing his hand on William's shoulder, Grayson said, "Don't worry, we will get her back."

"Hmm…" said William, looking out of the lake and wondering where Fredrik would have taken Violette and if he would eventually kill her.

"Sire… can Adrian help with finding Violette?" asked Grayson.

Looking into Grayson's eyes, it dawned on William that Grayson could be right.

"You may be onto something there."

Taking his phone out of his pocket William dialled Adrian's number.

"Quickly… let's get her into the van," said Fredrik to his two soldiers, as the portal closed behind him.

"Michael…" murmured Violette, as her eyes opened and closed, when they loaded her into the van.

"Give her some more of that serum," said Fredrik, as he slammed shut the sliding door.

"Yes, master," said the soldier.

"Beyer, I want you to locate where this multi-coloured beauty lives," demanded Fredrik.

"Yes, Fredrik," said Beyer, knowing he must do as he was told, otherwise Fredrik would kill his family.

Climbing into the back of the van, Beyer pulled a strand of Violette's hair from her head and placed it in the palm of his hand. As he chanted a locating ritual in his mind, and his eyes became a clouded mist, Beyer not only saw the house and street signage, but also the weapons room. Scribbling the location on his arm, Beyer's vision then returned to the van.

"Well…" said Fredrik, realising Beyer had stopped chanting.

"Fredrik… here is the address. Now will you release my family?" said Beyer.

"Once I have what I want and what is mine, then I will release them. Until then you are here at my beck and call. Are you understanding me?" said Fredrik, his face not showing any compassion.

"Yes, Fredrik," said Beyer, bowing his head slightly.

"Take us to the Gramaze house, Beyer," said Fredrik.

"Yes, sire," said Beyer, as he opened up another portal.

"Where are you?" asked William to Adrian abruptly.

"Hello to you too, William," said Adrian taking the call.

"No time for niceties… Violette has been taken by the Debauched," said William.

"What... how...? Oh never mind. What can I do to help?" asked Adrian, his brow furrowed.

"As I said, where are you?" said William.

"We are on holidays in Los Angeles at the moment," said Adrian.

"Can you come to Berne, Switzerland straight away?" asked William.

"Yes, but that will take hours," said Adrian.

"Do you know much about portals?" asked William.

"Yes. Quite a bit in fact," said Adrian, wondering where William was going with this.

"Good. Portal here to Berne! Now!" said William.

"Yes. But you will need to give me an address," said Adrian, looking at Emily who had just walked in on his conversation.

"Who is it?" mouthed Emily.

"William," mouthed Adrian.

"Oh," said Emily nodding.

"I will text you the address. But I need you here now," said William, authoritatively.

"That is no problem, William. I can be there in seconds," stated Adrian.

Within seconds of hanging up, William and Grayson watched on as a new turquoise green portal opened at the end of the long jetty and Adrian and Emily walked through, hand in hand.

"Hello, my friend. What can I do to help?" said Adrian, as the portal closed.

"Can you create a portal to where Violette is being held?" asked William.

"Yes... but it's not that easy. Do you know where she is being held?" asked Adrian.

"No, and that is the problem. There must be a way for you to locate her, is there?" said William.

"Yes. But I will need a few items first," said Adrian.

"Like what?" asked William.

"A candle, and something of Violette's," said Adrian.

"Sire… maybe we should go to Susan's house. Violette has just been there and I am sure Susan will have a candle," said Grayson.

"Good call. I'll give Susan a ring now and let her know we are on our way. The others are going to need medical attention and healing anyway. So we can kill two birds with one stone," said William. "Can your portal carry eleven of us back to Susan's house?"

"Yes, that is no problem, at all," said Adrian.

Chapter Eighteen

The half-moon shaped turquoise green portal opened, and William and his coven stepped out from the shimmering water, along with Adrian and Emily.

"It looks like the locator spell has brought you back home, William," said Adrian, looking around the grounds of the Gramaze home.

"How could this be right?" said William, frowning. "Let's get inside." *Renee, is Violette here?*

There was no answer.

Renee... Samantha, has Violette returned? thought William, as he walked through the back door.

There was no answer from either of them.

"Fuck... something is wrong. Renee and Samantha are not answering," said William, hoping his life partner was alive.

Grayson gulped back his saliva when he couldn't sense Samantha either. This could only mean two things. She was either unconscious or worse yet, dead.

"Fucking Debauched, they will pay if anything has happened to my Samantha," grunted Grayson.

A cold shiver ran down William's spin. *The queen...shit.*

"Grayson, Deveron, follow me," said William. They ran through the house and down to the basement at vampire speed.

William reached the queen's room first. Stopping in his tracks, he walked in slowly. Glass crunched under his feet as he was faced with up turned, broken furniture. With drawers pulled out and papers strewn all over the floor, the room looked like someone was looking for something.

But the queen was nowhere to be seen.

Only a message scrawled in what looked like blood on the wall of her room.

YOUR QUEEN IS OURS LEPIDOPTERA.

My queen… are you all right? thought William, hoping she would hear his thoughts.

But there was no reply.

"FUCK…! Them Debauched bastards are going to pay. Let's go," said William, in a heated voice.

"Wait, William," said Adrian, now standing in the doorway and looking at the mess that was left behind. "I can do a locator spell to find her."

"Good idea. Whilst you do that, we will look around the house for Violette, Renee and Samantha," said William, indicating to Grayson and Deveron to follow him.

Adrian nodded quickly. "Leave it with me."

William, Grayson and Deveron raced up the basement concrete stairs at vampire speed and started their search of the entire house, along with Michael, Danielle and Christian. As they went from room to room in search of the four female Lepidopteras, they noticed most of the house wasn't even touched, except for the combat room. Walking down the stairs that led into the combat room, they realised from the broken glass on the combat mats, that the weapons had been taken out of the wooden cabinets, and only silhouettes remained of the swords that had previously been on the walls.

"FUCK…!" yelled William, clenching his fists beside his body.

Grayson's lips thinned as he looked around the bare room and became frustrated, knowing the Debauched had stolen their weapons and had violated their inner sanctum. Racing over to what looked like a storage cabinet, which had been ripped open with its doors touching the ground, Grayson moved the cabinet sideways to gain access to a secret room which held more weapons, bombs, and enough fire power to annihilate the Debauched.

"Thank fuck they haven't taken anything out of here," said William, standing next to Grayson and looking inside the secret room.

"I can't believe them Debauched bastards didn't find this room. I am just wondering how did they know about our house?" said Grayson, his eyes squinting.

"Good question, Grayson. But there is something more important to worry about at the moment. The females... it seems none of them are here. Hopefully, Adrian's locator spell will find them all in the same place. FUCK, if anything happens to any one of our females, those bastards will pay. I will hunt each and every one of them down personally," said William.

"Sire, what would you like me to do?" asked Deveron.

"Help pack up some of these weapons. Once Adrian has located the females we will..." said William.

"William..." said Adrian interrupting William and walking into the combat room. "I have located the queen."

"The queen... what about the others? You said Violette was here too. But she isn't and nor are Renee and Samantha. What is going on?" said William, suspiciously.

"Well... I just checked out your security tapes with Brock, and it shows Violette arriving with the Debauched via a portal and then the four women being taken by Fredrik and his henchman," said Adrian.

"It's true William, what Adrian is saying. But what he didn't tell you was that Violette and the queen put up a good fight. Unfortunately they were overpowered and knocked unconscious. It seems they all took another portal somewhere else, sire. But as Adrian said, he knows where to locate the queen, so the others are likely to be with her," said Brock, standing in the doorway.

"Excellent... let's pack up some of these weapons we need and go," said William. "Good work, Adrian and Brock."

Stepping out of the portal Adrian had created, and onto a property with a white wooden fence, and pine trees lining the roadway up to the house, William gave the orders to his family to spread out and look for the female Lepidopteras.

"Adrian, Emily, I don't want you to get involved in our battle. Best you stay here and wait for us to come back... just have the portal ready," said William, standing in front of Adrian and Emily.

"As you wish, William," said Adrian, nodding.

As Grayson, Katelyn, Deveron, and Annabelle, approached the house together, Grayson said, "She is here."

Samantha, are you all right? thought Grayson to his life partner, as they reached the front doors of the house.

There was no answer.

"Let's get inside and find our family," said William, turning the handle of the front door quietly, not knowing what was on the other side of the door.

"Yes, sire," they all said together, following him inside with each of their weapons drawn.

Brock, Temperance, Stephen... how are you going around the back of the house? thought William. He knew that they had fully recovered from the machine gun fire earlier tonight, but wanted to make sure his family were ready for any Debauched surprise attacks.

We come across four Debauched, but they were no match for us. Just about to enter the back of the house, thought Brock to William, as he looked down at his bloodstained sword.

Excellent… keep me up to date on what you find. Don't forget we are missing Daniel too, thought William.

Yes, sire. We are quite aware, thought Brock, pulling open the screen door.

Nicky, Sherrie… keep an eye on that front gate. We don't want any surprises, thought William.

Yes, sire, they both thought, as they crouched behind the bushes next to the front white wooden fence.

Michael, Danielle and Christian… anything happening down the back of the property, near the sheds? thought William.

Nothing here, sire, thought Michael.

Right, come back up to the house, thought William.

Yes, sire, they all thought together.

Sire… thought Grayson, pointing to the stairs as he heard voices above them.

When the Debauched noticed the four Gramaze Lepidoptera now standing in the foyer of their house, they jumped the railing on the staircase with their swords drawn, and landed with a thud on the marble flooring.

"If you know what is good for you Debauched, you will hand over our family," demanded William, with his sword drawn and his nostrils flaring.

"Finders keepers, Gramaze," teased the Debauched soldier, as he rushed at them with ease. The five other Debauched with him then joined in.

Grayson was in no mood for the Debauched, as he took his blow torch out and ignited it. Pointing it in the direction of the Debauched, he then released his finger from the trigger and lit them, one by one, on fire.

Annabelle, Katelyn, Deveron, and Grayson watched on as each of the six Debauched screamed, until each of them was beheaded and their burnt bodies disintegrated into ash.

Upstairs… gestured William to Annabelle, Katelyn, Deveron and Grayson. *Be careful, they would have heard all the commotion down here already.*

Landing on their feet as they jumped from the foyer to the top of the staircase, William gave the signal for Annabelle, Katelyn and Deveron to go to the left and for Grayson to continue onto the right with William, in search of their family.

As they continued to open each door that was connected to the balcony and search each room, their family was nowhere to be seen.

"Where the fuck are they?" said Annabelle to Deveron.

"I don't think they are up here," said Deveron.

Opening her mouth to speak, Annabelle stopped in her tracks and listened to what she thought was a faint sound coming from a closet. Gesturing to Deveron to keep guard, they walked over to the closed closet door and stood in front of it and listened again. Soon enough she heard the noise again.

Daniel, thought Katelyn.

Annabelle pulled opened the closet door quickly. But to her surprise, she found Daniel, bound and gagged on the floor of the closet, trying to wriggle free of his chained feet and hands.

"Daniel…" said Annabelle, kneeling in front of him and taking his gag off his mouth. "Are you Ok?"

"Yes," said Daniel. "Untie me."

"Where are Violette, the queen, Renee and Samantha?" asked Annabelle as she broke the chains away from his body.

"Not sure… they drugged me before I could see anything," said Daniel, getting to his feet. "Who else is here?"

"Everyone. No one is safe at our house. The Debauched paid us a visit and try to take all our weapons whilst we were in Switzerland," said Annabelle.

"Bloody fuckers. What can I do to help?" asked Daniel.

"Just stick by me," said Annabelle.

"William is saying we need to get down to the basement," said Deveron, interrupting their conversation. "And the best news of all is that they have found Violette, Renee and Samantha and all of them are OK."

"That is good news. Right, stay close to us, Katelyn and Daniel. We don't want you getting hurt, or worse yet, killed," said Annabelle. She then handed them both a long handled, thick knife which she retrieved from her belt buckle. "You may need this."

"Thank you," said Daniel, looking at his sharp blade.

"Hmm… thanks," said Katelyn, not knowing if she would be able to use it.

As they came out of the bedroom, Annabelle was sliced with a sword in the abdomen by a Debauched whom she hadn't noticed. "Arrr, fuck," screamed Annabelle as she clutched her stomach and bent over in pain.

Katelyn and Daniel stood back with their mouths open, not knowing what they could do to help, as Deveron swung his sword in the air righteously and beheaded the soldier, before he could behead Annabelle, and then watched as Deveron took out the second soldier, with one jab to his heart and then beheaded him too.

When the fight was over, Daniel jokingly said, "I must remember not to get on the bad side of you, Deveron."

"Don't worry, boy. I will teach you how to fight like this one day, and soon," said Deveron, with his hand on Daniel's shoulder.

Daniel smiled and nodded.

"You Ok, Annabelle?" asked Daniel.

"Yeah... those fuckers won't stop me. Let's go," said Annabelle, walking towards the staircase, as she ignored the pain coming from her stomach.

At the bottom of the staircase in the basement, Deveron, Annabelle, Katelyn and Daniel first noticed a large metal furnace which was usually used for hot water heating, with the door open and burning brightly. They then noticed Violette, Danielle, Christian, Renee, Samantha and Michael standing with William and Grayson next to the furnace.

"Where is the queen?" asked Annabelle, as she got to the bottom of the stairs and observed the sadness in each of their eyes.

"In there," said William sadly, as he gestured to the brightly burning furnace. "She is dead."

"NO!" screamed Annabelle. "It can't be." The tears welled in her eyes.

"I'm sorry dear... it's true," said Renee, as she hobbled over to Annabelle and gave her a hug.

Pulling away from Renee, Annabelle's wiped the tears from her face and nose. "William... these fuckers must pay. I want revenge for her death."

"I agree... Stephen, Brock and Temperance are upstairs now and they have the Debauched leader, Fredrik and a few of his soldiers held at bay," said William, looking at each of his family members. "Michael, are you up to a fight?"

"No, sire," said Michael weakly. He had been beaten badly by the Debauched for protecting his family when they were first taken from the aeroplane and hadn't fully recovered yet.

"Right, I want you, Daniel and Deveron to stay here with Danielle, Violette, Katelyn, Renee and Samantha and guard them. Whilst you are waiting for us to come back and get you all, I want you to retrieve the queen's body from the furnace and ready her for transport back to our home. Am I clear...?" said William.

'Yes, sire,' they all said.

"Annabelle, Grayson, Christian, come with me," said William, as he ran towards the stairs.

"So... you finally make an appearance, William," sneered Fredrik, as he watched the four Gramaze coven form a circle around him and his two soldiers.

"You will pay dearly, Fredrik, for what you have done to our queen," said William, his fist clenched by his side and his brow furrowed.

"Ah, you have found her. That is of no consequence to me," said Fredrik, matter-of-factly, with his head held high. "I got what I needed from her."

As soon as the words came out of Fredrik's mouth, William ran towards him and pushed his sword through his chest and then beheaded him. His head, still snickering with a half-smile, fell to the ground, and his body disintegrated.

Annabelle and Grayson soon followed suit and beheaded Fredrik's two soldiers with their swords.

"Take that, you fuckers... think you can kill our queen and get away with it," sneered Annabelle.

Brock... where are you? thought William.

I'm in a shed out the back of the property destroying any evidence these fuckers have left, thought Brock.

Once you have finished doing that, I want this place blown sky high, you hear me? thought William.

Yes, sire. All the charges have been laid already. I am just waiting for everyone to clear out, then I can do my stuff, thought Brock.

Excellent... thought William to Brock.

William heard footsteps coming from behind him and turned to see two of his coven carrying Talitha's burnt body on a stretcher towards him, whilst the others helped the injured depart the house and walk towards the portal that Adrian had now created outside. When Talitha's limp body passed by him and through the portal, William gulped back his saliva and took in a deep breath.

They will pay… thought William to himself. As his nostrils flared and his lips thinned, he remembered back to the first night he had met Talitha and how he willingly let her turn him into a Lepidoptera.

William was originally from a farming community which he inherited from his father. The land he inhabited grew wheat, oats and barley, which gave him and young family more than enough money to live on, even after he paid his taxes to the king. But when the king ordered his soldiers to take the plentiful land from William, and he refused to let this happen, the soldiers slayed his wife and two young children in front of him for his defiance. Clutching his wife and children's bloodied, limp bodies as he knelt next to them, William vowed to himself that the king would one day pay for what he had done to his family and that he would never allow his land to be taken from him, so he decided to burn every single field to the ground.

As he stood at the edge of his property holding the fuel-soaked, wooden torch, and watching his fields burn, he remembered looking up to see a young, brown haired woman, who had a colourful aura around her, standing on the other side of the fire and she was summoning him to come to her. In a trance like state, William approached her and when she touched his face with her supple hand he felt a calm, relaxing, almost mothering manner about her. With her regal manner, Talitha caressed his face gently and reassured him of a better world if he joined her coven. Grief stricken and convinced he had nothing left to live for because his family and land were gone, he agreed then and there to Talitha turning him into a Lepidoptera and to serving her for the rest of his life.

"Sire..." said Grayson, as he watched the sadness and yonder look in William's eyes.

William blinked slowly, and then looked into Grayson's eyes. "Yes."

"We must go through the portal," gestured Grayson to the portal doorway.

Looking around, William noticed that he and Grayson were the only two left to go through and that the house behind them was in flames. "Right... let's go."

Chapter Nineteen

Awakened by a familiar voice in his head, William quickly sat up in bed and looked around the darkened bedroom. Taking a deep breath, he pulled the cotton sheet from his naked body and placed his feet firmly on the hard timber flooring, only to notice the light coming into the room from under the closed door. Roughly jostling his brown hair with his fingers, William realised that he must have been dreaming, as he looked over his shoulder and saw Renee sleeping peacefully. Standing, William made his way over to the tallboy and picked up his mobile phone to check the time.

Hmm… its only 1.45am, thought William, as he placed the mobile back down on top of the tallboy and headed for the bathroom.

The hot water seemed to cascade over his head and shoulders nicely, as William's large hands rested against the tiled wall and his tired body relaxed, when he closed his eyes.

Help… William.

Opening his eyes, he quickly pulled his head out from under the water and stood to attention, and listened carefully. The voice was faint, but it was familiar.

"Renee… is that you?" asked William, as he turned off the faucet and stepped out of the shower onto a mat.

There was no answer.

William.

"Who the fuck is that? Show yourself," said William, authoritatively, looking towards the doorway.

But again, there was no answer.

Help.

Shaking his head, William grabbed a towel from the rack and dried himself off. Placing the towel around his waist, he then continued on into his bedroom closet and quickly got dressed. As he sat on the side of the bed and placed his black leather lace up boots on he heard the voice once again. This time, it was loud and clear.

William... come to me... now.

Frowning, William headed towards the doorway. As he placed his hand on the handle and opened the door, he heard the voice once again.

William.

"Fuck..." said William, as he raced towards the stairs.

Reaching the bottom of the stairs at vampire speed, William just about knocked over Michael and Grayson who were waiting for him.

"You hear it too, hey?" said Michael to William.

William nodded.

"Yeah, so do we," said Grayson, smiling. "But I think we are the only ones that can hear it."

"Can't be..." said William, as he walked towards the basement stairs.

William placed his hand on the handle and hesitated for a minute at the doorway. Looking from Grayson the Michael, he said, "One way to find out."

Opening the door to Talitha's room, William's eyes looked towards her bedroom doorway, where they had laid her body to rest on top of her four-poster Queen Anne bed-spread the previous day. They had intended to give her a full ceremonial service the next night, where she would be bathed in the earth's fruits, wrapped in white cotton sheets and her body lit by the fire of the Lepidoptera's next queen, Violette.

Rubbing his eyes, William had to look twice. Talitha's body was no longer on the bed. As he raced towards her bedroom doorway, Michael pulled him back.

"Wait…" said Michael.

Frowning, William turned to Michael and Grayson and said, "Where is she?"

"Violette is in there with her. Give it a minute," said Michael, with a furrowed brow.

"Like fuck…" said William, walking into Talitha's bedroom. "What the…"

Violette's eyes were closed and a pure ray of bright ultraviolet light was coming out of her hands which were hovering over Talitha's body. The light seemed to be penetrating into Talitha's body as she floated above the ground, and her body was no longer charred from the fire; instead she looked like the queen he knew and loved.

Violette was chanting the same words over and over.

"Ong, Ma Lee, Bae Mae, Hong."

It was an ancient Buddhist healing ritual, which William hadn't heard for many years, which symbolised healing.

Grayson and Michael stood in the doorway to Talitha's bedroom, with their mouths open, and watched Violette chant the healing ritual and then move Talitha's lifeless body back to her bed.

"Ong, Ma Lee, Bae Mae, Hong," chanted Violette.

William watched on in awe of Violette, as she set Talitha's body back down on the bed with ease. But as soon as the chanting stopped, Violette collapsed on the floor.

Michael rushed past William and Grayson and over to Violette's unconscious body and shook her violently. "My sweet girl… Violette!" screamed Michael, anxiously.

"Give her a minute," said Talitha, as she sat up. "She is exhausted from healing me."

"My queen... but how?" muttered William. Sitting beside her on the bed, and placing his arms around her body, William couldn't control his happiness, he was so honored to be in her presence again. "We thought you were dead."

"Well, I nearly was. When our coven pulled me out of the furnace I was barely alive," said Talitha, slowly pulling away from his embrace. "But once we went through the portal that Adrian created and you brought me back to my room, I seemed to be able to communicate with Violette. So I summoned her to try and heal me. I wasn't sure it was going to work. The rest is history."

"But it did work," said Violette, in a low voice.

"Violette. You are Ok?" said Michael, as he hugged her tightly.

"Once you gain your strength back my dear, you will be fine," said Talitha. "Thank you for healing me Violette. I am indebted to you."

Violette smiled and nodded once.

"Come on. Let's get you back to our room where you can rest," said Michael, picking Violette up in his muscular arms.

Violette nodded and cuddled into his shoulder as he carried her out the room.

"I will leave you both to talk, Sire," said Grayson, following Michael and Violette out the room.

"Thank you, Grayson," said William.

"Is there anything I can get you, Talitha?" asked William, looking over her regal facial features.

"Some blood would be good," said Talitha. "But first I want to speak with you about my security... how on god's earth did the Debauched find me?"

"The only thing I can think of is that they stumbled upon you by accident, my queen. Fredrik already had Violette, so I suppose it tied her to this house and then they would have found you by searching the house," said William.

"Hmm, that would make sense. But am I safe here now?"

"Yes, my queen. Fredrik and his men have all been neutralised and I am sure no one else knows you are here."

"How do you know this, William?"

"Well, not only did we kill them Debauched bastards, but I have also instructed Adrian to place some wards around the house and the grounds so that they won't detect you either."

"A very well thought out plan. Thank you, William."

"My queen... I want to ask you something."

"What is it, William."

"Well... I knew from our connection that you were dead when you were in the furnace. Well, that's what I thought... but... I am still wondering how you survived. It doesn't make sense."

"I am still trying to piece it together myself, William. When our coven carried me through the portal, something in my body felt a surge of energy. I am thinking it was the portal's energy... and... then once I entered this house I could feel my body trying to heal itself. But I needed Violette to do the rest. Because we are mother and daughter, our connection... it's unbreakable, especially as she now has all her powers."

"She does? I wasn't aware of that, my queen."

Talitha nodded. "She is powerful, William, and you need to protect and keep her safe at all times. But what I am most afraid of is that she will not like to be cooped up like me. She is young, but still reckless. I don't think she actually appreciates how valuable she is to our kind. Even though she has been told."

"Yes, I would say you are right, my queen. I will have a word to her and Michael."

"Knock, knock," said Annabelle, standing in the doorway.

"Come," said Talitha, looking up.

"Here you go," said Annabelle, walking into the room and handing a glass of blood to the queen.

"Why, thank you, Annabelle," said Talitha, taking the glass from her hand.

"You're welcome. Is this anything else I can get you, my queen?" asked Annabelle.

"No, my dear," said Talitha, smiling.

"I will leave you then," said Annabelle, slightly bowing her head. "It's so good to have you back."

"Thank you, dear," said Talitha.

"Thanks, Annabelle," said William, as he watched her walk out the room.

Once Annabelle was out of earshot, Talitha said, "William, actually there is something that I wanted to speak with you about."

"What is it?"

"Daniel and Katelyn."

"What about them?" asked William, frowning.

"They are siblings. From Talon. You remember Talon?" said Talitha, picturing Talon's face. She then took a gulp of the blood from the glass.

Williams eyes widened. "Hmm… that would explain a lot. But, they don't know this?"

"No, they don't. And considering what has just happened to me in the past twenty-four hours, I would like to see them both, to explain everything," said Talitha, with a furrowed brow.

"I will get that organised," said William.

"Well… I need my rest, William. Bring Daniel and Katelyn in later on today and I will speak with them."

"Yes, my queen," said William, standing. "Is there anything you need before I go?"

"If I need anything I will summon you."

William nodded once and walked towards the door. "It's good to have you back, my queen."

'Thank you."

Talitha watched William pull the door closed and this seemed to jog her memory of the day that William had first introduced her to Talon. He had initially brought Talon to meet Talitha to speak with her about the dream walker community forming an alliance with the Lepidoptera's. From the moment Talon had walked into her apartment, Talitha had felt some sort of connection with him that excited her inner core.

As she lay her head on the pillow and stared at the white ceiling, all her memories of Talon and their on-and-off relationship came flooding back. Since Talon lived in Switzerland and she in France, they only saw each other sporadically, but when they did come together, the electricity between them ignited. Their many dinners, secret meetings at the 'Crestwell Hotel' in Switzerland, going to the theatre, enjoying each other's company, the thirst for sex. But what seemed to be at the forefront of her mind now was when she gave birth to Katelyn and then Daniel and how she dealt with the situation.

Closing her eyes, Talitha took a deep breath and tried to calm herself. Out of the many children she had given up over the years, Katelyn and Daniel had been the hardest to let go. And she wasn't proud of herself for the way she had handled their father, Talon. The pain of what she had done to protect her coven and its children was the only thing on her mind back then.

When her body finally relaxed and gave into sleep, Talitha dreamed of a younger Talon Donovan and of happier days together.

William's load felt lighter, now that the queen was still alive, as he walked up the staircase to his bedroom. As he reached the top of the stairs he was greeted by Adrian.

"Hello, my friend. What are you doing up this time of the morning?" asked William.

"Actually, Emily and I are just getting ready to leave," said Adrian.

"To go home or back to LA?" asked William.

"Back to LA. I still have a business to run there."

"Right. How did you go with the wards?"

"They are all in place. No Debauched will ever get in here again, let alone detect any of you, especially the queen and Violette."

"Thank you, my friend. I appreciate everything you have done for me and my family over the past twenty-four hours. I won't ever forget your commitment and selflessness."

"You are welcome, my friend," said Adrian, placing his right hand in front of him to shake William's hand. "I am just going to say goodbye to Violette and Danielle and then we will be on our way. We will be in contact soon."

"Right... we will speak with you soon, Adrian," said William, placing a hand on Adrian's left shoulder and shaking his hand.

As William placed his head on the pillow, Renee turned over and said, "Hello, my love."

"Hello... did you hear what has happened?"

"Yes. How is she?"

"Much better. She's resting at the moment. But I have a lot to sort out later on today."

"Oh... yes I see," said Renee, listening to Williams thoughts.

"Come here, my love," said William, placing his arm on her pillow for Renee to cuddle into the crook of his arm.

"Don't worry William, it will all work out," said Renee, snuggling into his shoulder.

"Always the optimist," said William, placing his arm around her stomach and pulling her in tight.

"William, now that things are back to normal, well, semi-normal, there is something I want to tell you," said Renee, looking up to his face.

"What is it, my love?"

"I am with child," said Renee.

"What... how is this possible?" said William, looking into her blue eyes.

"I don't know..." said Renee, resting her hand on the side of her face as she turned on her side. "I thought only the queen could have children."

William sat up slowly, and then looked down at Renee. "Apparently not." Shaking his head in disbelief. "It's just... wow... I am going to be a father."

"You sure are," said Renee, smiling, pushing a loose strand of her brown hair behind her ear. "I tried to work out how far along I am, and I think I am about six weeks."

"Right. Six weeks," said William, raising his eyebrows. "We will have to alert the queen to the situation."

"So... I am a situation?" She sat up and sighed.

"No, my love... after the day I have had, it just seems that a lot of unexplained things seemed to be happening here that I don't have any answers for," said William, placing his arm around Renee and kissing the side of her temple. "We will approach the queen together on this when she is feeling better today."

Renee nodded.

"So you are happy."

"Yes, my love. Ecstatic."

"Then why do I feel you are not telling me everything?"

"Renee... I don't want you going out on patrol any more, and I would be a lot happier if you took it easy. This child is important to me and I don't want anything or anyone taking that away for me," said William, placing his hand on Renee's stomach.

"Don't worry, I feel the same way." Renee leaned into William and kissed his lips.

"How are you feeling, Violette?" asked Michael, as he watched her drink a cup of blood.

Catching her breath from gulping the blood down so fast, Violette then said, "Better."

"That's good. Violette... I..."

"I know... I should have told you that my abilities had increased. It's just... well... you know I don't want to be tied to this house yet. I like to enjoy my freedom," said Violette, with her brow furrowed.

"Yeah I know. But... you don't seem to understand..."

Violette put her pointer finger to his lips and shook her head.

"I do understand, and that's the problem. All my abilities have kicked in and yes, I have been secretly practicing them. And now that the queen and William know I have all my abilities, they will put a stop to me leaving the house entirely. I don't want this life, Michael," said Violette, as the tears formed in her eyes.

Michael sat on the bed and gave her a hug.

"Shhh, it will be all right."

"I don't see how. Especially now they know," said Violette, slowly pulling away from his embrace.

"I can talk with William and maybe we can work something out."

"Thank you, Michael. Good luck with that. But I don't think that is going to help."

"Let's not worry about that now."

"How are you feeling now?" asked Violette.

"I am fully recovered. Them Debauched bastards can't keep me down," said Michael. "Would you like some more blood?"

"Yes please," said Violette.

"You lie down and I will go and fetch some from the kitchen."

"Ok," said Violette, pulling the covers back and slipping into the bed.

"Knock, knock," said Emily.

"Come in," said Violette, sitting up in bed.

"Hello, sweetheart. How are you going?" asked Emily, as she sat on the bed with Adrian.

"I'm Ok. I just need to rest. Michael has gone to get me some more blood," said Violette.

"Oh, that's good dear. Well… we have come to say good-bye," said Emily.

"You are leaving so soon?"

"Sorry Violette, we have a business that is requiring attention back in LA. But we are only a call away," said Adrian.

"It's Ok. I understand. Have you said goodbye to Danielle?" asked Violette.

"Yeah, just now. If you need anything whilst we are gone, you know you only have to call and we will return," said Emily.

"So you're going back via the portal again?"

"Fastest way to travel. Hate plane food too," said Adrian, smiling.

"Yeah me too," said Violette. "Give me a hug then, both of you."

As Emily and Adrian were giving Violette a hug, Michael walked back in the room.

"Oh, hello Emily and Adrian," said Michael, placing the cup of blood on the side table next to Violette.

"Hello Michael. I see you are looking after Violette well," said Adrian, indicating to the cup of blood.

"Yes, sir. I believe you are both going back to LA today," said Michael.

"Yes, we are leaving now. Just came to say goodbye to our girl," said Adrian, standing.

"Well it was great to see you both again. It's a pity the circumstances weren't a bit more positive. But nonetheless, it was good that you were able to help us with the Debauched once again," said Michael.

"It was good to see you too again, Michael. Look after our girl for us, won't you?" said Emily, standing. She then gave Michael a hug goodbye.

"I will."

"Goodbye Michael. We will see you in a few months' time," said Adrian, holding his hand out to shake Michael's hand.

"That you will," said Michael, shaking his hand.

"Bye, love," said Emily to Violette, as she kissed her forehead.

"Take care of yourselves. I miss you already," said Violette, looking from Emily to Adrian.

"Come on, let's get you settled back into bed," said Michael to Violette, as he watched Emily and Adrian walk towards the door.

Chapter Twenty

Violette.

Yes, my queen, thought Violette sitting up in bed.

Come to my apartment.

At vampire speed, Violette slipped quietly out of bed, trying all the while not to disturb or wake Michael, and ran down the stairs to the queen's basement apartment. As she reached the doorway, the door opened slowly for Violette to go on into the room.

"Come in, my dear," said Talitha.

"Are you all right?" said Violette, walking into the room.

Talitha nodded and said, "Come sit with me, dear." She patted the seat next to her.

Violette continued on into the room and took her place next to Talitha on the couch.

"How are you feeling this morning?" asked Violette.

"Much better. Thank you for asking… but I didn't summon you to talk about me. I want you to see something."

Nodding slowly, Violette said, "Oh, Ok. What is it?"

"Sit back and I will show you," said Talitha.

Violette sat back against the couch.

"Close your eyes, dear," said Talitha.

Violette trustingly nodded and closed her eyes.

Placing her hands either side of Violette's head, Talitha closed her eyes as well and was able to show Violette visions she had from the past.

When the fog cleared in her mind, Violette wondered where Talitha had taken her. The room looked familiar, but different somehow.

Where am I?

In my basement apartment, dear.

In the vision, Talitha led Violette over to a white cradle which was located in her bedroom. When she looked into the cradle a baby was swaddled firmly in a pink, blue and yellow striped baby blanket. Wondering why Talitha was showing Violette this vision, she then watched Talitha pick the baby up and kiss her forehead, lingering for a moment, to take in the sweet smell that only babies have.

Good bye, my sweet child. I love you dearly. I hope we get to meet again one day.

Violette realised through their connection, that the baby was her.

With her eyes opened wide, Violette asked, "Why are you showing me this?"

But before the queen could answer, the vision changed.

Violette was now standing at the entrance of what looked like a church with rows of long wooden seats either side of the room and a white marble altar at the front. As she continued to walk down the middle, she noticed three people standing to the side. But as she got closer a cold chill ran down her body as the faces became familiar.

Mom, Dad. Why am I here? thought Violette, as she looked to Talitha, who was standing beside her, for answers.

Just watch and listen.

Violette then watched on as Sister Mongose handed over a baby to her parents.

"Is that me?" asked Violette, as she looked into Talitha's eyes and frowned.

Talitha nodded and placed her finger to her lips.

Violette turned her attention back to her parents and listened to the conversation.

"You realise this baby is like your other child?" said Sister Mongose.

"Yes," said Mr. Castell.

Mrs. Castell nodded, as she cuddled the baby.

"The only difference is this child will only turn when she meets her life partner," said Sister Mongose.

"Right. Either way, she will be kept safe, sister," said Mr. Castell.

"Good," said Sister Mongose. "When is your flight back to LA?"

"No flight, this time. We are taking a portal back," said Mr. Castell.

Sister Mongose looked at her wrist watch. "Well anyway, you had better be on your way then. It's nearly seven o'clock, and we don't want the Debauched knowing she is alive."

"Right. Well… thank you again, sister.

Portal.

Violette looked at Talitha with a furrowed brow.

My parents… they were supernatural creatures too?

Yes, dear. Fae.

Unbelievable… we never knew, thought Violette as she shook her head slightly.

All of a sudden the visions ended and Violette was back in Talitha's apartment.

As Talitha took her hands away from Violette's head, she said, "This was why they were killed, my dear. The Debauched worked out that they were Fae and they were the ones that carjacked them."

"It's all starting to make sense. Stephen said that it was Debauched that had killed them."

"It was also Stephen who had you committed to the children's home."

"Hmm… what do you mean?" asked Violette, her brow furrowed.

"Well… when your parents died, they left you to be cared for by an aunt. Correct?"

"Yes. But we were told she couldn't look after us because she was poor. So we were then turned over to the home."

"That was just a story we made up, my dear. You see, we asked Stephen to mind control your aunt into saying that she couldn't look after you. And in fact, anyone else in your family who wanted to take you and Danielle in, Stephen did the same to them as well."

"You mean that we had family that wanted to take us in?" Violette remembered back to how unhappy she and Danielle had been at that time. Not only did they have to deal with their parents' death, but also the fact that their world had been turned upside down when they were taken to the home.

"Yes, my dear. But I couldn't let someone else foster you or care for you. Especially as you could transition anytime. So I organised for Emily and Adrian to foster you both."

"Oh my god…" said Violette, standing.

"I needed to keep you safe. Do you not understand that?" said Talitha, standing.

"I don't know what to think. I need to get out of here," said Violette, walking towards the doorway.

"Don't leave, Violette. I need to show you more."

"I don't think I want to see more. I…" Violette ran out of the room quickly. As the tears formed in her eyes, she ran up the concrete stairs. As she reached the top of the stairs, Stephen was waiting for her.

"Violette," said Stephen, as he tried to stop her running off.

"Let go of me," said Violette, trying to wriggle free from his hold. "I can't believe you have known this all this time and have never said anything. How dare you…?"

"I was sworn to secrecy. What was I meant to do?" said Stephen, who had overheard the conversation between Violette and the queen.

"You were meant to tell me the truth," said Violette, still wriggling.

"How else do you think we would have made contact again?" said Stephen, holding her still by her upper arms and looking into her tear-filled eyes.

"I don't know! Let me go, Stephen!" screamed Violette, as she tried to punch his chest hard.

"No… not until you see reason," said Stephen, pulling her in close and wrapping his arms around her.

"I order you to let me go," said Violette, heatedly.

"Not listening…"

Violette tried to wriggle free once again. But Stephen kept a tight hold on her.

As her hot tears overflowed onto her face, she gave in and sobbed into his chest.

"Shh… come on. At least you still have me and Danielle," said Stephen, enveloping her in his arms.

Violette continued to sob into his chest.

"Everything all right here, Violette?" said Michael, from behind Stephen.

"Yes, Michael. Just some sibling squabbling," said Violette, pulling away from Stephen's hold.

"As long as you are Ok."

"Yes, I am fine. Would you mind leaving me and Stephen to talk?"

"Ok," said Michael. Taking a deep breath, he continued down the stairs to the combat room.

"Let's go for a walk," said Stephen.

"Ok," said Violette, wiping her face and following Stephen out to the back yard.

Ever since the last attack by the Debauched, Talitha felt that she needed to let some of her children know about their past connections. She didn't want to die knowing she had kept the truth from them, ever.

One down, two to go, thought Talitha.

"Knock, knock," said Daniel, as he and Katelyn stood in Talitha's open doorway.

"Come," said Talitha, as she gestured to them to take a seat at her round table.

"I believe you wanted to speak with us both," said Katelyn, as she sat at the table.

"Yes… sit down. I have some important information I want to speak with you both about," said Talitha. She just hoped her meeting didn't go as bad as the one she had with Violette.

"What can we do for you, my queen?" said Katelyn.

"Firstly… do you both feel like you have a connection with one another?"

"Well… yes. But I only thought that was because we have the same mother," said Katelyn.

Daniel didn't say a word, he just continued to listen.

"Yes, it is because you have the same mother, but you also have the same father as well," said Talitha.

Daniel and Katelyn looked at each other in shock.

"Wait on, how could that be?" said Katelyn.

Daniel's neck jerked backwards and his brow furrowed.

"I first met Talon Donovan, your father, about twenty-four years ago. He came to me to discuss an alliance between the Dream Walker community and the Lepidopteras. After our initial meeting, he asked me on a date. At first I said no, because I didn't date dream walkers. But Talon being Talon kept persisting, so eventually I said yes. We seemed to get on well together. But when he had to return to Switzerland, I couldn't follow him, because of my coven business here. Our friendship did continue over the phone for weeks, until I organised with William to go and see Talon where he was living in Switzerland at the 'Crestwell Hotel'."

"But..." interrupted Katelyn.

Talitha held up her hand.

"Just let me finish... anyway, at first, I was going to visit Talon at least once a week, but it soon became logistically too hard to keep me safe when I was with him. So when I became pregnant with you Katelyn, I already knew Talon couldn't provide the type of security that I needed for a female Lepidoptera, and that's when I decided to foster you out. Plus, as you know, I have always fostered my children out so they could live a normal life with humans. Talon was not happy about our child being fostered out, nor was he ready to be a parent either. When you were born, I arranged with Sister Mongose at the local church, to come and collect you and organise some foster parents. On the night when Sister Mongose collected you, she was run down by the Debauched and you both were injured. She ended up getting better, but you were left paralysed, so I decided to place you in a home for disabled children. I knew the Debauched would never look for you there either. Plus I had a warlock put up some wards so they couldn't detect you anyway."

"This doesn't make sense. If you knew a warlock that could put up some wards, then why didn't you just let my father look after me. I would have been safer too, by the looks of it," said Katelyn.

"Talon wasn't ready to bring a child up by himself. And I knew it. He was too reckless," said Talitha, seeing Talon's face in her mind.

"Right..." said Katelyn, staring straight through Talitha and wondering what her life would have been like if she just could have stayed with her father.

"But hang on… why was I able to stay with my father and Katelyn wasn't?" asked Daniel.

"That's a good question," said Katelyn, her brow furrowed.

"Well… by the time I got pregnant again with you Daniel, it was about five years later. Your father, Talon… he had become stable and was rising up in the ranks by then. So I decided that he could look after you. And well you know the rest," said Talitha. "By the way, I was sorry to hear of your father's passing."

"Thank you, but why didn't you stay together?" asked Daniel.

"With me in France and him in Switzerland, it all became too hard," said Talitha.

Daniel nodded and turned to Katelyn.

"So… I have a full blood sister," said Daniel.

"Hmm… seems so. It would explain our connection too," said Katelyn.

"Yeah," said Daniel.

"Well it looks like you two will have a lot of things to talk about. Is there anything you wanted to ask me before you leave?" said Talitha.

"I can't think of anything at the moment," said Katelyn.

"Me neither," said Daniel, standing.

"Is there anything we can get you before we leave?" asked Katelyn, as she stood up.

"No thank you, my dear. I just need to rest," said Talitha. "Come by and see me If you have any questions later on."

They both nodded and left her room.

Daniel and Katelyn walked up the concrete stairs in deep thought. As they arrived at the top of the stairs, Katelyn said,

"It's a pity I have to go back home today. I think I would like to stay longer so I can get to know you better, Daniel."

"Yeah… even though it's a bit of a shock now knowing I have a sister, I too would like to get to know you more."

"Do you reckon William could release you for a couple of days, or weeks? I mean, you could always come and stay in Zurich with me for a while. Even though I have university, I would be able to see you at night and on weekends. That way we could get to know each other better. What do you think?"

Daniel nodded and said, "I would love to. Do you reckon Susan would be in agreeance to this as well?"

"I can't see why not. Why don't you go and ask William now and then if he says yes, I can ring my Mom and see what she says."

"Ok. I will go and find him now and ask," said Daniel, hoping for a good outcome.

His world had suddenly gone from not having any family at all, except for the Lepidoptera family, to having a full blooded sister. And his mother was still alive too. What more could he ask for?

Daniel found William sitting with Renee in the front lounge room.

"Afternoon, Daniel," said Renee, as she watched him walk into the lounge room and sit across from her.

"Renee, William," said Daniel.

"How did you go with Talitha?" asked William.

"Hmm, unbelievable. I now have a mother and a sister… it's just… well… I didn't think I would ever have a family again. Not blood related anyway, that made me feel safe, and loved, like my father had. And… well, I would like to ask your permission if I could go and live with Katelyn and Susan for a while?" said Daniel, tapping his foot nervously on the ground.

William looked at Renee and then back to Daniel. "Do you feel you have your transition under control?" asked William.

"Yes, sire."

Raising his eyebrows, William said, "Hmm... I can't see that being a problem. But I will check it out with Susan first and let you know." Taking his phone out of his top pocket of his jacket, he dialled the number.

"Thank you, William." Walking out the room, Daniel felt excited and hopeful for his future.

"Well... don't keep me in suspense, what did William say?" asked Katelyn, meeting him in the hallway.

"He said yes," said Daniel, smiling. "William is ringing Susan now to confirm that I can come and live with you for a while."

"Excellent... I can't see Mom saying no, anyway. Pack your bag bro," said Katelyn, smiling as she gave him a warm hug.

Daniel smiled and hugged Katelyn back.

Daniel, Katelyn and Deveron, come and see me in the lounge room, summoned William.

As soon as they both heard William summon them, Daniel and Katelyn released their hold on each other.

"Looks like we are about to find out if I can stay at your place," said Daniel.

"Yeah. Come on, let's get this over and done with. The suspense is killing me," said Katelyn.

Walking into the lounge room, Daniel and Katelyn noticed that only William and Deveron were waiting for them.

"Sit down," commanded William.

"Yes, sire," said Daniel, taking a seat across from William.

Katelyn quickly sat next to Deveron.

Deveron smiled at Katelyn and placed his hand in hers.

"After a discussion with Susan and our coven this evening, we have decided that the three of you will move into Susan's house straight away. Susan has stated that she will require more soldiers to guard her house from the Debauched, now that Katelyn has transformed and from my point of view, I think it will be a good idea for siblings and life partners to be together, instead of apart. Are you in agreeance?"

"I think this will be a good opportunity for Katelyn and I to get to know each other. Plus I am originally from Switzerland, so having knowledge of the Debauched there and the area should be of some advantage. I believe I could be a great asset to Susan's coven," said Daniel. "Thank you for the opportunity William. You won't regret your decision."

"I had better not," said William, authoritatively.

"Yes, I am in agreeance, William. And thank you for releasing me from your coven so I can be with my life partner. I, too, think I will be a good asset to Susan's coven and will do my best to protect Katelyn as well," said Deveron, looking from William to Katelyn.

"What about you Katelyn? How do you feel about all this?" asked William.

"Thank you, William, for organising all this. I am still in shock, to say the least, about all that has happened to me over the past couple of months. From meeting you and your coven, to finding my life partner, to walking, to then finding my brother. Life sure has been good to me, and I do appreciate everything I now have," said Katelyn, as the tears of happiness formed in her eyes.

"Indeed, it sure has changed," said William, remembering the day a shy Katelyn first arrived at the house and was wheelchair-bound. "Well... I need you three to go and pack up your belongings and I will organise for our jet to take you back to Zurich tonight. The sooner you get settled in there, the better."

They all nodded in agreeance.

Chapter Twenty-One

"There you are," said William to Renee, standing in the doorway to the queen's room. "By the look on both your faces, Renee has told you about the baby?"

Renee nodded and looked down into her lap.

"Yes, and I am trying to piece together just how this has happened. As you know, in the past I have been the only one who has had children in our Lepidoptera covens," said Talitha, her brow furrowed. "It's been so long now, but I am trying to remember when Renee first joined our coven and the circumstances that brought her to us. Maybe that has something to do with it. Not sure…"

Renee remembered it all too well.

From an early age, Renee grew up in the southern parts of Sweden on a farm with her family that harvested and traded vegetables and silage. With her mother dying at a young age of diphtheria and then her father passing away not long after, from heart problems, Renee, who was in her early twenties, was left to look after the farm with her older brother, Samuel.

Soon after the death of their parents, and with the economy not going so well, Renee and Samuel were forced to sell the land that had been handed down to them through many generations of their ancestors and leave Sweden to find work.

Ending up in France by passenger ship, they eventually found work on a wheat farm in northern France and were lucky enough to be able to stay together. But not long after they arrived in France, Samuel was struck down by cholera, and months later passed away in Renee's arms.

After Samuel's funeral, Renee fell into a deep depression and eventually lost her job on the wheat farm. Ending up on the streets of Paris, she begged for food and money. With nothing left to live for, Renee decided she was going to end her life by climbing the Arc De Triomphe and throwing herself off and into oncoming electric trams.

Renee stood on the side of the roof top of the arc looking out over the foreign land. With the wind and rain pushing her about, she then jumped off, with open arms, and seemed to float down to the roadway slowly below. When her body hit the ground with a hard thump, she groaned in agony and finally passed out.

When her eyes opened, Renee was no longer laying on the roadway near the Arc De Triomphe, instead she was in a beautiful French house, in a low-lit bedroom. Sitting up quickly, her eyes darted around the room, until she noticed a man, dressed in black leather clothing, sitting at the foot of the bed on a stool, watching her every move.

"Where am I?" asked Renee, as she pulled the blankets up to her chin.

"You are safe. How are you feeling?" asked the man.

"Ok, I suppose. But… how am I still alive?" said Renee, remembering back to her jumping off the Arc De Triomphe.

Standing, he came over to the side of the bed and said, "May I sit down?"

She nodded.

Placing his hand out in front of him, he said, "My name is William. What is yours?"

"Renee, but you didn't answer my question." She shook his hand.

"Well… that is a bit of a story and one for another day. Would you like a drink?" asked William, gesturing to a cup with a lid next the bed.

"Yes please," said Renee, picking up the cup. As she took a sip and swallowed it down she said, "Aww… what is that? Tastes disgusting."

"It's what you need right now," said William, with a furrowed brow.

Taking the lid off she looked inside the cup. Gulping she said, "Is this what I think it is... blood?"

He nodded yes.

"Why would you give me blood?" said Renee, placing the cup on the bedside table.

"Because you are in transition," said William.

"Transition... what are you talking about?"

"You know, vampire. I turned you so that you could live."

"What...?" said Renee, jumping out of bed and backing away from him.

William then explained how he had listened to her thoughts when she was on top of the Arc De Triomphe and how he couldn't get to her in time to stop her from killing herself, but instead turned her before she died.

"Renee..." said William, watching her stare into space.

"Hmm, yes," said Renee, slipping back into reality.

"You Ok?" asked Talitha.

"Yes, I am fine. I was remembering back to when I was a human. Seems like many moons ago now," said Renee.

"Ah, yes. I remember the day William introduced you to me. He was nervous, because you were the first one he had turned," said Talitha, looking from Renee to William. "Hmm... and maybe that's it. You could be pregnant because you were originally a human."

"Yeah... that would make sense," said Renee.

"Anyway, no matter how it happened. The best thing I could have ever done was to turn you into a vampire. Especially as I got to meet my life partner," said William.

Renee looked up at William and smiled.

"And now you are with child. Certainly a turn up for our kind," said Talitha, with raised eyebrows. "Renee... I don't want you leaving the house. Do you understand me?"

"Yes, my queen," said Renee, bowing her head slightly.

"You won't be safe out there. The Debauched will pick up on your baby's scent," said Talitha. "Believe me, I know. William, I would like for you to organise an obstetrician to come and see Renee. Use the same one we regularly go to, Dr. Collins."

"Yes, my queen. Is there anything else you would like me to do?" asked William.

"No. That is all for the moment."

"Well, I have some other news. Deveron and Daniel are leaving our coven. They have asked if they can live with Susan and Katelyn in Zurich and I have said yes. I have organised for them to fly to Switzerland tonight," said William.

"Obviously Susan has agreed to this as well?" stated Talitha.

"Yes. She is happy for them to come and live with her. She needed more guards anyway for Katelyn, now that she has transitioned," said William.

Talitha nodded. "Excellent."

"Are you Ok, my love?" asked William to Renee.

"Yeah... just a bit queasy in the stomach, that's all. How did you know?" asked Renee.

"I can feel it in my stomach too," said William. "Morning sickness?"

"Yeah, I would say so," said Renee.

"You need your rest, Renee," said Talitha, placing her healing hand on Renee's arm.

"Hmm... I might go have a lie down," said Renee, standing. "Oh, and thank you for the healing, Talitha. I feel a bit better already."

"You are welcome, my dear. Take care of her William," said Talitha.

"I will," said William, picking Renee up in his muscular arms and walking towards the doorway.

As Talitha watched Renee and William leave her room, she sat wondering about how a baby would fit into the Lepidoptera way of life in the Gramaze household and how over her lifetime she had to give up each and every one of her children when they were born. Things certainly had changed over time for her coven and she wasn't entirely sure if it was going in the right direction. Talitha knew she would need to keep an eye on everything from now on for her coven to survive.

Michael woke to find Violette thrashing around aggressively beside him. Realising she was dreaming, he shook her gently to try wake her up.

"Violette... Violette!" called Michael.

"No...no... Michael... I will kill each and every one of you sick motherfuckers," said Violette, her speech slurred.

Michael shook her once more, but vigorously this time. "Violette."

Violette opened her eyes wide. When she noticed Michael, she sat up quickly and hugged him tightly. Tears welled in her eyes as she remembered the bad dream she had just witnessed.

"It's Ok, Violette. It was just a dream. You are safe," said Michael, listening to her heartbeat accelerate.

"Oh, Michael... you had been killed by the Debauched. It was awful. I know it was just a dream, but it felt real."

"Shhh. I am not going anywhere," said Michael, hugging her firmly.

"It just felt so real..." sobbed Violette.

Slowly pulling away from her embrace, Michael wiped the tears from her face and said, "Come on… let's go outside for some fresh air."

Violette smiled briefly and nodded yes.

Sitting on the back limestone steps, Michael said, "How are you feeling… you need a drink?"

"Yes please," said Violette, looking into his blue eyes.

"Ok. I will be right back," said Michael, standing up and walking inside.

Staring straight ahead and out into the low-lit back gardens, next to the gazebo, Violette frowned when she noticed a shadow of a large man walking towards Renee who was sitting by herself inside the gazebo.

William. I might go inside and give them some privacy, thought Violette.

As she stood up, and turned to go inside, she heard Renee's thoughts and then her scream. Looking back over her shoulder, Violette's lips thinned when she realised that a Debauched soldier had a knife to Renee's throat.

Fuck.

"Be quiet, bitch. Otherwise, I will kill your child," said the Debauched soldier to Renee.

"Please… don't hurt my baby. I will do whatever you want," pleaded Renee, trying to appease the Debauched soldier.

Violette ran down the limestone steps at vampire speed and stood at the entrance to the gazebo. "LET… HER… GO."

"Ah… princess. I was wondering if you were here," said the Debauched soldier smelling her scent, as he pressed the blade of the knife into the skin of Renee's neck, and piecing her skin slightly.

"I said, LET HER GO!" shouted Violette, placing one hand out in front of her and curling her fingers towards the middle of her palm.

The Debauched soldier started to choke, but held the knife firmly against Renee's neck.

"One more move and I will kill this bitch and her baby." His voice was low and uneven.

As the words came out of the soldier's mouth, Violette summoned the elements. Within seconds it had become stormy and the winds were fierce beyond imagination. It then became almost impossible for the soldier to stand upright holding Renee, let alone breathe from the hold Violette had on his throat. Releasing his firm hold on Renee only for a second to get his balance, he lost control and Renee struggled free.

Running towards Violette, her hair flattened by the fierce winds, Renee stumbled and fell to the ground. As she rolled over clutching her stomach and breathing heavily, she watched the Debauched soldier out of the corner of her eye, throw the knife he was holding her against her will with, straight for her. Placing her arm up to deflect the knife, she then watched it stop about an inch from her head and float in the air. Looking back at the princess, Renee watched on as Violette instinctively moved her hands suddenly in a circular motion. The knife had turned in the direction of the Debauched soldier.

His eyes widened when the Debauched soldier realised what was about to happen.

With one swift move forward of her hand, Violette motioned the knife towards the Debauched vampire's throat, making a cutting motion with her hand as she went to cut his throat and behead him. His body dropped to the ground and disintegrated.

With the Debauched soldier obliterated, Violette calmed her mood and slowed the elements down. The cloud and wind soon died down.

"Are you all right?" asked Violette, as she knelt next to Renee, who was still on the ground.

"My baby... I think something is wrong," said Renee, clutching at her stomach. "The pain... I am in a lot of pain, Violette."

Baby.

"You're pregnant?" said Violette.

"Yes... help me, Violette," said Renee, tears forming in her eyes as she curled into a ball on the ground.

Violette placed both her hands on Renee. "Let me heal you."

Renee rolled over onto her back and grabbed for Violette's hands to place them on her lower abdomen. Looking into Violette's eyes she said, "I don't want to lose this baby."

Violette felt a swoosh of wind and looked up to find William and Michael standing next to them with their weapons drawn.

"Can you help her, Violette?" said William, as he knelt beside Renee, placed his gun on the ground and held Renee's hand.

"Yes. But I need one of you to keep guard. My senses tell me that there was more than one Debauched here. I think we have an audience from afar," whispered Violette, as she tilted her head, with her eyes following to the right.

But it was too late. Just as Violette spoke, four more Debauched came running at them at vampire speed, firing their weapons instinctively.

Michael tried to deflect the bullets as he stood in front of Violette to protect his life partner and princess. One bullet nicked the left side of his abdomen, but kept going cleanly through his skin and out the other side. Michael flinched, but kept his stance, as the blood spurted from his wound.

Quickly standing behind Michael, Violette grabbed for the two long steel swords he had inserted into the back of his belt.

These fuckers just don't give up, thought Violette.

Once again, Violette used her abilities and summoned the elements. Feeling the sky rumble under her feet, she looked up to see a bolt of lightning hit the ground and then smoke smolder from the hole it made in the grass.

"William… stay with Renee!" shouted Violette, as she ran forward towards the four Debauched soldiers, with the swords drawn in front of her.

William nodded and pulled out his automatic rifle from his leather jacket. He hovered in front of Renee and their unborn child to protect them, whilst he watched Michael and Violette run towards the Debauched.

"Arrr… you fuckers are gonna die!" shouted Violette, as she ran towards the Debauched and deflected the bullets showering her and then beheading the first one with Michael's Grikohr sword. The look in her crimson, fully dilated eyes was one of kill or be killed to the other Debauched that stood before her and she was not taking any prisoners. Violette was there to do one thing and that was to protect her family.

Michael pulled his semi-automatic shot gun from his leg gun holster and fired it rigorously at one of the Debauched vampire's legs. As the vampire let out a screech, he fell to his knees and then Violette beheaded him with her ruby stone handled sword.

"Two left. Let's get these mothers!" shouted Michael, as he ran towards one of them and fired his shot gun into the Debauched vampires leg.

"Arrr…," shouted Violette, as she ran towards a kneeling Debauched and watched the lightning strike his body, whilst she ran the sword through his neck and beheaded the soldier.

As the remaining Debauched watched his last brother fall and disintegrate, he was set upon from behind by Annabelle, who jumped on his back and tore off his head in a rage.

"Bloody fuckers seem to think that they can hurt my family. Well, they have another think coming," said Annabelle, with her hands on her hips, as she watched the wind blow away the ash from the Debauched body.

"Where did you come from?" asked Michael.

"I had just come back from patrol, when I heard all the commotion out here. I thought Adrian put up wards around the house and perimeter?" asked Annabelle.

"Well I thought he did too," said Violette.

"Violette..." called William.

Violette looked in his direction and saw Renee still on the ground, but she was unconscious.

Renee... shit, no.

*V*iolette ran back to Renee and knelt down beside her limp body. Placing her open palmed hands on her stomach area, Violette chanted.

When nothing seemed to be happening, Violette said, "William, let's get her inside off this cold concrete flooring."

William scooped up Renee quickly in his arms and ran with vampire speed inside to their bedroom. Laying her down on their bed, he then pulled the covers over her cold body.

Violette stood at the doorway and watched William stroke his life partner's forehead. Walking in, she said, "Here... let me have another go at healing her."

He nodded and stepped away from the bed, only to watch from behind Violette his beloved Renee lying all the while, unconscious.

As the seconds ticked by, all seemed lost.

But as Violette chanted her healing ritual, Renee's eyes opened and tried to focus.

"Renee... how do you feel?" asked Violette, keeping her hands on Renee's lower abdomen.

Taking a deep breath, Renee said, "I'm Ok. Is the baby all right?" Her eyes search Violette's for answers.

"I don't know," said Violette.

But just as Violette said this, the queen walked into the room.

"Step aside everyone," said Talitha, as she came around to the side of the bed and sat down next to Renee.

"My baby…," said Renee, with tears forming in her eyes.

Talitha placed her hand on Renee's stomach and put a finger to her mouth. "Shhh."

Renee's brow furrowed and her eyes opened wide as she watched Talitha place her ear to Renee's stomach.

Talitha then sat up straight and said, "There is a heart-beat." Smiling, she then placed her healing hands on Renee's stomach.

"Oh, thank goodness," said Renee, looking from Talitha to William.

William smiled and breathed a sigh of relief as he looked to his life partner with adoration.

"Thank you, my queen," said Renee.

"You are most welcome, my dear," said Talitha, standing. "William, a word outside."

William nodded and followed Talitha out of the bedroom. Closing the door, he left Violette to sit with Renee.

"How were those Debauched able to get in here, let alone sense Renee was outside?" said Talitha, her nostrils flared and hands on her hips.

"I am not sure, my queen," said William. "I don't under-stand how this happened."

"Well you damn well need to find out then, don't you? If you can't keep us safe, I will need to find someone who can. William, you assured me that Violette and I were in good hands here, but I don't see that happening," said Talitha pacing up and down the landing.

Bowing his head William said, "My apologies. This won't happen again, my queen."

"It had better not. I want you to contact Adrian and see why his wards have not worked. I don't care what it takes, I want Adrian here within the hour to sort this out. Am I making myself clear?"

"Yes, my queen."

"Well get moving then," said Talitha, heatedly.

William bowed slightly and walked away from Talitha with a knot in his stomach and clenched fists by his side. He had worked hard to keep this coven together, and he too wanted answers. But William felt her comment about giving the coven to someone else just wasn't called for. He knew she wouldn't find anyone else so loyal as him.

"Hmm, that doesn't sound too good," said Violette, as she and Renee listened to Talitha chastising William.

"It's not the worst I have heard. Talitha is pretty damn hard to keep happy. I am sure William will work through it. He has to," said Renee, looking up at Violette.

"What will happen if she puts someone else in place of William?" asked Violette.

"Let's not go there. I am sure it will all get worked out," said Renee, as she sat up.

"You feeling better?"

"Yeah. Feeling good actually. But I think I might go down to the kitchen for some blood. Just feeling a bit antsy at the moment."

Violette stood up next to the bed and placed her hand out front. "Come on. I'll go with you."

"Thank you, Violette... for everything. If it wasn't for you... well... the Debauched would have taken me. Goodness knows what would have happened to my baby. I am so thankful to you for saving us."

"No need to thank me. But you are welcome anyway. So… you are pregnant. Wow… like, how many weeks are you?"

"I think about six weeks," said Renee as they reached the bottom of the staircase.

"Renee… when the baby is born… umm… do you have to give it up for adoption? You know, like what happened to me."

"We haven't discussed it with the queen yet." *I don't care what Talitha says, I am keeping my baby. Even if it means having to leave here.*

"Oh, right," said Violette, as they entered the kitchen.

Renee walked over to the fridge and pulled out a bag of blood. "Did you need one, Violette?"

"Yes, please," said Violette, taking a bag of blood from Renee. Taking some cups out of cupboard Violette poured the blood into the two cups. "Here you go."

"Thanks, Violette… so… how are you feeling now?" said Renee, taking a seat at the island bench.

"Not bad," said Violette, as she took the seat next to Renee. "Do you know where Michael is? I saw him take a bullet when he was fighting the Debauched, and just want to make sure he is Ok."

"No," said Renee.

"I'm here," said a familiar voice from behind them.

Jumping up out of her seat, Violette raced over to Michael and placed her arms around his waist and planted a kiss on his lips.

How's the wound? thought Violette to Michael, as she pulled away from their embrace slowly and looked into his eyes.

It's already healed.

Violette smiled and noticed from his alluring smell, that he had already showered as well.

Looking over at Renee, Michael said, "How are you going, Renee?"

"I'm fine now… thanks to Violette," said Renee, as she poured some more blood into a cup. "What about you?"

"My wound has healed already," said Michael, lifting his shirt to show Renee and Violette his side. As he pulled his shirt back down, he asked, "Where is William tonight?"

"I think he may be in the operations room. I am not sure… the queen gave him a bit of a dressing down," said Renee.

"Oh, right. Is everything all right? said Michael.

"Time will tell. I might head back up to my room to rest and give you both some privacy," said Renee, standing.

"Would you like some help up to your room, Renee?" asked Violette.

"No… but thanks for asking. I will see you both later," said Renee, walking out the kitchen towards the front of the house.

"So much for a quiet night," said Michael, with a furrowed brow. "I still can't believe what went on here tonight. And you… you were awesome."

"I don't know about awesome… I couldn't even believe it myself, just how powerful I am. It's actually a bit scary knowing how much power I have inside of me," said Violette.

Chapter Twenty-Two

William stormed through the operations doorway, pushing the door hard against the wall as he entered.

Brock turned around from his laptop screen to see what the commotion was.

"Everything all right, William?" asked Brock, as he tried to read William's thoughts.

"There is just no pleasing some people."

Raising his eye brows, Brock said, "Hmm, I heard what happened."

"Yeah, I don't know how they got into our compound or how they detected that Lepidopteras live here. I need to give Adrian a ring to sort this out."

"Right… seems a bit odd. I hear Violette is a force to be reckoned with," snickered Brock.

"She is a real asset to our coven. Her abilities have well and truly kicked in. You should have seen her out there… unbelievable," said William, picturing how powerful she was and how she took control of the situation without hesitation. "Actually, Brock… there is something you can do for me tonight."

"What is that?"

"Organise for security cameras to be placed all around the front yard, starting at the front fence and up to the house, and then the same with the backyard, up to the house. I don't want them Debauched fuckers getting that close to the house ever again, without us knowing about it."

Yes, sire."

"And I want it monitored 24/7. I will leave you to organise who and when for the monitoring. In fact, I want you to also set up some distractions as well. Say like an electric fence around the perimeter."

"No problem. That is easy enough. I will start on this tonight and by tomorrow it will be finished."

"Excellent. Keep me updated on the progress and I will inform our coven on what is happening. Now… I must make a phone call to Adrian."

Brock nodded and returned to his laptop screen to organise better security for the house.

The phone rang once before Adrian picked it up. "Adrian."

"Yes, William."

"You need to return to our house. The wards you have put in place are not working. We were attacked tonight. They nearly took Renee, who by the way, is with child."

Adrian took in a deep breath. *Fuck.* "I will be there in a few minutes, William," said Adrian, shaking his head.

As Adrian walked through the portal doorway at the Gramaze household front door, William was standing at the entrance with his hands on his hips.

"Adrian."

"I am sorry about this William. I have been thinking about how this could have happened and I think I know what went wrong. You say Renee is pregnant? By the way congrats, man. Emily and I are happy for you," said Adrian.

"Thank you. Yes, we think she may be about six weeks along," said William, smiling proudly.

"The wards I put up were for Lepidopteras, not anything else."

William frowned.

"You see… the baby is not a Lepidoptera yet."

Rolling his eyes, William said "Now that makes sense. Can you rectify this with your wards tonight?"

"Yes. I have brought with me my potions," said Adrian, showing William his brown leather backpack. "Where can I set up?"

"Let's get you set up in the operations room. Come this way, my friend."

Adrian followed William through the house to the operations room.

As the door swung open, Brock turned to see William and Adrian walking in.

"Good evening, Adrian, William," said Brock.

"Hello Brock," said Adrian, placing his bag down on the long wooden table.

"Sire, can I have a word?" said Brock. *We have a problem.*

Williams eyes widened and his nostrils flared.

"I will leave you to set up Adrian. Let me know when it's done," said William, signalling Brock to follow him into the corridor.

"No problem, my friend," said Adrian, opening his bag.

Brock carried his open laptop out to the corridor.

"What's going on?" asked William.

"Sire, there seems to be a huge Debauched presence down at Loire Valley," said Brock, showing William the satellite image on his laptop.

"Can you bring up that image any closer?" said William, focusing on how many soldiers were present.

"Give me a minute."

The view became clearer on the screen and William and Brock watched on in horror at how the Debauched were drinking from humans and then discarding their drained, limp bodies into a fiery pit, which was behind an old chateau.

William felt sickened as he watched the slaughter of many humans, some even children. His nostrils flared as he looked up and took a deep breath. "Come with me."

William strode towards the operations room. *When is this madness going to end?*

Gramaze coven... I order you to come to the operations room, NOW, summoned William to his family authoritatively.

"How are you going in here, Adrian?" asked William as he entered the room.

"I'm done," said Adrian, looking up and sensing something was wrong from the fierce look on William's face. "Everything all right?"

"No..." said William, as he then watched his coven file in one by one.

Adrian swallowed hard, gathered up his bag and stepped to the back as he watched the room become crowded with the Gramaze Lepidopteras who towered near him.

William stood at the head of the wooden table and looked around at the faces before him as he spoke. "Gramaze... we have a serious problem tonight. It sickens me to tell you this, but the Debauched are, as we speak, slaughtering humans in the Loire Valley tonight... Brock bring up the images."

A hum came over the room as each Gramaze Lepidoptera watched the screen in shock. Each of them knew that it was going to be hard to explain this type of slaughter to the authorities, when so many humans had gone missing.

"Adrian... where are you?" asked William, looking around the room.

"Here..." said Adrian, looking from the screen to William.

All the Gramaze Lepidopteras turned towards Adrian, who was still standing at the back of the room.

"I need your help... can you stay longer?" said William.

"Whatever you need, I am here," said Adrian, standing strong.

"Right… do you think that you would be able to portal all of us to this location?" asked William.

Adrian looked around the room. "Yes. I can't see that being a problem."

"Right. Let's get ready, Gramaze coven, and organise our combat gear ready for battle. I want these fuckers stopped. We meet out in the backyard in ten minutes."

"Yes, sire," they all chanted and quickly filed out the operations room, leaving only William, Brock and Adrian standing there.

"Brock, I need you to stay here and monitor the screens."

"Yes, sire."

"Adrian, let's get you set up outside for the portal."

"No problem, my friend."

When Michael entered his and Violette's bedroom, he was glad to find Violette still sleeping soundly. She hadn't previously heard the summoning from William. He knew she would want to come along to this battle, but he couldn't afford to let her come because she was too valuable to the Gramaze coven. Moving around the room stealthily, he changed into his battle gear and then quickly headed towards the doorway, only looking back once, at his sleeping life partner and smiling before he shut the door to their room.

"She sleeping?" asked Danielle, as she and Christian met Michael in the hallway.

"Yeah. You two ready?" asked Michael.

They both nodded and watched as Grayson and Samantha came out of their bedroom doorway.

"Let's go," said Grayson, as he held Samantha's hand and they all jumped down to the landing below.

Entering the combat room, they noticed that Temperance, Sherrie and Nicky were already standing at the cabinet and taking weapons of choice out to hook onto their belts and to carry.

"You girls ready?" asked Grayson authoritatively.

"We were born ready," said Temperance, tucking a sword into her belt.

Nicky and Sherrie agreed.

William, Adrian, James, Taiven and Annabelle stood at the entrance to a turquoise coloured portal that had just been opened by Adrian and watched the others walk towards them.

"Right... once we arrive on the other side, I will give you all your orders," said William, looking around at each of their faces. "Stephen and Sharina are staying here to protect the queen, Violette and Renee. Now let's go."

As the last Gramaze coven member walked through, Adrian closed the watery looking portal and stood next to William awaiting his orders.

"The plan is to stop these bastards. I don't care what you have to do. Just stop them... if there are any humans alive, I want you to erase their memories, heal their injures and I will organise for them to be sent back to their homes. Stay together in pairs at all times. I don't want any heroics here. Are we clear?" said William, looking at each member of his coven.

"Yes, sire," they all said together quietly.

William walked in a horizontal line with his coven towards the front of the chateau. As they all got closer, it appeared that they were too late. No Debauched or humans were in sight. Instead the night air was still. William put his hand up to stop his coven walking any further. Taking his phone out of his jacket pocket, William rang Brock.

"Brock… what's going on? There are no Debauched or humans here at this chateau."

"What… I don't understand? Are you at the right chateau? Because I can still see them clearly on my satellite imagery."

William frowned. *What the fuck. I know we are at the right chateau. What's going on here?*

"Yes, we are at the right chateau, but…" But William didn't finish his sentence. Instead he watched as the air seemed to shimmer. Frowning, he shook his head and blinked a few times to check his vision. "I'll call you back."

William looked at Adrian, who was standing next to him. "Did you see that? What's happening?"

Adrian shrugged his shoulders and frowned. Looking forward towards the old building in front of him, he too noticed the air shimmering.

"Humph… they have glamoured the place and its grounds. Give me a minute," said Adrian, smirking. Waving his hand through the air, it then became apparent. The stench of blood in the air and the burning smell of bodies. The slurping sound of Debauched drinking, the screams of scared humans being slaughtered.

As the view became clearer, each Gramaze coven member couldn't believe what they were seeing.

Debauched gorging themselves on humans.

With their swords drawn, they ran with vampire speed towards the unsuspecting Debauched. But as they got closer to the action, they were hit by what seemed to be an invisible wall, which stopped them fast in their tracks. Each Gramaze coven member fell to the ground stunned.

Adrian watched each member smack straight into what seemed like thin air. Realising that the Debauched must have a warlock in the vicinity holding up the wards, he looked around aimlessly. He then spotted one of his oldest enemies whom he hadn't seen since World War One, and heard was dead. Gardon.

How dare you help these blood suckers? thought Adrian to Gardon.

Looking around to find the owner of the voice of who had spoken to him, Gardon spotted Adrian on the other side of the wall.

Ah... Adrian. We meet again, my warlock brother, thought Gardon.

I am not your brother. How could you let this happen? thought Adrian as he looked from Gardon to the Debauched who were literally sucking the life out of humans.

Easy. They pay and I do my magic. But this is not any of your business, thought Gardon as he came closer to the invisible wall.

You will be reported to the council for your evil ways, Gardon, thought Adrian, as he came closer to the wall, with his fists clenched.

Gardon's nostrils flared. *Humph...you dare.*

Yes. Take this wall down or I will, thought Adrian as he looked Gardon in the eyes.

William and his coven had recovered somewhat from hitting the wall and were now standing next to Adrian in a horizontal line with their teeth bared, ready to pounce as soon as the wall was gone.

Good luck with that. We will be gone by the time you try your sorcery, brother, thought Gardon.

"Stop this chatter, Adrian. Just take the wall down, NOW!" shouted William, angrily.

With a wave of his hand Adrian tried to break through the barrier Gardon had set up. But it didn't work.

"Try again," said William, watching the wall shimmer in the moonlight.

Adrian placed both hands in front of him and summoned the wall to disappear. But it held firm.

Gardon laughed. *Humph... goodbye brother. Hope to see you again one day*, he thought, as he walked away from the wall.

"Let me have a go," said a familiar voice from behind them all.

William turned to see Violette standing behind them, dressed in battle gear.

"No, Violette. You must return home," said William. *How did she get here so quick?*

"Portal."

William frowned.

"Never mind. Let's see if we can bring down his wall together, Adrian," said Violette, as she walked over to him.

Adrian smiled at his foster daughter, who was now standing beside him.

Joining their hands together, they chanted a spell of release and moved their arms towards the invisible wall in a circular motion.

Gardon watched on from afar as the wall instantly came down, and the Lepidopteras stormed towards the Debauched, beheading each and every one of them as they went. The battle lasted for twenty minutes before each and every one of the Debauched vampires were beheaded and had disintegrated.

When the battle was over, Adrian looked around for Gardon, but he was nowhere to be found. But he knew the next time he saw Gardon it would be a battle to the death.

William looked around to see who of his coven were still alive. As he paced throughout the grounds, he couldn't see three of them.

Sherrie… Nicky… Temperance, where are you girls?

There was no answer.

"Grayson, Annabelle, I need you to go look for the three girls," said William, standing with his hands on his hips.

"Yes, sire," they both said together.

"Danielle, Christian, Michael, Samantha, James and Taiven, I want you all to clean up this mess. Burn the bodies and get rid of the bones of the dead, then cover over this hole. We don't want the authorities knowing what went on here," said William, looking at each of their faces.

"Yes, sire," they all said together.

William searched around the grounds to see if there were any humans alive. Bending down to each one, he placed his hand on their bodies to ascertain if they were alive or dead. But to his dismay, the Debauched had drunk each and every one of them dry. Sucking in a deep breath, he then helped his family load the bodies into the burning fire.

As he stood at the mouth of the fire pit, William couldn't believe the carnage the Debauched had inflicted on the humans here tonight. *Why now? I haven't seen this happen for centuries.*

Sire… come down to the river, thought Grayson to William.

"What is it?" asked William, as he came to stand by Grayson and Annabelle near the edge of the water.

"We have searched the entire property and can't locate the female Lepidopteras, sire. But we have found their swords," said Grayson, pointing to the swords on the bank, near the edge of the water.

William's nostrils flared and he raked his hand through his hair when he realised what must have happened.

"Fuck…"

Taking his phone out of his jacket, William called Brock.

"Yes, Sire," answered Brock. "What can I do for you?"

"I need you to rewind the satellite view you have down to the banks of the river behind the chateau. I think Temperance, Sherrie and Nicky have been killed. Ring me back and let me know what you find," said William, kneeling down where the swords lay on the green grass, only to find ashes covering the palm of his hand as he touched the ground.

"Yes, sire." Brock hoped William was wrong as he punched in the co-ordinates.

William hung up his phone and placed it back in his jacket.

"Now that all the evidence has been concealed, I need you to round everyone up, Grayson. Let's get the fuck out of here," said William, standing.

"Yes, sire."

"Annabelle, take these three swords back home, until we find out for sure if the girls are dead," said William, passing the swords to Annabelle.

"Yes, sire."

William phone vibrated in his pocket. He took a deep breath as he pulled it out.

"Yes."

"You were correct, sire. Temperance and Sherrie were beheaded by two Debauched from behind. But as for Nicky... well... it looks like she was... god, how do I say this?... she was cut in half when the portal was closed on her as she was halfway through. Bloody fucking bastards. They are gonna pay for what they have done, William. I vow this," said Brock, saddened by the screen images he had frozen in front of him on the laptop.

"Thank you, Brock. We will be returning soon."

William stood silent, as he placed his phone in his jacket pocket once again and then sighed as he shook his head.

May you rest in peace knowing we will take retribution for your deaths, thought William.

Violette, thought William.

"Yes, sire."

William breathed a sigh of relief, as he looked in her direction of where she was standing with Adrian, near the back of the chateau. He hadn't seen her since the battle with the Debauched started.

"Create a portal back home… by the way, I will deal with you later."

Defiant child, thought William to himself.

Violette gulped hard, and did as she was told.

Epilogue

It had been six months since the Gramaze coven had stopped the Debauched soldiers massacre of human life in Loire Valley and so far the new wards that Adrian had placed around the house had been working well. There had been some minor incidents on the streets of France, like drug trafficking, but nothing of great significance had happened that William and his coven couldn't deal with. But word on the streets was that there was a new leader coming into town and if the intel was right, this Debauched leader was bringing a new breed of vampire, which was stronger, faster and more powerful than anything the Lepidoptera vampires had seen previously.

Talitha and William were not usually perturbed by the intel because their coven was not only powerful, but also committed to humans and vampires existing together peacefully in society. But something about this new leader that they were hearing about intrigued them. Especially as this new leader was a female, who was claiming to be a First One. Talitha knew she was the only First One alive, as all of her family members had been slaughtered thousands of years before.

"Humph, First One… I don't think so… this bitch sure has a nerve calling herself a First One. I want to you to find out her whereabouts and who she is," demanded Talitha, with her nostrils flared as she paced in front of William with her hands on her hips.

"Yes, queen." William nodded once in her direction. "I don't think we have much to worry about, though."

"Time will tell." Talitha took a deep breath and sighed. Taking a seat at her table, Talitha's eyes lingered as she looked upon an old sepia-coloured photo, which was tattered with age, of her family in their suits and gowns. It was the only remaining photo she had of her family prior to their deaths that had survived over the years.

"Was there anything else you wanted to discuss, my queen?" asked William, noticing Talitha rubbing her finger over the photo.

Talitha looked up from the photo and said, "No... just make sure you find out who this new leader is. I want a picture."

"Yes, my queen."

"You can go now," said Talitha, gesturing for William to leave the room with her hand.

William bowed his head once and headed for the doorway.

William looked up to see his heavily pregnant life partner standing at the top of the basement stairs.

"Hello, my love."

"Everything all right?" asked William, watching Renee rub her belly.

"Yes, everything is good, William. I wanted to see if you have a minute for a chat."

"Sure."

Taking his hand in hers, Renee said, "Let's go for a walk."

Renee felt secure as William placed his arm around her waist and she lay her head on his shoulder and they walked around the back gardens.

"William... I think we need to talk about the obvious... you know, the baby and when it's born," said Renee.

"Everything will work itself out, my love. You'll see."

"Well, now the queen has said we can keep the baby here... yes, that is all sorted out."

William frowned, not knowing what else could be wrong.

"I am talking about the birth of our baby. You know… the delivery."

"Oh, right. So what's the problem?"

"I want a specialist to come to the house and deliver our baby."

"Listen, I don't know why you are worried. I have helped deliver heaps of Talitha's babies, and nothing has gone wrong."

"Yes, I am quite aware of your expertise," sighed Renee, as she rolled her eyes. "But as I said, I want a specialist to bring our baby into the world. This baby is different, William, and I don't want any complications."

William listened whilst Renee rabbited on about all the things that could go wrong.

"Ok, Ok. I get it now. I will organise a specialist. But I still want to be there for the birth," said William, releasing his hold on her and looking her in the eyes.

"Of course; that is a given, William. You are the father and I want our child to come into this world with both of us there. Oh, thank you William," said Renee, smiling. Placing her arms around William's waist she gave him a hug.

"Anything for you, my love," said William. "Oh, I forgot to tell you… I heard from Susan today. She was saying that Daniel and Deveron have fit in really well at her house. Apparently guarding Katelyn from the Debauched and helping with patrol is working out too. She was saying that Katelyn and Daniel have fully embraced their Lepidoptera ways and abilities and things seem to be going well for them all."

"I am glad that that has already sorted itself out. One less thing for you to worry about," said Renee. "Aww… give me your hand." Taking William's hand, she placed it on her stomach.

"Feel that?" said Renee, looking into William's eyes.

Nodding quickly, William smiled, kept his hand on Renee's stomach and felt the baby's body move about under his palm. "Yeah. Unbelievable." Bending down he placed his ear next to Renee's stomach.

"I am looking forward to meeting you," he said to the baby.

Renee smiled.

Violette sat on the back step with Michael listening to Renee and William's conversation.

"Look at them two. It's nice to see they can work things out," said Violette.

"Hmm... yeah," said Michael, placing his arm around Violette's shoulders and pulling her in close.

"You Ok?" asked Violette, looking up. She could sense from their connection that he was sad.

"Yeah... I was thinking about Temperance, Sherrie and Nicky, and how in the last year we have lost so many of our coven," said Michael, staring off in the distance. "I have missed having them all around."

"I miss them too. I have lost way too many people in my life. I suppose in a way it has taught me to appreciate every day and the people I have in it."

"Hmm..." agreed Michael, watching Danielle and Christian walk towards them in their battle gear. "Hi guys... how was it out there tonight?"

"Pretty quiet actually," said Danielle, taking a seat on the ledge with Christian.

"Yeah... you can definitely sense something is going on, but not sure what. Fuckers are gonna die a horrible death when I catch up with them next for what they have done to our coven lately," said Christian, his nostrils flared and arms crossed over his chest.

"For sure, man," said Michael.

"What you guys gonna do for the rest of the night?" asked Violette.

"Besides a well-earned shower, we were discussing on the way back that we might get something to eat and watch a movie," said Danielle.

"That sounds good. We might join you, if you don't mind," said Michael, looking from Violette to Danielle and Christian.

"Sure... hey, what are Stephen and Sharina up to tonight?" asked Danielle.

"Not sure. Maybe we can all hook up," said Violette. "Whilst you both have showers, we can go and find them and see if they want to join us."

"Ok. We won't be long," said Danielle, standing with Christian.

"See you later on then," said Michael, as he stood up with Violette.

"Yeah, bro. We shouldn't be too long," said Christian walking towards the back doorway.

As Michael and Violette entered the kitchen they found Stephen, Sharina, James and Taiven all seated at the island bench chatting.

"Hey guys. What you all up to?" asked Michael.

"Not much, bro," said James. "We all just came back from patrol. Pretty quiet out there. What about you two?"

"We are gonna watch a movie with Christian and Danielle. You all want to join?" asked Michael.

Stephen looked at Sharina and said, "Sounds good. We are in."

"Hmm, yeah sure," said James.

"What about you, Taiven?" said Violette.

"Sounds like a plan," said Taiven. "Let's go and see what we can download to watch."

"I might get a drink and meet you all in there," said Violette.

"Sure, sis. No problem," said Stephen, standing.

As the movie started and they all were seated in the theatre room, Violette took her seat next to Michael and cuddled into his shoulder. Looking around the room, Violette's thoughts wandered back to when she first met the Gramaze family and how they all made her feel welcome and loved. Then when she found Stephen and how Danielle became a Lepidoptera. And how she had found out she was a princess and had now gained all her abilities. Times sure were different now for Violette. But what most of the Lepidopteras in this room didn't realise was how Violette had become so in tune with most of them. She seemed to feel all their feelings and their pain and could read their thoughts and basically felt a part of them all.

Considering how many coven members she had lost already over the past twelve months, she didn't want to lose any other family members. Violette knew she would need to speak with William and Talitha about what their plan of attack was and how they would be able to keep their coven safe. Her basic plan was to eradicate the Debauched and anyone who was associated with them.

Check Susan's website for when the fourth book in this series will be published. www.susanhoddy.com

For the latest news on Susan Hoddy visit:-

Facebook susanhoddyauthor

Twitter @susan_hoddy

Instagram susanhoddy

If you would like a group or book club reading done of some chapters and/or a book signing in your store, please contact Susan via her website susanhoddy.com to organise an appointment.

ALSO BY SUSAN HODDY

BOOK ONE
OF THE LEPIDOPTERA VAMPIRE SERIES

BOOK TWO
OF THE LEPIDOPTERA VAMPIRE SERIES

Acknowledgements

In some ways, this book was the hardest book for me to write. So many twists and turns and characters evolving. But even though it's been hard, I have thoroughly enjoyed writing it.

This book would not be here, resting in your hands, or on your e-reader if it weren't for the following people. I owe all of them my deepest appreciation.

My daughter, Samantha Hoddy, and my fiancée, Michael Houston. You have always given me time and space to write my books and have been interested in what I am writing. I could not have written this without your continued advice, support and love. Thank you Michael and Sam.

My editor, Rebecca Freeman, whose continued advice and support has provided me with a much needed calming strength to keep going. Thank you, Rebecca.

Several friends, and family members, whom have read my manuscript and gave me feedback on what they wanted to see in the storyline and book cover. Thank you all.

My book cover designer, Lily from Winter Editorial Design, who worked tirelessly to provide me with a truly awesome cover design. Thank you, Lily.

About the Author

Susan Hoddy is an Australian, American and French young-adult fiction writer, best known for her Lepidoptera Vampire Series. Susan was born in Perth, Western Australia in 1966, and enjoys a good chinwag with family and friends, cups of tea, day-dreaming and writing.

Susan has always worked in many facets of an office during her life, but in 2012 she decided life was too short and wanted to make a start on her passion, which was writing. After acquiring her novel writing diploma from the Australian College of Journalism, she continues to create worlds where fantasy and romance exists, with her books.